P9-DCD-742

THE
Three Musketeers

THE
Three Musketeers

By ALEXANDRE DUMAS

A NEW TRANSLATION BY JACQUES LE CLERCQ

EDITED AND ABRIDGED BY THE TRANSLATOR

ESPECIALLY FOR

The Illustrated Junior Library

ILLUSTRATED BY

Norman Price AND *E. C. Van Swearingen*

Illustrated Junior Library

GROSSET & DUNLAP PUBLISHERS NEW YORK

Contents

EDITOR'S NOTE

The distinguished artist, Norman Price, had done a great deal of research in preparation for the illustrations in this book before his death on August 2, 1951. He had nearly completed some of the paintings for the color illustrations. However, a great deal of research was still to be done and additional drawings to be made. We commissioned the well-known artist, Mr. E. C. Van Swearingen, whose style and technique were developed in the same school of painting, to complete the assignment, and we feel that Mr. Van Swearingen has been singularly successful.

Author's Preface

*Wherein it is proved that despite their names ending in
-os and -is, the heroes of the history we are about to relate
have nothing mythological about them*

ABOUT A YEAR AGO, while I was engaged in research in
the Royal Library for my *History of Louis XIV*, I chanced
upon a volume called *The Memoirs of Monsieur d'Artagnan*.
Like most works in a period in which authors could not tell
the truth without risking a more or less lengthy sojourn in
the Bastille, it was printed at Amsterdam. The publisher
was one Pierre Rouge. The title fascinated me; I took the
book home (with the permission of the Librarian, of course)
and I devoured its pages.

I do not intend to give a minute account of this curious
work here; I merely indicate it to those of my readers who
enjoy pictures of a given period. In it they will find a gallery
of portraits penciled by a master; and, though most of these
sketches may be traced on barracks doors or on the walls of
taverns, yet they present the figures of Louis XIII, of Anne
of Austria, of Richelieu, of Mazarin and of most of the
courtiers of the period quite as vividly and faithfully as
Monsieur Anquetil does in his *History of France*.

Now, as everybody knows, what strikes the capricious
mind of the poet does not always impress the mass of readers. So while I admired, as others doubtless will admire, the

details I have just cited, my main preoccupation concerned a matter to which no one had paid the slightest attention previously.

In his *Memoirs,* Monsieur d'Artagnan relates that, on his first visit to Monsieur de Tréville, Captain of His Majesty's Musketeers, he met in the antechamber three young men belonging to the illustrious corps in which he was soliciting the honor of enrolling. Their names were Athos, Porthos and Aramis.

I must confess these three foreign names struck me. I immediately decided that they were pseudonyms under which D'Artagnan disguised names that were perhaps illustrious. Or else, perhaps, the bearers of these names had themselves chosen them on the day when, thanks to a whim, or discontent, or exiguity of fortune, they donned the uniform of a ranker in the Musketeers.

From then on I knew no rest until I could find some trace in contemporaneous works of these three names which had aroused my passionate curiosity.

The mere catalogue of the books I read with this object in view would fill a whole chapter, which might prove highly instructive to my readers but would certainly not amuse them. Suffice to say that, just as, discouraged at so much fruitless investigation, I was about to abandon my quest, I at last found what I was after. Guided by the counsels of my illustrious and erudite friend, Paulin Pâris, I consulted a manuscript in folio—Number 4772 or 4773, I forget which, in the catalogue of the Royal Library—entitled *Memoirs of Monsieur le Comte de la Fère,* concerning some events in France toward the end of the reign of Louis XIII and the beginning of the reign of Louis XIV.

The reader may imagine my immense joy when in this manuscript, my last hope, I came upon the name of Athos on Page 20, of Porthos on Page 27, and of Aramis on Page 31.

The discovery of a completely unknown manuscript, at a period in which the science of history has progressed to such an extraordinary degree, seemed to me to be almost miraculous. I therefore hastened to ask for permission to print it in order to present my candidacy to the Académie des Inscriptions et Belles Lettres on the strength of another's work in case I could not enter the Académie Française on the strength of my own—which is exceedingly probable! I must add that this permission was graciously granted. I do so in order publicly to refute the slanderers who maintain that we live under a government scarcely favorable to men of letters.

It is the first part of this precious manuscript which I now offer to my readers, restoring the fitting title that belongs to it.

Should this first part meet with the success it deserves (of which I have no doubt) I hereby undertake to publish the second part immediately.

In the meantime, since godfathers are second fathers, as it were, I beg the reader to hold myself and not the Comte de la Fère responsible for such pleasure or boredom as he may experience.

This being understood, let us proceed with our story.

THE

Three Musketeers

CHAPTER 1:

Our Hero Sets Forth

THE town of Meung was used to disturbances of one sort or another because of the troublous times. But on the first Monday in April, 1625, it appeared as though pandemonium had broken loose. The citizens, bolstering up their uncertain courage, rushed to an inn called *The Jolly Miller*.

Panics were frequent in France at that period. There were the nobles fighting among themselves, the King making war upon the Cardinal, and Spain battling against the King. There were brigands, beggars, wolves and knaves who attacked all comers.

And today, what was the cause of the riot? No armies, no brigands, no beggars, no wolves. Only a simple young man called D'Artagnan, who came out of the deep South of France. He boasted a steed so noteworthy that no man could fail to take note of it. A nag, it was, twelve or fourteen years old, with a yellow coat and hairless tail, and not without swellings on its legs. This fact proved all the more painful to our hero, because he knew how ridiculous such a steed made him. Indeed, he had heaved a deep sigh as he accepted this gift from his father. But the words accompanying the gift were beyond all price.

"My son," said the old Gascon gentleman, "this horse was born in your father's house some thirteen years ago. Never sell it! If you go to Court, remember you are a nobleman and have a right to do so. Endure nothing from anyone save the Cardinal and the King. Nowadays a gentleman makes his way by his courage. Never avoid a quarrel: seek out the hazards of high adventure."

After a pause, D'Artagnan's father went on:

"I have nothing to give you, my son, except fifteen crowns, my horse and the advice you have just heard. To these, your mother will add a recipe for a balsam which she acquired from a gypsy woman. It possesses the miraculous virtue of curing all wounds which do not reach the heart. Take advantage of everything that comes your way; live happily and long!" Then: "One word more," the old man added. "I would wish to propose an example for you. I mean Monsieur de Tréville. He was formerly my neighbor. As a child, he had the honor of being the playmate of our King, Louis XIII, whom God preserve! He is Commanding Officer of the Regiment of Musketeers. Go to him with this letter. And model your behavior upon his. Accomplish what he has accomplished."

Leaving his father, the young man went to his mother's apartment where she awaited him with that sovereign balm which he was to use so often in later days.

Madame d'Artagnan wept copiously, and he, too, shed tears.

And now, far away from his parents, the youth was in the town of Meung, and already had started a riot. It all happened like this:

At the inn he spied, through an open window on the ground floor, a gentleman of fine figure and proud, though sullen, mien. This person was talking to two others. The

*"Go to him with this letter. And model
your behavior upon his."*

gentleman was discussing D'Artagnan's horse. The audience was laughing.

D'Artagnan first wished to examine the insolent fellow who dared make mock of him. His haughty glance fell upon the stranger, a man of forty, pale of complexion, with piercing black eyes, a nose boldly fashioned, and a black, impeccably trimmed mustache. D'Artagnan had a presentiment that this stranger was to exercise a powerful influence on his future.

The man kept on mocking him and the man's two auditors roared with laughter. This time, there could be no doubt whatsoever: D'Artagnan had been truly insulted. Convinced of it, he pulled his beret down over his eyes and stepped forward, his right hand on the hilt of his sword.

"Look here, Monsieur!" he cried. "Look here—yes, I mean *you*— Look here! Tell me what you are laughing at!"

"I am not aware that I was addressing you, Monsieur."

"Never mind," countered D'Artagnan, "*I* was addressing *you!*"

The stranger eyed him again, smiled fleetingly as before and, withdrawing from the window, walked slowly out of the inn.

Seeing him approach, D'Artagnan drew his sword a full foot out of its scabbard.

"Upon my word, this horse is certainly a buttercup!" observed the stranger.

"Laugh all you will at my horse," said D'Artagnan angrily. "I dare you to smile at his master!"

"As you may judge from my features, Monsieur, I do not laugh frequently," the stranger replied. "But I intend to laugh when I please."

"As for me," cried D'Artagnan, "I will allow no one to laugh at *me!*"

"Well, Monsieur, I dare say you are right." The stranger edged away. But D'Artagnan was not the type of youth to suffer anyone to escape him, least of all a man who had ridiculed him so impudently. Drawing his sword at long last and for cause, he ran after the stranger, crying: "Turn about, turn about, Master Jester! Must I strike you in the back?"

"*You* strike *me?*" The stranger surveyed the young man with astonishment and scorn. "Come, lad, you must be crazy." Then, in subdued tones, as though talking to himself, "What a bore!" he sighed.

He had barely finished speaking when D'Artagnan lunged at him so impetuously that this jest might have been his last. The stranger drew his sword, saluted D'Artagnan and took up his guard. But suddenly, at a sign, the two onlookers, backed up by the innkeeper, fell upon D'Artagnan with shovels, tongs and an iron pot. While this sudden onslaught held D'Artagnan, the stranger sheathed his sword as readily as he had drawn it.

"A plague upon these Gascons!" he muttered. "Put him back on his orange nag and away with him!"

"Not before I kill you!"

"Another Gascon boast! Really, these Gascons are incorrigible! Keep up the dance then, since that is what he wants! When he is tired, we will cry quits."

But D'Artagnan was never one to knuckle under. So the fight went on for a few seconds more, until D'Artagnan, exhausted, dropped his broken sword. Simultaneously, a cudgel struck him squarely on the forehead, bringing him to the ground bloody and almost unconscious.

It was at this moment that the citizenry of Meung came flocking from all sides to the scene of action. The host, fearing a scandal, carried the wounded man into the kitchen where some trifling attentions were administered.

As for the stranger, he had resumed his stand at the window whence he stared somewhat impatiently upon the mob.

"Well, how is this madman doing?" he inquired as the host poked his head through the door.

"He is better now. He fainted quite away, but before he fainted, he gathered all his strength to challenge and defy you!"

"Why, this fellow must be the devil in person!"

"Oh no, Your Excellency, he is no devil." The host shrugged his shoulders disparagingly. "We searched him and rummaged through his kit. All we found was one clean shirt and twelve crowns in his purse, which didn't stop him from cursing you roundly."

"Come, come, my dear host, while your young man was unconscious, I'm sure you did not fail to look into his pocket. What did you find?"

"A letter addressed to Monsieur de Tréville, Captain of the Musketeers."

"Indeed! Where is the fellow?"

"Upstairs in my wife's room. They are dressing his wounds."

"Did you take his rags and kit up? Did he remove his doublet?"

"All his stuff is downstairs in the kitchen. But if this young fool annoys you—"

"He annoys me very much. He has caused an uproar in your hostelry, a thing which respectable people cannot abide. Go upstairs, man, make out my bill, and summon my lackey."

"What! Is Monsieur leaving us already?"

"Of course. I told you to have my horse saddled. Have you done so?"

"Yes indeed, Your Excellency," the host said and, examining the stranger, "Can he be afraid of this stripling?" he wondered.

An imperious look from the stranger sent him about his business and, bowing humbly, he withdrew.

"Milady must on no account be seen," the stranger mused. "She will be passing through here soon; I daresay I had better ride out to meet her. If only I knew what was in this letter to Tréville." Mumbling to himself, he made off for the kitchen.

Meanwhile the host, certain that the youth's presence had driven the stranger from his hostelry, ran upstairs to his wife's room. There he found D'Artagnan, who had at last come to. Suggesting that the police would handle the youth pretty roughly for having picked a quarrel with a great lord, he persuaded D'Artagnan, weak though he was, to get up and be off.

D'Artagnan rose. He was still only half-conscious, he had lost his doublet, and his head was swathed in a linen cloth. Propelled by the innkeeper, he worked his way downstairs. But as he reached the kitchen, the first thing he saw was the stranger standing with one foot on the step of a heavy carriage.

He was chatting urbanely with a lady who leaned out of

the window of the coach to listen. She must have been about twenty-five years of age. D'Artagnan was no fool; at a glance, he perceived that this woman was young and beautiful, her beauty the more striking because it differed so radically from that of the South, where he had always lived. She was pale and fair, with long curls falling in profusion over her shoulders; she had large blue, languishing eyes, rosy lips and hands of alabaster. She was talking vivaciously to the stranger.

"So the Cardinal orders me—?"

"To return to England at once. Should the Duke of Buckingham leave London, you are to report directly to the Cardinal."

"Any other instructions?" the fair traveler asked.

"They are in this box here. You are not to open it until you reach England."

"Very well! And you? What will you do?"

"I go back to Paris."

"Without chastising that insolent youth?" the lady objected.

The stranger was about to reply. But before he could open his mouth, D'Artagnan, who had heard all, bounded across the doorsill.

"That insolent youth does his own chastising," he cried, "and this time, I trust, chastisement will not escape him!"

"Will not escape him?" the stranger echoed, frowning.

"With a woman present, I dare hope you will not run away again."

The stranger grasped the hilt of his sword. Milady, seeing this, cautioned, "Remember that the least delay may ruin everything."

"You are right, Milady. Let us go our several ways!"

Bowing to the lady, the stranger sprang into his saddle. The coachman whipped up his horses and galloped off in one direction; the stranger tossed a purse to the landlord and cantered off in the other.

"Oh, you coward! you wretch! you bogus gentleman!" cried D'Artagnan, springing forward. But his wounds had left him too weak to bear the strain of such exertion. A giddiness swept over him, a cloud of blood rolled over his eyes, and he fell in the middle of the street, crying, "Coward! Coward! Coward!"

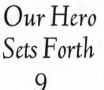

"A coward he is!" mine host agreed as he went to D'Artagnan's aid.

"Ay, he's a coward, a base coward!" D'Artagnan murmured. "But the lady! How beautiful she was!"

"Who?"

"Milady!" D'Artagnan faltered, as he fainted once again.

D'Artagnan rose next day at five o'clock, went down to the kitchen unaided, and requested several things. First, he asked for certain ingredients, the nature of which has not been transmitted to us. Then he asked for wine, oil and rosemary, and, his mother's recipe in hand, he concocted a balsam with which he anointed his numerous wounds. Thanks to the efficacy of the gypsy salve, the young man felt practically cured on the morrow.

D'Artagnan prepared to settle his score. In his pocket he found only his worn velvet purse and the twelve crowns which it contained. As for the letter to Monsieur de Tréville, it had vanished.

He began to search for it with utmost patience . . . to turn his pockets inside out . . . to rummage in his bag . . . to ransack his purse, opening it, closing it, and opening it again and again. Then, convinced at last that the letter was not to be found, he flew for the third time into such a fit of fury that he might easily have required a fresh supply of wine and aromatic oils. Mine host saw this young firebrand on the rampage and heard him vow to tear down the establishment if his letter was not forthcoming. Immediately he seized a spit, his wife seized a broom, and his servants the same cudgels they had used two days before.

"Give me my letter!" D'Artagnan kept shouting. "Give me my letter or I'll run you through like birds to be roasted."

"But where is that letter?" said mine host, lowering his spit.

"Ay, where *is* that letter?" D'Artagnan repeated. "Let me tell you that letter was addressed to Monsieur de Tréville. It *must* be found and if it isn't, Monsieur de Tréville will know the reason why!"

This threat completed the intimidation of the innkeeper.

After the King and the Cardinal, Monsieur de Tréville was probably the most important figure in the realm, a constant subject of discussion among soldiers and even citizens.

Throwing down his spit and ordering his wife and servants to cast away their respective weapons, the innkeeper himself inaugurated the search for the missing document.

"Was there anything valuable in your letter?" he asked.

"Good Heavens, I should say so!" cried the Gascon. Had he not been counting on this letter to speed his advancement at court? "It contained my whole fortune! Drafts on the Privy Treasury of His Majesty of France!" Having expected to enter the King's service on the strength of this recommendation, he believed himself justified in hazarding this somewhat misleading reply without incurring the dishonor of lying.

"God help us all!" wailed the host.

"It is of no moment!" D'Artagnan said with true Gascon calm. "It is of no moment! Money means nothing to me!" He paused. "But that letter meant *everything!* I would rather have lost one thousand golden coins than that letter!"

Just as the innkeeper, finding no trace of the letter, was about to commit himself to the devil, a ray of light pierced his skull.

"That letter is not lost," he said. "It was stolen from you!"

"Stolen? Who stole it?"

"The gentleman who was here the day before yesterday. He came down here to the kitchen and was alone here for quite a while. I'll wager he stole your letter."

"You think so?" D'Artagnan asked.

"Sure as I stand here! I told him you had a letter for this illustrious gentleman. He asked me where the letter was and went straightway down to the kitchen."

"He's the thief, then!" D'Artagnan scowled. "I shall com-

plain to Monsieur de Tréville, and Monsieur de Tréville
will complain to the King."

Majestically, he drew two crowns from his purse, handed
them to the innkeeper, and made for the gate. The yellow
nag awaited him; he leaped into the saddle and rode off.
His steed bore him without further misadventure to Paris,
where its owner sold it for three crowns. The dealer to
whom D'Artagnan sold it did not fail to make it clear that
he was disbursing this exorbitant sum solely because of the
originality of the beast's color.

So D'Artagnan entered Paris on foot, carrying his kit under his arm, roaming the city until he found a room suited
to his scanty means. It was a sort of garret situated in
Gravediggers' Row, near the Luxembourg Palace.

Having paid a deposit, D'Artagnan took possession of his
lodging and spent the rest of the day sewing. His specific
task was to stitch onto his doublet and hose some ornamen-
tal braiding which his mother had ripped off an almost new
doublet of her husband's and given to her son secretly.
Next he repaired to Armorers' Quay to have a new blade
put to his sword. Then he walked back toward the Louvre,

the Royal Palace, to ask the first musketeer he met where Monsieur de Tréville's mansion was. It proved to be quite close to where D'Artagnan had taken a room. The circumstance appeared to him to augur well for the success of his journey. Next day D'Artagnan would call on Monsieur de Tréville.

Monsieur de Tréville had begun life exactly as D'Artagnan. He had marched on the capital without a sou to his name; but he possessed a wealth of audacity, shrewdness and intelligence. His insolent bravery sped him to the top of that difficult ladder called Court Favor.

Monsieur de Tréville was a friend of the reigning king, Louis XIII, who venerated the memory of his father, Henry IV. Now, Monsieur de Tréville's father had served Henry IV with unfailing loyalty during the Wars of Religion, and when he died he left his son his sword and his motto as sole inheritance. Thanks to this double gift and the spotless name that accompanied it, Monsieur de Tréville was admitted into the household of the young prince. There he made such good use of his sword and proved so faithful to his motto that King Louis XIII had a genuine liking for Tréville and appointed him Captain of the Musketeers, who were fanatically loyal to Louis XIII.

Monseigneur Cardinal, Duc de Richelieu, did not lag behind the King in this respect. Seeing the impressive elite Louis XIII had recruited, the Cardinal, who was the actual ruler of France, determined to have his own private guard too. Thus there were two corps of guards, the King's and the Cardinal's, and these two powerful rivals vied with each other in attracting the most celebrated swordsmen. Over their evening games of chess, Cardinal and King argued the merits of their respective soldiery. Officially, they condemned all duels, but privately they incited their henchmen to quarrel, deriving immoderate pleasure in victory or acute chagrin in defeat.

Loose in their ways, battle-scarred, the Musketeers roamed the city. They were to be seen lounging in the taverns or strolling in the public walks shouting, twirling their mustaches and rattling their swords. They took immense pleasure in jostling the Guards of Monseigneur Cardinal when they met. Then they would draw their swords in the open street, amid a thousand jests, as though it were all the greatest sport in the world. Sometimes they were killed, but they died certain of being mourned and avenged; often they did the killing, but they were certain of not languishing in jail, for Monsieur de Tréville was there to claim them.

Monsieur de Tréville employed his musketeers on behalf of the King and the King's friends in the first place, then, in the second place, on behalf of himself and his own friends. The Captain of the Musketeers was admired, feared and loved, a state which constitutes the zenith of human fortune.

Tréville's mansion resembled an armed camp. Groups of fifty or sixty musketeers appeared to replace one another in relays so as always to present an imposing number. They paraded ceaselessly, armed to the teeth and prepared for any eventuality. In quest of favors, the office-seekers of Paris sped up and down those colossal staircases; there were gentlemen from the provinces eager to enroll in the Musketeers, and flunkeys in brilliant, multicolored liveries. In the antechamber, on long circular benches, sat the elect, that is to say those fortunate enough to have been summoned. A perpetual buzzing reigned in this room from morning till night while Monsieur de Tréville, in an adjoining office, received visits, listened to complaints and gave his orders.

Entering through the massive door with its long, square studs, D'Artagnan walked into the midst of a troop of swordsmen crossing one another as they passed, calling out, quarreling and playing tricks on one another. He advanced with beating heart through this tumult and confusion, holding his long rapier tight against his lanky leg and keeping one hand on the brim of his felt hat. Having got past one group, he breathed more easily, but he realized that people were turning round to stare at him and, for the first time in his life, D'Artagnan felt ridiculous.

Things were still worse when he reached the staircase to be confronted with the following scene: Four musketeers were amusing themselves fencing. Three were on the bottom steps; a fourth, some steps above them, naked sword in

Our Hero Sets Forth

15

hand, prevented or attempted to prevent the three from ascending, as they plied their agile swords against him. Ten
or twelve comrades waited on the landing to take their turn
at this sport. At first D'Artagnan mistook these weapons for
foils and believed them to be buttoned, but he soon recognized by the scratches inflicted that every weapon was
pointed as a needle and razor-sharp. Incidentally, at each
scratch one of the fencers dealt an adversary, both spectators and the actors themselves roared with laughter.

At the head of the stairs, the musketeers were not fighting, they were exchanging crude jokes; in the antechamber
they were exchanging stories about the Court. On the landing, D'Artagnan blushed; in the antechamber he shuddered. If his love of decency was shocked on the landing,
his respect for the Cardinal was scandalized in the antechamber. There, to D'Artagnan's amazement, they were
loudly and boldly criticizing the policy which made all Europe tremble. What! Was it possible that the great man
whom Monsieur d'Artagnan the elder revered so deeply
served as an object of ridicule to musketeers? D'Artagnan
could scarcely believe his ears as he heard these soldiers
cracking jokes about His Eminence's bandy legs and His
Eminence's crooked back.

"Upon my word, these fellows will all be imprisoned and
hanged!" D'Artagnan thought. Needless to add, he dared
not join in the conversation. But he was all eyes and all
ears, jealous lest he miss the merest detail. Despite his faith
in the paternal injunction, his tastes and instincts led him
to praise rather than to blame the unheard-of things he was
witnessing.

Presently a flunkey went up to him and asked what he
wanted. D'Artagnan gave his name very modestly and requested a moment's audience. The servant, with a somewhat patronizing air, promised to transmit his request in
due time.

D'Artagnan, recovering from his first surprise, now had

leisure to examine the persons and costumes of those about him.

The center of the most lively group was a very tall, haughty-looking musketeer dressed in so peculiar a costume as to attract general attention. He was wearing a sky-blue doublet, somewhat faded and worn, and over it, a long cloak of crimson velvet that fell in graceful folds from his shoulders. Across his chest, from over his right shoulder to his left hip, blazed a magnificent shoulder belt, called a baldric, worked in gold and twinkling like rippling waters in the sun. From it hung a gigantic rapier.

This musketeer, who had just come off guard, coughed affectedly from time to time and complained of having caught a cold. That was why he was wearing his cloak, he explained to those around him, speaking with a lofty air and twirling his mustaches disdainfully.

"After all, baldrics are coming into fashion," said the musketeer. "It was wildly extravagant of me, but still they're the fashion! Besides, a man must spend his money somehow."

"Porthos, that baldric came from the heavily veiled lady I met you with two Sundays ago over by the Porte Saint-Honoré."

"No, by my honor, I bought it myself!" the man designated as Porthos protested. "I paid twelve pistoles for it." The general wonderment grew but the general doubt persisted. "Didn't I, Aramis?" he concluded, turning to still another musketeer.

The companion whose corroboration he invited offered a perfect contrast to Porthos. Aramis was a young man twenty-three years old at most, with a delicate and ingenuous countenance, black, gentle eyes and tenuous mustaches that marked a perfectly straight line over his upper lip. He seemed mortally afraid to lower his hands lest their veins swell up; he would pinch his ear lobes from time to time to preserve their smooth, roseate transparency.

Porthos and Aramis then began arguing about Court gossip, the former growing even more violent and explosive, the latter milder and more witty. Presently, conceding Aramis the victory, Porthos cried, "What a wit this lad Aramis is! What a pity you did not follow your early vocation! What a delightful abbé you would have made!"

"A temporary postponement!" Aramis answered, flicking an imaginary speck of dust off his sleeve. "Some day I *shall* be a priest! Why do you suppose I am going on with my theological studies?"

"My dear Aramis, make up your mind. Are you to be an abbé or a musketeer? Be one or the other, not both." Porthos paused. "You know what Athos told me the other day? He said you were all things to all men—and women."

Aramis raised his arm violently.

"Come, let us not get angry," Porthos urged.

Again Aramis made an impatient gesture.

"Good Heavens, don't bother to tell us about your luck with the ladies," Porthos said. "No one wants to discover your secret; everybody knows you for a model of discretion."

Aramis looked at his friend. He sighed. "Porthos," he declared, "you are vain as Narcissus. I have told you this before, I tell you again. You know how I loathe moralizing, unless Athos does it. As for yourself, my fine friend, your baldric is far too magnificent to chime with your philosophy. If I care to become an abbé, I shall do so. Meanwhile I am a musketeer. I am pleased to say that I find you very boring."

Their comrades hastily interfered: "Come, come, gentlemen. . . . Stop, Porthos. . . . Look, Aramis. . . . After all, he didn't mean it. . . . Now, now. . . ."

The door of Monsieur de Tréville's study flew open. A lackey stood on the doorsill.

"Monsieur de Tréville will receive Monsieur d'Artagnan," he announced.

CHAPTER 2:

Of a Shoulder, a Baldric and a Handkerchief

MONSIEUR DE TRÉVILLE greeted his young caller politely. D'Artagnan bowed to the ground and in his sonorous Gascon accent paid his profound respects. His southern intonation and diction reminded Monsieur de Tréville of his own youth and his country. But before bidding D'Artagnan be seated, Monsieur de Tréville stepped toward the antechamber and called three names: "Athos! Porthos! Aramis!"

At his summons, only two soldiers appeared, the musketeer of the golden baldric and the musketeer who would be an abbé. No sooner had they entered than the door closed behind them. Though they were not quite at ease, D'Artagnan admired their bearing; they were at once carefree, dignified and submissive. Monsieur de Tréville was pacing up and down in silence, his brows knit. The musketeers stood smartly at attention, as if on parade. Suddenly he stopped squarely in front of them, wheeled round to face them, and, surveying them angrily from top to toe: "Do you gentlemen know what the King said to me no later than yesterday evening?" he demanded.

There was a moment's silence. Then one of them replied, "No— No, Monsieur, we do not."

"He told me that from now on he would recruit his musketeers from among the Cardinal's Guards."

"The Cardinal's Guards!" Aramis asked indignantly. "But why, Monsieur?"

"Because His Majesty realizes that his inferior wine needs improving by blending it with a better vintage."

The two musketeers blushed to the roots of their hair. D'Artagnan, completely in the dark about what was happening and considerably embarrassed, wished himself a hundred feet underground.

"Ay," Tréville went on, growing angrier apace. "Do you know what happened yesterday evening when the Cardinal was playing chess with the King? Well, I'll tell you. The Cardinal looked at me with a commiserating air which frankly vexed me. Then he told me that my daredevil musketeers had made a night of it in a tavern and that a patrol of his guards had been forced to arrest the rioters."

Monsieur de Tréville paused for breath.

"Come now, you must know something about it!" he resumed. "My musketeers—arrested! And you were among them, don't deny it. Come, Aramis, tell me, why did you ask me for a musketeer's uniform when a cassock would have suited you so much better? And you, Porthos? Of what use is that fine golden baldric of yours if all it holds up is a sword of straw? And Athos—by the way, where *is* Athos?"

"Monsieur," Aramis explained mournfully, "Athos is ill."

"Ill, you say? What's the matter with him?"

"We're afraid it's chicken pox, Monsieur," Porthos improvised, determined at all costs to take part in the conversation.

"The pox! Chicken pox at his age! No, I know better. He was probably wounded or killed, I dare say."

Tréville began pacing his office again, then turned fiercely on the culprits:

"Gentlemen, I will not have my men haunting disreputable places. Above all, I will not have them make themselves the laughingstock of the Cardinal's Guards. These guards are decent fellows, they are law-abiding and tactful, they do not put themselves in a position to be arrested. They would prefer dying in their tracks to yielding an inch. Whereas self-preservation, flight and surrender," he sneered, "seem to be the watchwords of His Majesty's Musketeers."

During his long censure, Porthos and Aramis were shaking with rage. They would cheerfully have strangled Tréville had they not felt that the great love he bore them made him speak thus. Their ordeal was the worse because they knew that Monsieur de Tréville's voice carried over into the antechamber. In a trice, from the door of the captain's office to the gate on the street, the whole mansion was seething.

"So His Majesty's Musketeers are arrested by the Cardinal's Guards, eh?" At heart Monsieur de Tréville was as furious as any of his soldiers. "Six of the Cardinal's Guards arrest six Royal Musketeers! Ha! I know what to do now. I shall go straight to the Royal Palace and submit my resignation as Captain of the Royal Musketeers."

"I beg your pardon, Captain," said Porthos, flaring up, "but the truth is that we were not evenly matched, six to six. They set upon us treacherously and unawares; before we could even draw our swords, two of our men were dead and Athos was grievously wounded. Meanwhile, we did not surrender, we were dragged forcibly away. Anyhow, before they got us into jail, we escaped."

"And Athos?"

"Well, Monsieur, they thought Athos dead and what point was there in carrying off a corpse?"

"I assure you, Monsieur, that I killed one guardsman with his own sword," Aramis put in. "Mine was broken at the first parry. I killed him or stabbed him."

Monsieur de Tréville appeared to be somewhat mollified.

"I did not know all this," he admitted. "From what I now hear, I suppose the Cardinal was exaggerating."

Profiting by the fact that his commanding officer seemed to have calmed down, Aramis hazarded:

"I beg you, Monsieur, not to say that Athos is wounded. He would be desperately unhappy if the King should hear of it. The wound is a very serious one; the blade passed through his shoulder and penetrated into his chest. So it is to be feared that—"

Suddenly the door opened, the tapestry curtain was raised, and a man stood on the threshold. He stood at attention, his noble head erect, his shoulders squared. His features were drawn, his face white.

"Athos!"

"Athos!" Monsieur de Tréville echoed in amazement.

"My comrades told me you had sent for me, Captain," the newcomer said in a feeble, yet perfectly even, voice.

He was in regulation uniform, buttons ashine, boots glittering, belted as usual for duty, every inch a soldier. With a tolerably firm step, he advanced into the room. Tréville, deeply moved by this proof of courage, sprang to meet him.

"I was telling these gentlemen that I forbid my musketeers to expose their lives needlessly," he explained. "Your hand, Athos!"

And without waiting for the other's reaction, Tréville seized his right hand and pressed it with all his might. In his enthusiasm he failed to notice that Athos, mastering himself as he did, could not check a twitch of pain. Athos turned even whiter than before. Suddenly Tréville felt the hand of Athos stiffen and, looking up, realized that Athos was about to faint. At that moment, Athos rallied all his energy to struggle against pain, but he was at length overcome, and fell to the floor like a dead man.

"A surgeon!" Tréville ordered. "My surgeon or the King's! Anyhow, the best surgeon you can find. Unless you fetch a surgeon, my friend Athos will die."

At this, many of the musketeers outside rushed into Monsieur de Tréville's office (for he was too occupied with Athos to close the door upon them) and crowded around the wounded man. Elbowing his way through the throng, a physician approached Athos and asked that he be removed to an adjoining room. Tréville immediately opened the door and pointed the way to Porthos and Aramis, who carried off their comrade in their arms. Behind them walked the surgeon, and behind the surgeon the door closed.

An instant later, Porthos and Aramis reappeared, leaving only the surgeon and Tréville at their friend's side. Presently Tréville himself returned. Athos, he said, had regained consciousness and, according to the surgeon, his condition need not worry his friends; his weakness was due wholly to loss of blood.

Then all withdrew save D'Artagnan, who did not forget that he had an audience and who, with Gascon tenacity, sat tight.

"Pardon me, my dear compatriot," Tréville said with a smile, "pardon me but I had completely forgotten you. You can understand that. A captain is nothing but a father charged with an even greater responsibility than the father of an ordinary family. Soldiers are just big children. But as I insist on the orders of the King, and more particularly the orders of the Cardinal, being carried out—"

D'Artagnan could not help smiling. Observing this, Tréville judged that he was not dealing with a fool and, changing the conversation, came straight to the point.

"I loved your father dearly," he said. "What can I do for his son? Tell me quickly, for, as you see, my time is not my own."

"Monsieur," D'Artagnan explained, "I intended to request you to enroll me in the Musketeers. But after what I have seen here during the last two hours, I understand what a tremendous favor this would be. I am afraid I do not deserve it."

"It is indeed a favor, young man, but perhaps not so far beyond your hopes as you believe or affect to believe. But I am sorry to have to tell you that no one is admitted to the Musketeers unless he has fought in several campaigns or performed certain brilliant feats or served at least two years in some other regiment less favored than ours." D'Artagnan bowed without replying. "However, on account of my old comrade, your father, I want to do something for you, as I said. I dare say you haven't brought any too much money up with you?"

D'Artagnan drew himself up proudly; his expression indicated clearly that he accepted alms of no man.

"Very well, young man, I understand," Tréville observed. "I know those airs; I myself descended upon Paris with four crowns in my purse and I would have fought with anybody who suggested that I could not buy the Royal Palace!"

D'Artagnan drew himself up even more proudly as he realized that, thanks to the sale of his nag, he was beginning his career with three crowns more than Tréville had possessed in similar circumstances.

"You ought, I say, to husband your resources, however great they may be, but you ought also to perfect yourself in exercises befitting a gentleman. I shall write a letter today to the director of the Royal Military Academy and he will admit you tomorrow at no expense to yourself. You will learn horsemanship, swordsmanship of all sorts, and dancing. You will make desirable acquaintances there and you can call on me from time to time."

D'Artagnan could not help feeling a certain coldness in this reception.

"Alas, Monsieur!" he mourned. "My father gave me a letter of introduction to present to you. Now I realize how much it would have helped me."

And he proceeded to relate the adventure of Meung, describing the unknown gentleman with the minutest detail and with a warmth and truthfulness that delighted Tréville.

"This is all very curious," Tréville declared after a moment's reflection. "You mentioned my name aloud then?"

"Yes, Monsieur, I confess I committed that imprudence. But why not? A name like yours must needs serve me as a shield on my journey."

Flattery was very current in those days and Tréville loved incense as well as any king or cardinal.

"Tell me," he asked, "did this gentleman have a slight scar on his cheek?"

"Yes, the kind of scar he might have if a bullet had grazed him. . . ."

"Wasn't he a fine-looking man?"

"Yes, splendid."

"Tall? Fair complexion? Brown hair?"

"Yes, Monsieur, that's right, that's the man!"

"He was waiting for a lady?"

"Yes, and he left after talking to her for a few moments."

"Was this woman English?"

"He called her Milady."

"It is *he*, it *is* he!" Tréville murmured. "I thought he was still at Brussels."

"Oh, Monsieur, if you know this man, pray tell me who he is and where he comes from. It would be the greatest favor you could possibly do me. If you will, then I shall release you from all your promises, even that of helping me eventually to join the Musketeers. The only thing I ask of life is to avenge myself!"

"Beware of trying any such thing, young man," Tréville cautioned. "On the contrary, if you ever see him on one side of the street, make sure to cross to the other."

"That will not prevent me, if ever I meet him, from—"

Suddenly Tréville eyed D'Artagnan suspiciously. This theft seemed an improbable thing at best. Might not the Cardinal have sent this youth to set a trap for Tréville?

His eyes fixed upon D'Artagnan's, he spoke slowly: "My boy, your father was my old friend and comrade. I believe this story of the lost letter to be perfectly true and I should like to dispel the impression of coldness you may have remarked in my welcome. Perhaps the best way to do so would be to reveal to you, a novice as I once was myself, the secrets of our policy today."

He then went on to explain to D'Artagnan how the King and the Cardinal were the best of friends; their apparent bickering was only a stratagem intended to deceive fools. He assured D'Artagnan of his devotion to both these all-powerful masters; the Cardinal, he added, was one of the most illustrious geniuses France had ever produced.

"Now, young man, rule your conduct accordingly. If for family reasons or through your friends or through your own instincts, even, you entertain such enmity for the Cardinal as we are constantly discovering, then let us bid each other adieu. I will help you as much as I can but without attaching you to my person."

There was a long pause.

"I hope my frankness will at least make you my friend," Monsieur de Tréville said at last, "because you are the only young man to whom I have ever spoken like this."

"I came to Paris with just the intentions you advise me to harbor, Monsieur," D'Artagnan replied candidly. "My father warned me to follow nobody but His Majesty, the Cardinal and yourself—whom he considered the three leading personages in the realm of France."

(Monsieur d'Artagnan the elder had indicated only Louis XIII and Richelieu, but his son thought the addition of Monsieur de Tréville would do no harm.)

"You are an honest lad. But at present I can do for you no more than what I just offered. The Tréville mansion will always be open to you. In time, you will probably achieve what you desire."

"You mean, Monsieur, when I have proved myself worthy?" said D'Artagnan. And, with all the familiarity of Gascon to Gascon: "Well, you may rest assured, you will not have to wait long!"

Whereupon he bowed, to take his leave, as if he considered the future putty in his hands to shape as he willed.

"Wait, wait!" Tréville laid a hand on his arm. "I promised you a letter to the director of the Royal Academy."

Tréville left D'Artagnan in the embrasure of the window, where they had been talking, and moved to his desk to write the promised letter. Meanwhile, D'Artagnan drummed a tattoo on the windowpane, and amused himself by watching the musketeers.

The letter finished, Monsieur de Tréville sealed it. Suddenly, to his amazement, his protégé turned crimson with fury.

"What's the matter?"

D'Artagnan leaped across the room, crying, "By Heaven, he'll not slip through my fingers this time!"

"Who?"

"My thief!" D'Artagnan shouted as he rushed from the room. "Ah, coward! Traitor! At last!"

Mad with anger, D'Artagnan was darting toward the stairs when, in his furious rush, he collided head foremost with a musketeer. As D'Artagnan butted the man's shoulder, the other uttered a cry.

"Excuse me," said D'Artagnan, trying to start off again. "Excuse me but I am in a hurry."

He had scarcely gone down the first step when a hand of iron seized him by the belt.

"Oh! you're in a hurry, eh?" said the musketeer, blanching. "You're in a hurry, so you run right into me and you say 'Excuse me' and you expect me to take it? Not at all, my lad. You heard Monsieur de Tréville speak somewhat cavalierly to us today and you think we can take that sort of thing from anybody. Let me set you straight, comrade, you are not Monsieur de Tréville."

D'Artagnan recognized Athos, who, having had his wounds dressed by the doctor, was on his way home.

"I assure you I did not do it on purpose," D'Artagnan apologized. "As it was an accident, I said 'Excuse me.' Let me go, please, let me go about my business."

"Monsieur, you are far from courteous," Athos replied, loosing his hold of him. "It is obvious that you are newly come from some remote province."

D'Artagnan had already gone down several steps, but at this remark he stopped short.

"Monsieur," he growled, "I may come from a distance but I warn you, you are not the man to give me lessons in deportment."

"Perhaps."

"If I were not in such a hurry and if I were not chasing somebody—"

"Monsieur-the-gentleman-in-a-great-hurry, you can find me again without running after me, if you see what I mean."

"And where, if you please?"

"Near the Carmelite convent."

"At what time?"

"About noon."

"About noon. Very well. I shall be there."

And D'Artagnan set off as though borne by the devil, confident that he would overtake the man of Meung whom he had seen sauntering down the street. But at the main gate, he saw Porthos talking to the soldier on guard. Between the two of them there was just room for a man to pass. D'Artagnan, thinking he could whisk through, shot forward like an arrow between them. Unfortunately, he had not reckoned with the wind. As he was about to pass, a gust blew out the portly musketeer's long cloak and D'Artagnan landed right in the middle of it. Porthos doubtless had his own reasons for not wishing to abandon this essential part of his costume, for he pulled it toward him. D'Artagnan was thus rolled up inside the velvet by a rotatory movement attributable to the persistency of Porthos.

Hearing the musketeer swear, he tried to emerge from under the cloak which was blinding him and sought to find his way from under its folds. Above all he must avoid marring the virgin freshness of the baldric Porthos set such store by. Opening his eyes timidly, he found his nose glued between the musketeer's shoulders flat against the baldric.

Alas, like most things in this world which have but appearance in their favor, the baldric was aglitter with gold in front, but behind it was of ordinary buff. Vainglorious as he was, if Porthos could not afford a baldric wholly of gold, he would have at least one half of it. This explained the necessity of the cold he had complained of and the necessity for the cloak he sported.

"Confound it, you must be crazy to crash into people this way," Porthos grumbled as D'Artagnan kept wriggling behind him.

"Excuse me," said D'Artagnan, reappearing from under the giant's shoulder, "but I am in a great hurry. I was running after somebody and—"

"And you always go blind when you run, I suppose."

"No," D'Artagnan answered, somewhat nettled. "In fact, thanks to my eyes I can see a good many things other people don't."

And enchanted with his wit, he went off, still chuckling over the semi-golden baldric. Porthos, foaming with rage, was about to fall upon him.

"Later, later!" D'Artagnan admonished. "When you haven't your cloak on."

"At one o'clock, then, behind the Luxembourg Palace."

"Very well, then, at one o'clock."

D'Artagnan turned the corner of the street, looking care-

fully ahead and up and down the cross street. Then he inquired of passers-by if they had seen a person answering his enemy's description. He walked down as far as the ferry and came up again along other streets, but he found nothing, absolutely nothing. Yet this wild-goose chase helped him in a sense, for, fast as the beads of sweat ran down his forehead, his heart began to cool.

He retraced all the events that had occurred. In the first place, he had disgraced himself in the eyes of Monsieur de Tréville, who could not but consider his withdrawal somewhat rude; in the second and third, he had invited dangerous duels with two men, each capable of slaying three D'Artagnans—with two musketeers, in short.

"What a lunatic I was and what a clod I am! Poor brave Athos was wounded in the shoulder and I was fated to butt against it! Why he did not kill me then and there, Heaven only knows! As for Porthos—dear old Porthos!—my run-in with him was the drollest thing that ever happened to me!"

At the thought, the youth could not help roaring with laughter, but he looked very carefully about him to make sure lest his solitary laughter, unaccountable to any passer-by, be considered offensive. His mirth spent, he continued to talk to himself with all the amenity he believed to be his due:

"Look here, D'Artagnan my friend, if you escape (which seems to me highly improbable) you must learn to be perfectly polite in the future. To be mannerly and obliging does not make a man a coward. Look at Aramis, he is amiability and grace personified. Well, has anyone ever dreamed of calling him a coward? Certainly not, and I vow that from now on I shall take him as a model in everything. Ah, here he is!"

Aramis stood before the Royal Guards' headquarters chatting gaily with three gentlemen of the Guards. D'Artagnan, still full of his plans of conciliation and courtesy, approached the quartet. Aramis bowed his head slightly but did not smile. The four soldiers immediately broke off their conversation.

D'Artagnan at once perceived that he was intruding

upon them, but he was not familiar enough with the manners of the fashionable world to know how to extricate himself gallantly from a false position. He was racking his brains to find the least awkward means of retreat when he noticed that Aramis had dropped his handkerchief and,

doubtless by mistake, had placed his foot over it. Here, thought D'Artagnan, was a favorable opportunity to make up for his tactlessness. With the most polished air he could summon, he stopped and drew the handkerchief from under the musketeer's foot. Holding it out, he said, "Here, Monsieur, is a handkerchief I believe you should be sorry to lose."

Indeed, the handkerchief was richly embroidered and one of the corners bore a coronet and crest. Aramis, blushing excessively, snatched it from the Gascon's hand.

"Ah, ha, my most discreet friend," one of the guards said to Aramis, "will you insist you are not very fond of the charming lady who lent you one of her handkerchiefs?"

The glance Aramis shot at D'Artagnan was a declaration of mortal enmity. Then, resuming his usual suave air: "You are in error, gentlemen," he answered. "This handkerchief does not belong to me. As proof of what I say, here is mine in my pocket."

Whereupon he produced his own handkerchief. As he held it up, they could all see it was ornamented with a single cipher, its owner's.

But the others refused to be convinced by the musketeer's denial and teased him good-naturedly.

"The fact is," D'Artagnan hazarded timidly, "I did not see the handkerchief fall from the pocket of Monsieur Aramis. He had his foot on it, that is all. Seeing his foot on it, I thought it was his."

"And you were completely mistaken, Monsieur," Aramis replied coldly, indifferent to D'Artagnan's efforts at reparation.

As they all burst out laughing, the affair, as may be supposed, had no untoward sequel. After a moment or two, the conversation ceased, the three guardsmen and the musketeer shook hands cordially and went off in opposite directions.

"Now is my chance to make my peace with this gallant gentleman," D'Artagnan thought, and, agog with good intent, he hurried after Aramis.

"Monsieur, you will excuse me, I hope."

"Monsieur, allow me to observe that your behavior in this circumstance was not that of a gentleman."

"What, Monsieur! Do you suppose—?"

"I suppose you are not a fool, Monsieur. I also suppose that, though you come from Gascony, you must know that people do not step upon handkerchiefs without a reason."

"Monsieur," D'Artagnan replied, his naturally aggressive spirit gaining the upper hand over his pacific resolutions, "I am from Gascony, it is true; I need not tell you that Gascons are anything but patient. When a Gascon has begged to be excused once, even for a foolish act, he is convinced that he has already done once again as much as he should have."

"Monsieur, I am no bravo, thank Heaven! I am but a temporary musketeer. I fight only when I am forced to. This time you have involved a lady."

"*We* have involved a lady, you mean."

"Why were you so tactless as to give me back the handkerchief?"

"Why were you so clumsy as to drop it?"

"I said and I repeat, Monsieur, that the handkerchief was never in my pocket."

"Well, Monsieur, you have lied twice, for I saw it fall. Draw your sword at once, if you please!"

"Not here, Monsieur, we do not fight in the streets! And this building is filled with servants of the Cardinal!"

"I fight anywhere—"

"Monsieur is a Gascon?"

"Yes, this monsieur is a Gascon and he never postpones a duel through prudence."

"Prudence, Monsieur, is a somewhat useless virtue for musketeers, I know. But it is indispensable to churchmen. At two o'clock I shall have the honor of waiting for you at the Tréville mansion. There I shall let you know the best place and time we can meet."

The two young men bowed and parted.

"Decidedly, I shall not return from my duels," D'Artagnan mused. "But at least if I am killed, I shall be killed by a musketeer."

CHAPTER 3:

Musketeers and Guards

D'ARTAGNAN did not know a soul in Paris. He therefore went to his appointment with Athos without any friends to support him. He fully intended to offer the brave musketeer all suitable apologies, for he feared the usual outcome when a young, vigorous man fights against one who is weak from his wounds. If conquered, he doubles the value of his adversary's triumph; if victorious, he is accused of having taken an unfair advantage of a handicap.

Thinking over the different men he was about to fight against, D'Artagnan gained a clearer view of the situation. By offering a sincere apology, he hoped to make a friend of Athos, whose lordly air and austere bearing he admired immensely. Unless he were killed outright, he flattered himself that he could frighten Porthos with tales of the adventure of the baldric. As for the astute Aramis, D'Artagnan was not seriously afraid of him.

When D'Artagnan arrived, Athos had been waiting only five minutes. Twelve o'clock was striking.

Though Tréville's physician had dressed his wounds

D'Artagnan took off his hat and bowed deeply

afresh, Athos was still suffering. Seeing D'Artagnan draw near, Athos came courteously to meet him. D'Artagnan, for his part, took off his hat and bowed deeply.

"Monsieur, I have engaged two of my friends as seconds, but they have not arrived yet," Athos said.

"Monsieur," D'Artagnan answered, "I have no seconds. I arrived in Paris just yesterday. The only person I know in the city is Monsieur de Tréville."

"Monsieur de Tréville is the only person you know?"

"Yes, Monsieur."

"Look here, look here!" Athos grumbled. He was addressing D'Artagnan, yet half of what he said was for his own benefit. "If I kill you, I shall be taken for a child-slaying ogre."

"No one will say our fight was too one-sided," D'Artagnan protested. "After all, your wounds must be giving you considerable trouble."

"Ay, it is all very troublesome, I must confess. And you hurt me devilishly when you charged into me. But I shall fence with my left hand! I usually do so in such circumstances."

"Monsieur," said D'Artagnan, bowing again, "I assure you I am immensely grateful to you for your perfect courtesy."

"You are too kind," Athos replied, ever the gentleman. "Let us speak of something else, if you please." Then, as a twinge of pain seized him: "Oh!" he cried. "You certainly hurt me. My shoulder is on fire!"

"If you would permit me—" D'Artagnan ventured.

"What, Monsieur?"

"I have a wonderful balm for wounds. My mother gave it to me. I have had occasion to try it on myself."

"Well?"

"Well, after three days, when you are cured, I would still deem it a great honor to cross swords with you."

D'Artagnan spoke with a simplicity that did honor to his courtesy without casting the least doubt upon his courage.

"Upon my honor, Monsieur, there's a proposition I cannot but admire. But, however carefully we might try to guard our secret, people would learn we were about to fight and we would be prevented from doing so." Athos frowned as he looked at the horizon. "Confound it, will these fellows never come?"

"If you are in a hurry, Monsieur," D'Artagnan suggested in the same polite tone he had used before, "we might set to without your seconds."

"I like you for those words," said Athos, nodding graciously. "I see plainly that if we do not kill each other, I shall hereafter have much pleasure conversing with you." He had barely finished speaking when, looking up: "Here comes one of my friends!" he cried. To his surprise, D'Artagnan discerned the gigantic bulk of Porthos at the far end of the street.

"What! Is Monsieur Porthos one of your seconds?"

"Certainly. Does that disturb you?" He paused. Then, suddenly: "Look! here comes my second friend!" he said.

"What?" D'Artagnan cried, even more astonished than before. "Monsieur Aramis is your other friend?"

"Of course. Don't you know that we are the Three Inseparables?"

Meanwhile Porthos came up, waved his hand to Athos, then, noticing D'Artagnan, stopped short, gaping with surprise. Incidentally he had changed his baldric and left off his cloak.

"Well, bless me! What does this mean?" he asked.

"This is the gentleman I am to fight with," Athos explained.

"But *I* am going to fight with him too!"

"Not before one o'clock, Monsieur," D'Artagnan reminded him.

"And I too am to fight with this gentleman," Aramis announced, joining the group.

"Not until two o'clock," D'Artagnan replied as casually as before.

Aramis turned to Athos. "By the way, Athos, what are you fighting about?" he inquired.

"By my faith, I'm none too sure. As a matter of fact, he hurt my shoulder. What about you, Porthos?"

"I'm fighting—" Porthos blushed a deep crimson. "I'm fighting because I'm fighting!"

Athos, whose keen eye lost no detail of the scene, observed a faint sly smile steal over the young Gascon's lips.

"We had a slight disagreement about dress," D'Artagnan said.

"And you, Aramis?"

"Oh, ours is a theological quarrel." Aramis made a sign to D'Artagnan begging him to keep the cause of their difference a secret.

"And now that we are all here, gentlemen," D'Artagnan announced. "Allow me to offer you my apologies."

At the word "apologies," a cloud passed over the brow of Athos, a haughty smile curled the lips of Porthos, and a nod of refusal from Aramis proved more expressive than any words.

"Gentlemen, you do not understand me," D'Artagnan objected. "I am apologizing only in case I cannot settle my score with all three of you. Monsieur Athos has the first right to kill me, a fact which lessens the value of your claim, Monsieur Porthos, and makes yours, Monsieur Aramis, practically worthless."

With these words, accompanied by the most gallant gesture, D'Artagnan drew his sword. The blood had rushed to his head. It was high noon; the sun beat mercilessly down upon them. But at that moment D'Artagnan would cheerfully have tackled all the musketeers in the kingdom.

"It is very hot," Athos remarked, drawing his sword in his turn, "but I cannot take off my doublet. My wound has begun to bleed again."

"Well, then I will fight in my doublet, like yourself."

"When you please, Monsieur," said Athos.

"I was awaiting your orders, Monsieur," D'Artagnan replied, crossing swords. But the sound of the two blades clashing had barely died down when a company of the Cardinal's Guards turned the corner of the convent.

"The Cardinal's Guards!" Porthos cried. "Sheathe your swords, gentlemen!"

But it was too late; the combatants had been seen in a position which left no doubt of their intentions.

"Ho, there!" Jussac, the cardinalist leader, called. "Hallo, there, musketeers! So you're fighting here, are you? And the laws against dueling, what about *them?*"

"If we saw *you* fighting, I can promise you we would not try to interfere," Athos replied angrily. "Leave us alone!"

"Gentlemen," said Jussac, "we have our duty to accomplish. Sheathe, then, if you please, and follow us. And if you disobey," he warned, "we shall charge you."

"There are five of them," Athos said in a low voice, "and only three of us."

Athos, Porthos and Aramis huddled together as Jussac marshaled his men. This short interval was enough to convince D'Artagnan; he must choose between King and Cardinal and forever abide by his choice. To fight meant to disobey the law, to risk his head, to attract in one instant the enmity of a minister more powerful than the King himself. He perceived all this quite clearly and, to his credit, did not hesitate a second. Turning to the musketeers:

"Gentlemen," he said, "allow me to correct you. It seems to me that there are four of us."

"But you are not one of us," Porthos demurred.

"True, I wear no musketeer's uniform, but I have the

spirit of a musketeer and so I shall fight! Try me, gentlemen, and I swear on my honor that I will not leave this field if we are vanquished."

"Come along now, gentlemen, have you made up your minds to make up your minds?" Jussac asked.

"We are about to have the honor of charging you," Aramis answered, raising his hat with one hand and drawing his sword with the other.

At once the nine combatants rushed up to join battle furiously but not without method. Athos singled out a certain Cahusac, a favorite of the Cardinal's, Porthos paired off with Bicarat, and Aramis was faced with two adversaries. As for D'Artagnan, he was pitted against Jussac himself.

The young Gascon's heart beat as though it would burst —not with fear, for he welcomed danger—but with emulation. He fought like a furious tiger, turning dozens of times around his opponent and continuously changing his ground and his guard. At length these tactics exhausted Jussac's patience. Enraged at being held in check by an adversary he had dismissed as a mere boy, he lost his temper and began to make mistakes. Determined to have done with him, he sprang forward and lunged to the full extent of his reach, aiming a terrible thrust at D'Artagnan. The latter whipped his blade under Jussac's and lunged. Jussac fell like a log.

D'Artagnan then cast a swift, anxious glance over the field of battle. Aramis was able to look after himself. Bicarat and Porthos had just made counter-hits, but neither of these wounds was serious and they fought on ever more doggedly. Athos, wounded anew by Cahusac, grew increasingly pale but had not yielded an inch of ground.

D'Artagnan was therefore free to assist whom he pleased. While endeavoring to ascertain which of his comrades stood in greatest need, he caught a glance from Athos. Athos would have rather died than appealed for help, but he could look and, in that look, ask for assistance. D'Artagnan, divining what Athos meant, sprang to Cahusac's side with a terrible bound, crying:

"My turn, Monsieur le Garde; I am going to slay you!"

"No, no!" Athos cried to D'Artagnan, "don't kill him, lad! I have an old bone to pick with him. Just disarm him, make sure of his sword. That's it! Oh, well done, well done!" Athos cried, as he saw Cahusac's sword fly through the air and land twenty paces away.

Cahusac ran over to one of the guardsmen, whom Aramis had killed, seized his rapier and returned toward D'Artagnan. But on the way he met Athos, who had recovered his breath during the short respite. A few thrusts and Cahusac fell, pinked in the throat.

Meanwhile it was imperative to finish the fighting soon. There was danger of the watch coming by and picking up all the duelists, wounded or not, royalists or cardinalists. Athos, Aramis and D'Artagnan, surrounding Bicarat, called on him to surrender. Though one against four and wounded in the thigh, Bicarat was determined to hold out. Jussac, rising on his elbow, cried out to him to yield.

"They are four to one," Jussac remonstrated. "Leave off, I command you."

"Oh, if you command me, that's another thing," Bicarat agreed. "You are my superior officer, it is my duty to obey you."

And, springing backward, he broke his sword across his knee to avoid having to surrender it, threw the two pieces over the convent wall and crossed his arms, whistling a cardinalist air.

Bravery is always honored even in an enemy. The musketeers and D'Artagnan saluted Bicarat with their swords and returned them to their sheaths. Next, D'Artagnan, with the help of Bicarat, the only adversary still on his feet, carried Jussac, Cahusac and the guardsman Aramis had wounded, under the porch of the convent, leaving the dead man where he lay. Finally they rang the convent bell and, taking along four cardinalist swords as trophies of victory, they set out, wild with joy, for Monsieur de Tréville's mansion.

"If I'm not a musketeer yet," D'Artagnan told his new-found friends as they swung through the gateway of the Tréville mansion, "at least I've begun my apprenticeship, don't you think?"

The affair caused a sensation. In public Monsieur de Tréville scolded them roundly, but he congratulated them in private. That evening he went to the King's gaming table. His Majesty was winning and, being very miserly, was in an excellent humor. Seeing Tréville at a distance, the King cried:

"Come, come here so I may chide you. Do you know that the Cardinal has been complaining again about your musketeers, Captain? These musketeers of yours are devils incarnate and gallowsbirds all!"

Tréville hastened to deny the accusation. On the contrary, he insisted, his soldiers were kindly creatures and meek as lambs. He would personally warrant that they had but one desire, namely to draw their swords only in His Majesty's service.

"Hark at Monsieur de Tréville," the King commented. "Hark at the man! Anybody would imagine he was speaking about the members of a religious order."

Presently, luck at the gaming table turned against the King. As his winnings began to shrink, he was not sorry to find an excuse whereby to leave the table.

"Take my place," he told a courtier, "for I must speak to Monsieur de Tréville." Then, turning to Tréville, he walked toward the window.

"Well, Monsieur, how did it happen? Tell me all about it."

"Well, Sire, it was like this. Three of my best soldiers, Athos, Porthos and Aramis, decided to go on a jaunt with a young fellow from Gascony, so they decided to meet at the Carmelite convent. Here they were molested by De Jussac, Cahusac, Bicarat and two other guardsmen who certainly did not go there without intending to flout the laws against dueling. I do not accuse them, Sire. But I leave Your Majesty to judge what five armed men could possibly want in so deserted a place as the convent garden. Seeing my musketeers, the cardinalists changed their minds; their private grievances gave way to party hatred."

"So the Cardinal's Guards picked a quarrel with the King's Musketeers?"

"That probably happened, but I cannot swear to it, Sire."

"Your three musketeers were not alone. They had a youth with them."

"True, Sire, but one of the three was wounded. Thus the Royal Musketeers were represented by three soldiers, one of whom was wounded, plus a mere stripling. They stood up to five of the Cardinal's stoutest guardsmen and laid four of them low."

"What a victory for us!" The King beamed. "Four men, you say . . . one of them wounded . . . and a mere lad . . . his name?"

"D'Artagnan, Sire, the son of one of my oldest friends, the son of a man who served throughout the Civil War under His Majesty, your father. He is little more than a boy. But, Sire, Your Majesty can be proud of that lad. He pinked De Jussac, to the Cardinal's vast annoyance."

"I want to see him, Tréville, I want to see him. If anything can be done, we shall make it our business. . . ."

"When will Your Majesty deign to receive him?"

"Tomorrow at noon, Tréville."

"Shall I bring him alone?"

"No, bring all four of them, I wish to thank them at once."

"We shall report at noon tomorrow, Sire!"

"Good!" the King said. Then, fidgeting nervously: "Er—the back staircase, Tréville, come up the back staircase. There's no point in letting the Cardinal know—"

At eight o'clock next morning D'Artagnan called on Athos. As their audience was not till noon, Athos had arranged to play tennis with Porthos and Aramis. He invited D'Artagnan to join them.

Porthos and Aramis were already on the court, playing together; Athos, who was an excellent athlete, with D'Artagnan as a partner, challenged them. But though Athos played with his left hand, his first shot convinced him that his wound was still too recent to permit of such exertion. D'Artagnan therefore remained alone. Suddenly a smashing ball from Porthos just missed hitting D'Artagnan in the face. Had it done so, D'Artagnan would have been compelled to forego his audience with the King. So he bowed politely to Porthos and Aramis, declaring that he would not resume the game until he knew enough about it to play with them on equal terms. Then he returned to a seat in the gallery close to the court.

Unfortunately for D'Artagnan, one of the Cardinal's Guards was among the spectators.

"I am not surprised this youth is afraid of a tennis ball," he drawled. "He must surely be a 'prentice musketeer."

"Your words are too clear to require a commentary," D'Artagnan said. "I beg you to follow me out of here."

"Do you know who I am?" the other asked.

"What *is* your name?"

"Bernajoux, at your service."

"Well, Monsieur Bernajoux, I shall wait for you at the door."

Bernajoux was surprised that his name had made no impression on the Gascon, for he was known to everybody everywhere as an instigator of daily brawls. When they met at the door, D'Artagnan said:

"Upon my word, though you may be called Bernajoux, it is lucky you have only a 'prentice musketeer to deal with. But never mind, I shall do my best. On guard, please!"

"This is no place to fight," the other objected. "We would be better off elsewhere."

"Unfortunately, I have very little time to spare; I have an appointment at twelve sharp," D'Artagnan objected. "On guard, then, Monsieur, I beg you."

Bernajoux was not the man to entertain two requests to draw; an instant later, his sword glittered in the sunlight and he swooped down on D'Artagnan. D'Artagnan, fresh from a spectacular victory and fired by hopes of favors soon forthcoming, was determined not to budge an inch. So the two swords were hilt to hilt and, as D'Artagnan stood his ground, it was Bernajoux who had to retreat. In doing so, Bernajoux's sword deviated from the line of guard; D'Artagnan at once freed his blade by passing it under his adversary's, and lunged, pinking Bernajoux on the shoulder. Then D'Artagnan stepped back and, according to the rites of dueling, raised his sword to salute his defeated foe.

But Bernajoux would have none of it. Assuring D'Artagnan that he was unscathed, he rushed blindly at him, actually spitting himself upon the Gascon's sword. As he had not fallen, he refused to declare himself conquered. Instead, he kept retreating toward the mansion of the Duc de la Trémouille, in whose service he had a relative. By now the noise from the street had reached the tennis court. Two fellow-cardinalists rushed out, sword in hand, and swept down upon the Gascon. Close at their heels came Athos, Porthos and Aramis, and just as the cardinalists attacked D'Artagnan, the three musketeers intervened to drive them back. Bernajoux suddenly fell, exhausted. Since there were now four royalists against two cardinalists, the latter cried for help:

"To the rescue! To the rescue!"

Immediately, all those in the Trémouille mansion, coming to the aid of the cardinalists, fell upon the victors. Our four friends set up an antiphonal cry: "Musketeers, to the rescue!"

This appeal was widely and briskly heeded, for the musketeers, notorious foes of His Eminence, were correspondingly popular. The melee became general. Very soon, the musketeers and their allies prevailed; the Cardinal's guardsmen and Monsieur de la Trémouille's servants beat a hasty retreat into the Trémouille mansion, slamming the gates just in time to prevent their pursuers from entering after them. As for Bernajoux, he had been picked up and conveyed to safety early in the battle; his condition was critical.

Excitement was at its height among the musketeers and their supporters. Somebody suggested that they set fire to the Trémouille mansion to punish Monsieur de la Trémouille's servants for their insolence in daring to make a sally against the Royal Musketeers. But suddenly the clock struck eleven. D'Artagnan and his friends recalled their audience with the King, and because they could not fight it out then and there, they prevailed on their friends to retire. The royalists decided to hurl some paving stones against the gates, but the gates were too solid and they soon tired of the sport. Besides, the leaders of the enterprise had left the group and were on their way to the Tréville mansion. Arriving there, they found the Captain of Musketeers awaiting them; he had already been informed of their latest escapade.

"Quick, to the Royal Palace," he said. "We must get there before the King has been influenced by the Cardinal. We will describe this business as a consequence of yesterday's trouble and pass the two off together."

Accordingly the four young men and their commanding officer set off for the Royal Palace. To Tréville's amazement, he was told that the King had gone stag hunting in the forest of Saint-Germain.

"Did His Majesty see the Cardinal?" Tréville asked.

"Most probably, Your Excellency," the valet answered. "I saw the Cardinal's horses being harnessed. I asked where he was going and they told me to Saint-Germain."

"The Cardinal has stolen a march on us," Tréville told his protégés. "I advise you to return home to await further developments."

For his part, Tréville determined that he had best register an immediate complaint. He therefore despatched a servant with a letter to Monsieur de la Trémouille.

The two nobles met and exchanged polite greetings.

"Monsieur," said Tréville, "each of us believes that he has cause for complaint against the other. I have come here to attempt to clear up our misunderstanding."

"I am perfectly willing, Monsieur, but I warn you that I have made inquiries and that the fault lies wholly with your musketeers."

"How is Monsieur Bernajoux, your esquire's kinsman?"

"Very ill indeed."

"Is he still conscious?"

"Certainly."

"Can he talk?"

"Yes, but with difficulty."

"Well, Monsieur, let us go to his bedside and call upon him to tell us the truth."

La Trémouille thought the matter over for a moment, and agreed. Together he and Tréville repaired to the sickroom.

The upshot of it all was exactly as Tréville had foreseen. Hovering between life and death, Bernajoux made a clean breast of everything that had occurred. This was all that Tréville desired. Wishing Bernajoux a speedy convalescence, he took leave of La Trémouille, returned to his mansion and immediately sent word to the four friends, inviting them to dinner.

Toward six o'clock, Monsieur de Tréville announced that it was time to go. The hour of the audience granted by His Majesty was long since past. Still the King had not returned from hunting. The courtiers and others waited for about a half-hour. Suddenly all the doors were thrown open and an usher announced His Majesty the King. D'Artagnan trembled with anticipation; he was thrilled to the core, for he felt that the next few minutes would probably decide the rest of his life.

Louis XIII appeared, his henchmen in his wake. He was clad in dusty hunting dress; his high boots reached over his knees and he held a riding crop in his right hand. At first glance D'Artagnan realized that he was vexed.

"Things are going badly," Athos commented, smiling. "We shall not be appointed Knights of the Royal Order this time."

"Wait here for about ten minutes," Tréville told his protégés. "If I do not return by then, it will be useless to stay on."

Obediently they waited ten minutes, fifteen, twenty; finally, apprehensive of what might be happening, they withdrew.

Tréville marched boldly into the King's rooms to find a very glum Majesty, ensconced in an armchair, beating his boots with the handle of his riding crop. This did not prevent Tréville from inquiring after the royal health.

"Bad, Monsieur, bad as can be. I am bored stiff!"

"What? Bored? I thought Your Majesty had been hunting."

"Hunting, Monsieur? Fine pleasures indeed! I don't know whether it's because the game leaves no scent or because the dogs have no noses, but everything is wrong. Ah, I am a very unhappy monarch, Monsieur."

"Indeed, Sire, I understand your discomfort."

"And the Cardinal will not give me a moment's respite, what with his talk about Austria, about England, about Spain. Ah, speaking of the Cardinal, I am much annoyed at you."

Here was the chance Tréville had been waiting for.

"Have I been so unfortunate as to incur Your Majesty's displeasure?" Tréville asked, feigning the greatest astonishment.

"Is this how you perform your duties, Monsieur?" the King continued. "Did I appoint you Captain of Musketeers so that your men should assassinate a soldier, disturb a whole quarter and try to set fire to Paris, while you stand by without opening your mouth?" The King paused a moment, then added judiciously, "But perhaps I am too hasty in rebuking you. Doubtless the rioters are in prison and you have come to tell me that justice has been done."

"Sire," Tréville answered calmly. "On the contrary, I have come to ask *you* for justice."

"Against whom?"

"Against slanderers."

"Well, well, here is something new! I suppose you are going to tell me that your three musketeers, plus your lad from Gascony, did not fall upon poor Bernajoux like so many maniacs? Come now, can you deny this?"

"Who told you this fine story, Sire?"

"The prop of the State, my only servant, my only friend, the Cardinal!"

"The Cardinal is not infallible, Sire."

"Do you propose to tell me that the Cardinal is misleading me? Come, speak up!"

"Sire, I say that the Cardinal has been misled."

"The accusation comes from La Trémouille himself. What do you say to that?"

"Sire, I know La Trémouille to be an honorable gentleman. I therefore refer the whole thing to him—but on one condition, Sire!"

"Which is—?"

"That Your Majesty will summon him here and that you will question him in private."

"La Chesnaye!" the King called. "La Chesnaye!" The monarch's confidential valet, who never left the door, entered the room. "La Chesnaye," said the King, "send somebody immediately to find Monsieur de la Trémouille. I wish to speak to him this evening."

As the valet withdrew, Tréville turned to the King:

"Your Majesty promises not to see anyone else in the meantime?"

"I promise."

"Tomorrow, then, Sire?"

"Until tomorrow, Monsieur."

"If my musketeers are guilty, Sire, the culprits shall be delivered into Your Majesty's hands for you to dispose of them at your pleasure. Does Your Majesty require anything further?"

"No, Monsieur, no. I am not called Louis the Just without reason. Tomorrow, then, Monsieur, until tomorrow."

"Till then, and God preserve Your Majesty."

On the morrow, in the King's private antechamber, Tréville learned from La Chesnaye that they had not been able to reach La Trémouille at his mansion the night before, that he had only just arrived, and was even now closeted with His Majesty. Tréville was pleased at this news, for he could be certain that no foreign suggestion could insinuate itself between La Trémouille's testimony and himself. In fact, after some ten minutes, the door of the King's closet opened and La Trémouille came out.

"Monsieur de Tréville," said the duke, "I told the King the truth, namely that the fault lay with my people and that I was ready to apologize."

"Monsieur le Duc," Tréville replied, "I was so confident of your honor that I asked for no other defender before His Majesty. I see that I was not mistaken; I thank you."

Suddenly the King appeared upon the threshold.

"Well, Tréville," he asked, "where are your musketeers?"

"They are downstairs, Sire, and with your permission La Chesnaye will bid them come up."

"Yes, let them come up immediately."

The duke saluted and retired. As he opened the door, the three musketeers and D'Artagnan appeared.

"Come in, my brave lads," the King called. "Come in, I am going to scold you."

The musketeers advanced bowing, D'Artagnan close behind them.

"Seven of His Eminence's Guards crushed by you four in two days!" the King exclaimed. "One man, now and then, I don't mind much; but seven in two days, I repeat, is too many, far too many."

"As Your Majesty sees, my men have come, contrite and repentant, to make their apologies."

"A fig for their contrition and repentance," the King said. "I place no confidence in their hypocritical faces, particularly that Gascon face over there! Come here, Monsieur."

D'Artagnan, aware that the compliment was addressed to him, and assuming a most shamefaced air, stepped forward.

"Why, you told me he was a young man! This is a boy, Tréville, a mere boy! Do you mean to say it was he who dealt Jussac that master stroke?"

"Yes, and he accounted for Bernajoux as well."

"And besides this," Athos put in, "had he not rescued me from Bicarat, I would certainly not have the honor of making my very humble obeisance to Your Majesty at this moment."

"La, this lad from Gascony is a very devil! I suppose this sort of work involves the slashing of many doublets and the breaking of many swords. And Gascons are always poor, are they not? La Chesnaye, go rummage through all my pockets and see if you can find forty pistoles; if you do, bring me the money. And now, young man, tell me exactly how all this came about."

D'Artagnan related the adventure of the day before in full detail.

"That is what I fancied," the King murmured. "Your account agrees in every particular with La Trémouille's. Poor

Cardinal! Seven men in two days, and his very best men, too! But that will do, gentlemen, you hear, that will do. You have taken your revenge for the tavern brawl and even exceeded it; you ought to be satisfied."

"If Your Majesty is, then so are we," said Tréville.

"Yes, I am quite satisfied." Taking a handful of gold from La Chesnaye and putting it into D'Artagnan's hand: "Here you are!" the King said. "Here is proof of my satisfaction.

There," His Majesty added, looking at the clock, "there, now, it's half-past eight, you may withdraw. Thank you for your devotion, gentlemen; I can continue to rely upon it, I feel sure."

As they retired, he turned to Tréville and added, in a low voice, "I know you have no room in the Musketeers, so

I beg you to place this young man in the company of Royal
Guards commanded by Monsieur des Essarts, your brother-
in-law."

The Captain of Musketeers nodded affirmatively.

"Ah, Tréville, I rejoice to think of the face His Eminence
will make when he finds this out. He will be furious; but *I*
don't care."

CHAPTER 4:

A Court Intrigue

Having divided his money into four equal shares, D'Artagnan consulted his friends on what use he might best make of his portion. Athos suggested he order a good meal at an excellent tavern; Porthos urged him to engage a lackey; Aramis proposed he invite his three friends to a sumptuous banquet.

The banquet took place that very day, with the lackey serving them at table, for Athos had ordered the meal and Porthos had furnished the lackey. D'Artagnan's domestic was called Planchet; he hailed from Picardy. Porthos had picked him up by the river side, where he was leaning over the parapet watching the rings that formed as he spat into the water.

Athos, for his part, had a valet named Grimaud whom he had trained to serve him in a singularly original manner.

Although Athos was barely thirty years old, strikingly handsome and remarkably intelligent, he was never known to have had a sweetheart. His reserve, his severity and his silence made almost an old man of him. He had accustomed Grimaud to obey his slightest gesture or a mere movement of his lips. He spoke to him almost never.

Though Grimaud entertained a strong attachment to his master's person, he feared him as he feared fire. Sometimes, the silence and aloofness of Athos seemed almost inhuman.

Porthos was by character quite the opposite of Athos. Porthos not only talked much but he talked loudly and, to do him justice, without caring whether anybody was listening to him or not. He talked for the pleasure of talking. Less distinguished in bearing and manner than Athos, he was conscious of his inferiority.

An old proverb says: "Like master, like man." Porthos had a valet called Mousqueton, a Norman who agreed to serve Porthos on condition he be merely clothed and lodged, but handsomely; in return, he worked elsewhere two hours a day at a job which provided for his other wants.

As for Aramis, his lackey was named Bazin. Because his master hoped to take Holy Orders, the servant was always clad in black, as becomes the domestic of a churchman.

Athos had an apartment which consisted of two small rooms, agreeably furnished. The walls of his humble abode shone with vestiges of past splendors. There was, for instance, a richly embossed sword which obviously belonged to the age of François I; its hilt, studded with precious stones, was alone worth two hundred pistoles, then the equivalent of about eight hundred dollars. Yet in his moments of direst need, Athos had never sought to pawn or sell it. There was also a portrait of a nobleman of the time of Henry III, dressed with the greatest elegance and wearing the blue ribbon of the Order of the Holy Ghost, doubtless an ancestor of Athos.

Porthos lived in an apartment of vast dimensions and very sumptuous appearance. Whenever he chanced to stroll by with a friend, he would point to his windows, at one of which Mousqueton was certain to be standing, dressed in full livery, and, raising head and hand, exclaim sententiously:

"That is where I live!"

As for Aramis, his modest abode consisted of a study, a dining room and a bedroom, all on the ground floor, overlooking a tiny garden, green, cool, shady and safe from the eyes of prying neighbors.

D'Artagnan, curious like most enterprising people, did his best to discover the key to the real names of Athos, Porthos and Aramis. But Tréville alone possessed this secret. Vainly D'Artagnan sought to pump Porthos for information about Athos and to draw out Aramis on the subject of Porthos. All he could find out about Athos was that Athos had suffered crosses in love and that a tragic betrayal had poisoned his life.

The life of Porthos, except for his real name, was an open book; his vanity and indiscretion made him as transparent as crystal.

Aramis, while appearing anything but reserved, was a very repository of secrets; he replied meagerly to the questions asked him about others and he eluded those concerning himself.

"I'm only a temporary musketeer," he used to say, "a musketeer in spite of myself."

The life of the four young men was pleasant enough. Athos gambled and as a rule, unluckily; yet he never borrowed a sou from his companions though his own purse was ever at their service.

Porthos was erratic. When he won, he was insolent and splendiferous; when he lost, he disappeared completely for several days to reappear with money in his purse.

As for Aramis, he never placed a wager.

Planchet, D'Artagnan's lackey, endured his master's prosperity with noble zeal. But when the winds of adversity began to sweep across D'Artagnan's home—in other words, when Louis XIII's gift was more or less gone—he launched into complaints which Athos considered nauseous, Porthos unbecoming, and Aramis ridiculous. Athos advised D'Artagnan to dismiss the fellow; Porthos agreed but insisted that Planchet be roundly thrashed before being dismissed; Aramis contended that a good master should heed only the compliments paid him.

In winter the musketeers and D'Artagnan would rise at eight o'clock, in summer at six, and report immediately at Tréville's to receive orders. Though not a musketeer, D'Artagnan performed this duty with touching punctuality; he mounted guard whenever one or another of his friends was on duty.

The three musketeers thought the world of him. They would all meet three or four times daily, whether for dueling, business or pleasure. Each was the other's shadow and from one end of Paris to the other, they were soon known as The Inseparables.

Meanwhile Tréville was working on D'Artagnan's behalf as keenly as he had promised. One fine morning the King ordered Monsieur des Essarts to admit D'Artagnan as a cadet in his company of Royal Guards. As he donned the Guardsman's uniform, D'Artagnan sighed, for he would have given ten years of his life to exchange it for that of a Musketeer.

Meanwhile, D'Artagnan a Royal Guardsman, what could Athos, Porthos and Aramis do but reciprocally mount guard with him when he was on duty? Thus Monsieur des Essarts' company, by admitting one D'Artagnan, found itself four men the stronger.

Like all good things in this world, Louis XIII's gift having had a beginning, came to its appointed end. At first, Athos supported the group for a while out of his own pocket; next Porthos succeeded him and kept them going a fortnight; next Aramis came to the rescue with good grace and a few pistoles he had obtained, so he said, by selling some theological books; next, as they had done so often, they appealed to Tréville, who advanced them some money on their pay.

Finally, realizing they were about to fall into dire want, they managed by a last desperate effort to raise eight or ten pistoles with which Porthos was despatched to the gaming table. Unfortunately, he lost every sou.

Athos was invited to meals four times, Porthos six times and Aramis eight times; each time all the friends shared their good fortune. D'Artagnan unearthed a priest from his own province who supplied a light breakfast with chocolate, and a cornet of the Guards who furnished a dinner at his home.

His plight gave him considerable food—for thought! He came to the conclusion that this coalition of four young, brave, enterprising and active men ought to have some other object than swaggering about the city, taking fencing lessons and playing practical jokes that were more or less funny.

He was racking his brain to find a direction for this single force four times multiplied, and the longer he meditated, the surer he became that Athos, Porthos, Aramis and D'Artagnan would succeed in moving the world. Suddenly there was a light knock at the door; D'Artagnan awakened Planchet and ordered him to open it.

A stranger entered, obviously a simple bourgeois. D'Artagnan requested him to be seated. The two men looked at each other appraisingly. Then D'Artagnan bowed.

"I have heard Monsieur spoken of as a very courageous young man," the stranger said. "This well-deserved reputation emboldens me to confide a secret to him."

"Speak, Monsieur, speak."

The stranger paused, then went on:

"I have a wife who is seamstress to Her Majesty the Queen. My wife is not lacking in either virtue or beauty. Though she brought but a small dowry, I was induced to marry her about three years ago because Monsieur de la Porte, the Queen's cloak bearer, is her godfather and befriends her. Well, Monsieur, my wife was abducted yesterday morning."

"By whom was your wife abducted?"

"I know nothing for certain, Monsieur, but I have my suspicions. Let me add this, Monsieur: I am convinced that politics is at the bottom of this business."

"Politics?" D'Artagnan murmured with a thoughtful air. "What do you suspect?"

"Monsieur, I believe my wife was arrested because of a lady far mightier than herself."

"The Queen?" D'Artagnan hazarded.

"Yes, Monsieur," his terrified visitor replied.

"And in what connection?"

"In connection with the Duke of—."

"The Duke of—?" D'Artagnan repeated, hiding his ignorance and bewilderment.

"Yes, Monsieur," the stranger interrupted, even more faintly than before.

"But how do you know all this?"

"I know it through my wife, Monsieur."

"And your wife? Where did she learn this?"

"From Monsieur de la Porte. Didn't I tell you my wife is his goddaughter? And isn't he Her Majesty's most confidential retainer? Well, Monsieur de la Porte placed my wife near Her Majesty in order that our poor Queen might at least have someone she could trust, abandoned as she is by the King, spied upon by the Cardinal, and betrayed by everybody."

"Ah, your story is taking shape!"

"Now, my wife came home four days ago, Monsieur. I

must explain that she visits me twice a week. Well, she told me that Her Majesty was frightened."

"Indeed?"

"Ay, the Cardinal, it would seem, pursues and persecutes the Queen more than ever. His feelings are stronger than hatred now; he is moved by the lust of vengeance. And the Queen believes that someone has written to the Duke of Buckingham in her name."

"In the Queen's name?"

"Ay, in order to persuade him to come to Paris."

"What a tale! But what has your wife to do with all this, Monsieur?"

"Her devotion to the Queen is well known. Somebody therefore wishes either to remove her from her mistress or, by intimidating her, to learn Her Majesty's secrets."

"That seems plausible," D'Artagnan agreed. "But what about the man who abducted her? Do you know him?"

"As I said, I think I know him."

"His name?"

"That, I do not know. But I do know he is a creature of the Cardinal's. I have seen him."

"What does he look like?"

"He is a nobleman of lofty bearing . . . black hair . . . a swarthy complexion . . . eyes piercing as drills . . . very white teeth . . . and a scar on his cheek. . . ."

"Why, that's my man of Meung!" D'Artagnan gasped.

"Your man, you say?"

"Yes, yes! Where can I find this man?"

"I'm sure I don't know."

"Would you happen to know where he lives?"

"No. One day when I was accompanying my wife back to the Royal Palace, she pointed him out to me."

D'Artagnan cursed. Then: "Look here, how did you hear your wife had been abducted?"

"Monsieur de la Porte told me."

"Did he give you any details?"

"He knew none himself."

"Did you obtain any other information?"

"Well, I—"

"May I ask what your name is?"

"Bonacieux, at your service."

"Your name sounds familiar."

"Possibly, Monsieur; I am your landlord."

"Ah," D'Artagnan sighed, half bowing to his visitor. Pertinently, Bonacieux added:

"I realize you have not paid any rent in the last three months. I have not bothered you for it. So I hoped you might do me a favor in return. May I go on—"

"Surely."

Bonacieux took a sheet of paper from his pocket and presented it to D'Artagnan. Unfolding the paper, D'Artagnan read:

Do not look for your wife. She will be sent back to you when her services have ceased to be useful. If you but take one step to attempt to find her, you are irremediably lost.

"That is positive enough," D'Artagnan remarked. "But after all, it is merely a threat."

"Ay, but a threat that terrifies me, Monsieur. I am no soldier or duelist, and I dread the Bastille."

"Hm! I'm no keener on the Bastille than you are. Were it but a question of dueling—"

"I have seen you constantly surrounded by musketeers; naturally, I supposed that you and your friends would be delighted to do the Queen justice and the Cardinal an ill turn."

"Undoubtedly, we—"

"I thought that if I were never to mention the rent again so long as you remain under my roof—"

"Very good! What else?"

"Well . . . to go further . . . I thought I would make bold to offer you, say, about fifty pistoles. . . ."

"So you are a rich man, my dear Monsieur Bonacieux."

"I am comfortably off, Monsieur, that's all. I have scraped together an income of something like two or three hundred thousand crowns from my haberdashery business. You can judge for yourself, then, Monsieur, how I—but look, look!"

"What?"

"Over there!" said the stranger, pointing through the window.

"Where?"

"In the street there . . . that man wrapped in a cloak."

Suddenly both recognized their man.

"It's the man I told you about!" said Bonacieux.

"It's the man I'm after!" cried D'Artagnan, springing across the room for his sword. "This time he will not escape me." And he rushed out of the apartment. On the staircase he met his three friends.

"What's up? Where are you off to? What's the matter?"

"The man of Meung!" D'Artagnan cried as he disappeared.

He had more than once told his friends about his adventure with the sinister stranger and the apparition of the beautiful English lady to whom his enemy had confided some important missive. The musketeers had long since formed their own opinions about the incident.

Athos and Porthos understood that D'Artagnan would either meet his man of Meung and despatch him promptly or he would lose sight of him; in either case, he would return home. Accordingly they continued to walk upstairs.

When D'Artagnan returned home he found his friends waiting in full force.

"Well?" asked Athos with pessimistic calm as D'Artagnan burst in, his brow bathed in perspiration, his face dark with anger.

"Well?" said Porthos jauntily.

"Well?" said Aramis in a tone of discreet encouragement.

"Well—" D'Artagnan threw his sword on the bed, "well, that man must be the devil in person. He vanished like a phantom, a shadow, a specter."

"Do you believe in apparitions, Porthos?" Athos inquired.

"I believe only in what I have seen. I have never seen an apparition, therefore I do not believe in apparitions."

"The Bible orders us by law to believe in them," Aramis remarked. "Did not the ghost of Samuel appear to Saul?"

"At all events, human or devil, body or shadow, illusion or reality, that man was born for my damnation," said D'Artagnan. Then, calling for his valet: "Planchet," he ordered, "go down to my landlord, Monsieur Bonacieux, and tell him to send up half a dozen bottles of Beaugency wine. It is my favorite tipple."

"So you have credit with your landlord, eh?"

"Yes, I established credit today. If his wine is bad, never mind; we will send him to find something more palatable."

Impetuously, D'Artagnan told his friends all that had passed between his landlord and himself, concluding with the startling information that Madame Bonacieux's abductor and D'Artagnan's enemy from Meung were one and the same man. Also that Bonacieux had hinted at money to be made.

Having sampled the wine like a connoisseur, and nodded to indicate that he found it good, Athos declared:

"You are in luck, D'Artagnan, your worthy landlord seems good for fifty or sixty pistoles. The only question to debate is whether these fifty or sixty are worth the risk of four heads."

"You forget there is a woman in the case," D'Artagnan protested, "a woman who was carried off, a woman who is probably being threatened and perhaps even being tortured, and all because she is faithful to her royal mistress."

"Careful, D'Artagnan! I feel you are overzealous about Madame Bonacieux's fate," Aramis cautioned.

"I'm not worried about Madame Bonacieux," D'Artagnan answered, "but about the Queen. The King neglects her, the Cardinal persecutes her, and her friends are being killed one after the other."

"Why does she love what we hate most in the world, the Spaniards and the English?"

"Spain is her native land," D'Artagnan explained. "It is quite natural that she should love the Spaniards; are they not her fellow countrymen? As for your second reproach, I have heard it said that she does not love the English, but rather one Englishman."

"Upon my faith," said Athos, "that Englishman deserves

to be loved. I never saw a man of nobler aspect in all my life."

"And he dresses better than anyone in the world," Porthos added. "I was at the Louvre the day he dropped his pearls. I picked up two that I sold for ten pistoles apiece."

"If I knew where the Duke of Buckingham was," said D'Artagnan, "nothing could prevent me from taking him by the hand and leading him to the Queen's side, if only to enrage the Cardinal."

"Did your haberdasher say the Queen believed that Buckingham came to Paris on the strength of a forged letter?" Athos asked.

"That is what the Queen fears. I am convinced," D'Artagnan said, "that the abduction of the Queen's seamstress, my landlord's wife, is connected with what we have been discussing and perhaps even with the presence of Buckingham in Paris."

"That Gascon is full of ideas!" Porthos said admiringly.

"I like to hear him speak," said Athos. "His accent delights me."

"Gentlemen, please listen to what I am about to tell you," Aramis broke in.

"Go ahead!"

"We are listening!"

"We are all ears."

"Yesterday," said Aramis, "I happened to be at the house of a learned doctor of theology whom I sometimes consult about my studies. This doctor has a niece."

"Ah, he has a niece!" said Porthos teasingly.

"A very fine young lady," Aramis insisted. "This niece I mentioned often calls on her uncle; she happened to come yesterday while I was there, and I had to offer to see her into her carriage. Suddenly I saw a gentleman, a tall dark man very much like your man of Meung—"

"Perhaps it was my man!"

"It may well have been," Aramis agreed. "Anyhow, he advanced toward me, followed at a distance of ten paces by five or six men. 'Monsieur . . .' he said courteously to me, and 'Madame . . .' to the lady on my arm. '. . . Monsieur, Madame, will you be good enough to step into this carriage without offering the slightest resistance or making the least noise?'"

"He took you for Buckingham!" D'Artagnan exploded.

"I rather believe so."

"But the lady?" Porthos persisted.

"He took her for the Queen," D'Artagnan said.

"Exactly," Aramis assented.

"Gentlemen," D'Artagnan urged, "let us look for the haberdasher's wife. She holds the key to the riddle."

"Do you really think so, D'Artagnan?" Porthos curled his lip contemptuously. "A woman of such humble standing?"

"She is the goddaughter of La Porte, cloak bearer to the Queen. Didn't I tell you that? Besides, on this occasion Her Majesty may deliberately have sought the support of a person of modest station."

"The first thing to do," Porthos counseled, "is to drive a bargain, and a good one, with your haberdasher."

"That's unnecessary," D'Artagnan replied. "I have an idea that if Bonacieux fails to pay us, we shall be paid handsomely by another party."

Suddenly footsteps resounded on the stairs, the door flew open and the luckless haberdasher rushed in.

"Save me, gentlemen, for the love of Heaven, save me!" he wailed. "There are four men downstairs who came to arrest me. Save me, save me!"

Porthos and Aramis sprang to their feet; D'Artagnan intervened hastily:

"Not so fast, gentlemen!" He motioned to them to sheathe their half-drawn swords. "It is not courage we need now, but prudence—"

"Are we to stand here," Porthos stormed, "and allow—"

"You will allow D'Artagnan to do as he thinks best," Athos declared. "He is the brainiest of us."

Suddenly four bailiffs appeared at the door of the antechamber, but, seeing four musketeers standing there, fully armed, they seemed somewhat hesitant about entering.

"Come in, gentlemen, come in," D'Artagnan called to them. "This is my apartment and we are all faithful servants of the King and of the Cardinal."

"So you have no objection to our carrying out our orders."

"On the contrary, we would assist you if that were necessary."

"What on earth is D'Artagnan saying?" Porthos muttered.

"You're a simpleton!" Athos whispered. "Silence!"

The wretched haberdasher protested in a whisper, "But you promised me—"

"We can save you only by remaining free ourselves," D'Artagnan whispered. "If we appeared eager to defend you, we would be arrested too."

"All the same, it seems to me—"

"Come, gentlemen, come," said D'Artagnan, aloud. "I have no reason to defend Monsieur here. I saw him today for the first time in my life. He can tell you in what circumstances we met; he came to collect the rent for my lodgings."

"That is quite true," the landlord answered. "But Monsieur has not told you—"

"Not a word about me, not a word about my friends, and above all, not a word about the Queen, or you will ruin everybody without saving yourself!" D'Artagnan cautioned Bonacieux. Then aloud to the bailiffs: "Come, gentlemen, take this fellow away!"

The myrmidons of the law, mouthing their thanks, took

away their prey. But just as they were about to go downstairs, D'Artagnan clapped their leader on the shoulder.

"Come, I must drink to your health and you to mine!" he said jovially, filling two glasses with the wine he owed to Monsieur Bonacieux's liberality.

"Here's to your health, Monsieur," said the bailiff.

"But first and foremost, above all healths," cried D'Artagnan, as if carried away by his enthusiasm, "I drink to the King and the Cardinal!"

Had the wine been bad, the bailiff might have questioned D'Artagnan's sincerity; but the wine was good, and he was convinced.

"What devilish villainy have you been up to?" Porthos inquired after the bailiff had joined his companions. "Shame on us, shame! We have just stood by without moving a finger and allowed an unfortunate fellow who called for help to be arrested under our very noses! And the gentleman responsible for all this has to hobnob with a bailiff!"

"Look here, Porthos," Aramis said. "Athos has already told you that you are a simpleton. May I add that I completely share his opinion?"

"Well, I *am* in a maze," Porthos exclaimed. "Do you mean to say you approve of what D'Artagnan did?"

"Why, of course I do!" Athos told him. "I not only approve of it but I offer him my heartiest congratulations."

"And now, gentlemen," said D'Artagnan. "*All for one and one for all*—that is our motto, is it not?"

And, with one voice, the four friends repeated the slogan dictated by D'Artagnan: "*All for one and one for all!*"

CHAPTER 5:

A Seventeenth-Century Mousetrap

THE invention of the mousetrap is not a modern one. Long ago, when human societies, in the process of formation, invented the police, the police invented the mousetrap.

When in a house of any kind a person suspected of a crime has been arrested, the arrest is kept secret. Four or five policemen are posted in ambush in the front room of the prisoner's apartment. The door is opened to all who knock but, as it closes, the visitor becomes a prisoner. Monsieur Bonacieux's residence, then, became a mousetrap; whoever appeared was seized and investigated by the Cardinal's men. However, as a special passage led to the second floor, where D'Artagnan lodged, his callers were exempt from molestation.

The musketeers reported that they had all made careful independent investigations but to no avail. Athos had even gone so far as to question Monsieur de Tréville, a step which, in view of his usual reticence, had much surprised his captain. But Tréville knew nothing save that the last time he had seen the Cardinal, the King and the Queen, the Cardinal looked very anxious, the King seemed worried and the Queen's bloodshot eyes betrayed either a sleepless night or much weeping.

As for D'Artagnan, from the watchtower of his windows, he saw all who, entering the house, walked into the trap. He also removed a plank of the flooring and cleared enough of the foundation so that there was but a mere ceiling between him and the inquisition room below.

Those arrested were first submitted to a minute search of their persons. Then, almost invariably, they were asked:

"Has Madame Bonacieux given you anything to deliver to her husband or to another party? Has Monsieur Bonacieux given you anything to deliver to his wife or another party? Has either of them confided anything to you by word of mouth?"

"If they knew anything they would not question people in this manner," D'Artagnan mused. "Now what do they want to find out? Exactly this: whether the Duke of Buckingham is in Paris and whether he has had or is due to have an interview with the Queen."

On the day after Monsieur Bonacieux's arrest, late in the evening, someone was caught in the mousetrap!

D'Artagnan leaped to his listening post and lay flat on his belly, his ear to the ground. Soon he heard cries, then moans which someone was apparently trying to stifle.

"It sounds like a woman!" D'Artagnan thought.

In spite of his prudence it was all D'Artagnan could do not to interrupt the scene.

"But I tell you I live here, gentlemen," cried the unhappy woman. "I tell you I am Madame Bonacieux; I tell you I belong to the Queen."

"You are exactly the lady we were awaiting."

The voice grew more indistinct, then a series of bumps shook the wainscoting; no doubt the victim was struggling as fiercely as a lone woman could struggle against four men.

"Gentlemen, gen—" murmured the voice. Then it lapsed into inarticulate sounds.

"They have gagged her, they are going to drag her away." D'Artagnan sprang to his feet. "My sword! Planchet!"

"Monsieur?"

"Go fetch Athos and Porthos and Aramis. Tell them to come here at once, fully armed."

"But where are *you* going, Monsieur?"

"I'm going down through the window, it's quicker. You put back the boards, sweep the floor, go out by the front door and be off to where I told you."

"Oh, Monsieur, you are going to get killed."

"Hush, idiot!" said D'Artagnan. Vaulting over the windowsill, he clung to it for a moment, then dropped without mishap to the ground, which fortunately was no very great distance. A second later, he was knocking at the street door.

The sound of his knock brought the tumult within to an abrupt halt. Steps were heard approaching, the door opened and D'Artagnan, sword drawn, rushed into Monsieur Bonacieux's apartment. This door clicked shut upon him.

Immediately the whole neighborhood heard loud cries, a stamping of many feet, a clash of swords, and a prolonged smashing of furniture. Those who, surprised at this bedlam, went to their windows to ascertain its cause, were rewarded by seeing the street door flung open again and four black-clad men emerging. These did not walk or run, they actually flew out like so many frightened crows.

Left alone with Madame Bonacieux, D'Artagnan turned toward where the poor woman lay back, deep in an armchair, half-conscious. One swift glance revealed a charm-

"Oh, Monsieur, you are going to get killed."

ing woman of twenty-three or twenty-four, with dark hair, blue eyes and a slightly turned-up nose, glistening teeth and a complexion marbled with rose and opal.

While he was surveying Madame Bonacieux, he noticed a fine cambric handkerchief lying on the floor. True to habit, he picked it up. In one corner he recognized the same crest he had seen on the handkerchief which had almost caused Aramis to cut his throat.

He put it back in her pocket. At that moment, Madame Bonacieux recovered her senses.

"Ah, Monsieur, you saved me! Pray let me thank you—"

"Madame, you owe me no thanks. I did what any gentleman would have done in my place."

"Oh, but I do owe you thanks, Monsieur, and I hope to prove to you that you have not befriended an ingrate. But tell me . . . those men . . . What did they want with me? . . . And why isn't Monsieur Bonacieux here?"

"Madame, these men were agents of the Cardinal. As for your husband, he isn't here because he was picked up yesterday and taken to the Bastille."

"My husband in prison! Oh, what has he done?"

"What has he done?" D'Artagnan echoed. "I think his only crime consists in having at once the good fortune and misfortune to be your husband."

"But Monsieur, then you know—?"

"I know that you were abducted, Madame."

"Who did it, Monsieur? Do you know?"

"You were abducted by a man forty or forty-five years old, with black hair, a swarthy complexion, and a scar on his left cheek."

"Was my husband aware that I had been abducted?"

"He received a letter telling him about it."

"Does he suspect the reason for my abduction?" Madame Bonacieux asked.

"I believe he attributed it to political motives."

An almost imperceptible smile stole over the roseate lips of the comely young woman.

"How did you escape?" D'Artagnan asked.

"I took advantage of a few minutes when they left me alone. Then, thinking my husband would be at home, I rushed here."

"To put yourself under his protection?"

"No, no, poor dear man! I knew quite well that he was incapable of defending me. But I wished to talk to him."

"About what?"

"I cannot tell you that, because it is not my secret."

"In any case, Madame, this is scarcely a place for an exchange of confidences. The men I put to flight will soon return with reinforcements; if they find us here, we are ruined."

"Yes, you are right! Let us fly, let us escape!" Considerably frightened, she slipped her arm through D'Artagnan's and urged him forward.

"But where to?" D'Artagnan asked. "Where shall we fly to?"

"First let us get away from this house; afterwards we shall see."

Without bothering to close the door behind them, the young couple walked quickly down to the Place Saint-Sulpice.

"Now what shall we do?" D'Artagnan asked. "To what address may I accompany you?"

"I must own I am at a loss how to answer," she told him. "I intended to have my husband go to ascertain what has been happening at the Royal Palace for the last three days and whether I could safely go back there."

"Surely *I* can go to Monsieur de la Porte."

"Perhaps so. Still there is one drawback. They do not know you."

"But surely there must be a doorman at some wicket of the Palace who is devoted to you, and thanks to a password—"

Madame Bonacieux looked earnestly at the young man.

"Suppose I give you this password, will you promise to forget it as soon as you have used it?" she asked.

"I promise on my word of honor and on my faith as a gentleman," said D'Artagnan fervently.

"I believe you. You appear to be an honorable man. Besides, your services might well make your fortune."

"Without thought of reward, I shall do all I can to serve the King and the Queen. I am your friend."

"But I—where shall I go meanwhile?"

"Ah, I have it! We are but a few steps from the house of my friend Athos. . . ."

"Let us go to your friend's house. Where does he live?"

"Just around the corner."

As D'Artagnan had foreseen, Athos was out. D'Artagnan picked up the key, which was always given him, and introduced Madame Bonacieux into the little apartment.

"Make yourself at home," he said. "Stay here, bolt the door and let no one in unless you hear three raps."

"Good. Now, may I give you your instructions?"

"I am all attention," D'Artagnan assured her.

"When you reach the Royal Palace, go in at the wicket by the Rue de l'Echelle and ask for Germain."

"Yes?"

"When Germain asks you what you want, say two words: 'Tours' and 'Brussels.' Immediately he will place himself at your orders. Tell him to fetch Monsieur de la Porte, valet to Her Majesty."

"And when he has fetched him?"

"Ask Monsieur de la Porte to come here to me."

"That offers no difficulty. But where and how shall I see you again?"

"Do you wish very much to see me again?"

"Certainly."

"Then you may count on me. Meanwhile, do not fret."

"I depend on your word."

"You may do so unreservedly."

Everything happened just as Madame Bonacieux had indicated. Then, as La Porte bade D'Artagnan good-bye, he said, "You may get into trouble because of what has just happened."

"Really?"

"Yes. Have you by any chance some friend whose clock runs too slow?"

"Monsieur, I—"

"Go call on him. Let him testify that you were at his house at nine-thirty. In a court of justice that is what we call an alibi."

D'Artagnan, finding this counsel prudent, hurried off to Monsieur de Tréville's. But instead of going into the reception room he asked to be shown into the captain's study.

As he frequented the mansion assiduously, his request was granted. Five minutes later, Tréville was asking D'Artagnan what he could do to be of service and what occasioned a visit at so late an hour.

"I beg your pardon, Monsieur, I did not think twenty-five minutes past nine was too late to wait upon you."

(Left alone to wait for the captain, he had of course turned back Monsieur de Tréville's clock three quarters of an hour.)

"Twenty-five past nine!" cried Monsieur de Tréville, looking at his clock. "But that's impossible."

"Clocks don't lie, Monsieur."

"That's true. But I would have thought it was much later. Well, tell me what I can do for you?"

D'Artagnan made a trifling request and, as the clock struck ten, took his leave. Then, at the foot of the staircase, D'Artagnan suddenly remembered that he had forgotten his cane. He therefore ran upstairs again, returned to Tréville's office, and, with a turn of the finger, set the clock right again so that on the morrow no one would know it had been tampered with. Then, certain that he had secured a witness to prove his alibi, he sauntered out into the street.

D'Artagnan, deep in thought, took the longest possible way homeward. He was thinking of Madame Bonacieux. Pretty, mysterious, privy to almost all the secrets of the Court, her delicate features reflecting such charming gravity, she might be supposed not entirely indifferent to him. Did not his important service establish a bond of gratitude which might well assume a more tender character?

But what about Monsieur Bonacieux, whom D'Artagnan had delivered into the hands of the officers, betraying him publicly after his private promises to save him? It must be confessed that D'Artagnan did not vouchsafe him a thought, for love is the most selfish of all passions.

Dreaming thus, apostrophizing the night and gazing at

the stars, D'Artagnan suddenly decided to pay Aramis a visit to explain why he had dispatched Planchet to him. Also he thought that a visit to Aramis offered him a chance of talking about pretty little Madame Bonacieux, who at this point filled his heart.

For the past two hours Paris had been swathed in darkness and the streets were practically deserted. Eleven o'clock struck from all the clocks of the capital. The night was mild. Gratefully D'Artagnan breathed in the redolence of flower and grass and tree. Afar, muffled by stout shutters, echoes of drinking songs floated out from taverns scattered across the plain.

D'Artagnan could see the door of his friend's house, nestling under a clump of sycamores and clematis that formed a vast leafy arch above. Suddenly a shadow-like form issued from the end of the street. That form was wrapped up in a cloak, and D'Artagnan first thought it was a man, but the slenderness of the figure, the hesitancy of the gait and the insecurity of the steps convinced him that it was a woman. As if uncertain of the house she sought, she kept looking up to get her bearings, stopped, retraced her steps, and once again approached. D'Artagnan was seized with curiosity.

Meanwhile the young woman kept coming forward, counting the houses and the windows. D'Artagnan drew back, making himself as thin as possible, as he took his stand on the darkest side of the street near a stone bench set in a niche. The young woman continued to advance, betraying herself not only by her light step but also by a soft cough—a signal, thought D'Artagnan—which suggested a sweet voice. Then, with finger crooked, she rapped three times, at equal intervals, on the musketeer's shutter.

"It *is* Aramis!" D'Artagnan murmured.

Scarcely was the rapping done when the window opened

and a light appeared through the slats of the shutter. But to D'Artagnan's astonishment, the shutter remained closed, the light that had shown for a moment disappeared, and once again darkness reigned. D'Artagnan, sensing that this could not last long, kept his eyes peeled and his ears pricked up for the next move. He was right. After a few seconds two sharp raps were heard inside; the young woman in the street replied by a single rap and the shutter opened ever so slightly.

The young woman drew a white object from her pocket and unfolded it quickly into the shape of a handkerchief. D'Artagnan suddenly recalled the handkerchief he had found at Madame Bonacieux's feet, which in turn reminded him of the one he had pulled out from under the feet of Aramis.

From his point of vantage, D'Artagnan could not distinguish Aramis, but he felt certain it was his friend within conversing with the lady. Curiosity prevailed over prudence. Making the most of the couple's preoccupation over the handkerchief, he emerged from his hiding place and, swift as lightning, flattened himself against an angle of the wall, whence he could see into the room Aramis occupied.

Looking in, he almost cried out, so great was his surprise. It was not with Aramis the midnight visitor was conversing but with another woman! He perceived her clearly enough to recognize this by the clothes she wore.

The woman inside now drew a handkerchief from her pocket and exchanged it for the one the visitor had shown her. The two women spoke a few words more and presently the shutter was closed. The visitor turned back and passed within four steps of D'Artagnan, lowering the hood of her mantle. But her precaution was too late. D'Artagnan had recognized Madame Bonacieux.

Madame Bonacieux! Already when he had seen her draw the handkerchief from her pocket a suspicion had flashed through his mind, but he had dismissed it. Seeing the young man as he detached himself from the wall, like a statue walking out of its niche, and hearing his footsteps resound so near her, Madame Bonacieux uttered a little cry and fled. D'Artagnan came abreast of her before she was one-third of the way down the street. The unfortunate woman was exhausted not by fatigue but by terror, and when he laid his hand on her shoulder, she fell to one knee and cried in a choking voice:

"Kill me if you like, I shall not tell you anything."

D'Artagnan slipped his arm around her waist and drew her to her feet; as he felt that she was about to faint, he hastily comforted her by protestations of devotion. Despite her confusion, she thought she recognized that voice; she opened her eyes and gave a cry of joy.

"Oh, it is you! Thank God! Thank God!"

"Why were you tapping at the window of one of my friends?" he asked.

"Of one of your friends?"

"Come, come, you're not telling me you don't know Aramis?"

"This is the first time I have ever heard his name."

"So you weren't looking for Aramis?"

"You saw, I was talking to a woman."

"The woman is probably a friend of Aramis—"

"I don't know anything about that."

"Who is she?" he insisted.

"Oh, that is not my secret."

"My dear Madame Bonacieux, you are the most attractive and the most mysterious of women."

"Is what you call my mystery a handicap?"

"No. On the contrary, you are adorable."

"Give me your arm, then, and escort me; I have a call to make."

"Where?"

"Where I am going."

"But where *are* you going?"

"You will see because I shall ask you to take me to the door. And you will leave me afterward."

"Yes."

"Without waiting for me to come out again?"

"Yes."

"On your word of honor?"

"By my faith as a gentleman. Take my arm and let us go."

Half-laughing, half-trembling, she slipped her arm through his and together they strolled through the streets until she hesitated at a particular door she seemed to recognize.

"Now, Monsieur," she said, "I have reached my destination."

"Oh, come, Madame, please," he cried, seizing her hands and gazing ardently into her eyes, "please be more generous. Confide in me. Can you not see by my eyes that my heart is filled with sympathy and devotion?"

"Truly, I can. Ask me my own secrets and I shall hold nothing back. But you are asking me to divulge the secrets of others, which is a very different matter."

"No matter, I shall discover them."

"Beware of doing anything of the sort!" the young woman replied so earnestly that D'Artagnan gave an involuntary start. "Please, believe everything that I have told you. Do not bother about me; I no longer exist for you, it is as though you had never laid eyes on me! You say a friend of yours lives in that house?"

"I say and repeat: a friend of mine lives in that house and his name is Aramis."

"This misunderstanding will be cleared up later," the young woman murmured, "but for the present, Monsieur, please be silent."

"If you could see plainly into my heart, you would satisfy my curiosity at once. A woman has nothing to fear from the man who loves her."

"You speak very suddenly of love," she objected, shaking her head.

"That is because love has come upon me very suddenly, because I was never in love before and because I am only nineteen."

"Monsieur," the young woman implored, "Monsieur, in the name of Heaven, on the honor of a soldier and the courtesy of a gentleman, please, please be off. Hark! Midnight is striking, the hour of my appointment."

"Madame," said D'Artagnan, bowing, "I cannot refuse a request couched in such terms. Be content, I will go my way."

"Ah, I was sure of it, I knew you were a gentleman."

Seizing her outstretched hand, D'Artagnan kissed it ardently. Then, with that naïve bluntness which women often prefer to the affectations of politeness, he murmured, "Ah, would to God I had never seen you!"

"Well, well, I will not say the same about you!" Her voice was almost caressing and she squeezed the hand that still clung to hers. "Who knows, some day I may be free to satisfy your curiosity. And now go, go in Heaven's name! I was expected promptly at midnight and I am late."

As if it required the most violent effort to make himself release the hand he held in his, he sprang away from her and started running down the street while she rapped three times at regular intervals. When he reached the street corner, he turned around; the door had opened and shut again, Madame Bonacieux had disappeared.

D'Artagnan pursued his way. He had given his word not to watch her. Had his very life depended upon this visit of hers or upon the person who was to accompany her, D'Artagnan would nevertheless have returned home, because he had so promised. Five minutes later he was in his own street.

"All this is very strange and I am most curious to know how it will end," he mused.

"It will end badly, Monsieur," said a voice which he recognized as Planchet's. Soliloquizing as people so often will when they are preoccupied, D'Artagnan had turned into the alley that led to his staircase.

"What do you mean, badly? Explain yourself, idiot! What has happened?"

"To begin with, Monsieur Athos was arrested."

"Arrested? Athos arrested? What for?"

"He was found in your room. They mistook him for you."

"Who arrested him?"

"Guards brought by those men in black that you drove off."

"Why didn't he give them his name? Why didn't he tell them he knew nothing about the whole business?"

Planchet explained that Athos had drawn him aside and said, "Your master knows all about this, I know nothing; he needs his liberty, I don't need mine. The police will think they have arrested him; that should give him time. In three days I shall tell them who I am and they will have to let me go."

"Four of them took him away to some prison," the valet said. "Two stayed with the men in black, rummaging through everything and seizing all your papers."

"And Porthos and Aramis?"

"I could not reach them. They did not come."

"Well, you sit tight here, Planchet, and don't budge. If they come, tell them what happened. The house may be watched, it's too dangerous to meet here; tell them to wait for me at the *Sign of the Fir Cone*."

"Very good, Monsieur."

Then, fast as his legs could carry him, D'Artagnan sped

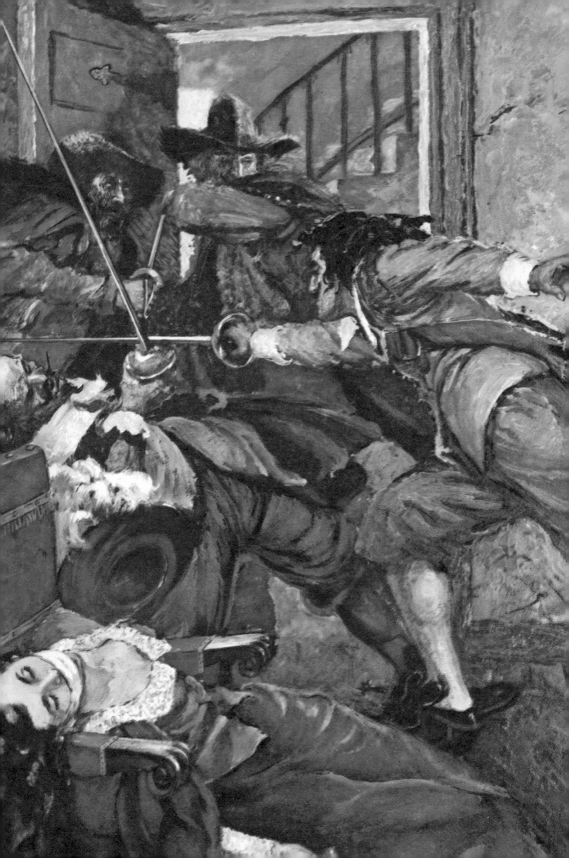

away. Tréville was not at his mansion; his company was on guard at the Louvre and he was with his company. D'Artagnan knew he must see Tréville, he must somehow try to enter the Louvre. Surely his uniform, identifying him as a guardsman, would serve him as passport?

As he reached the Quay, he saw two persons, a man and a woman. Their appearance struck him and, as he eyed them carefully, he realized that the woman looked very much like Madame Bonacieux and her cavalier like Aramis. They crossed the bridge, which was also D'Artagnan's road, since he was bound for the Louvre, he several paces behind them. D'Artagnan had not gone thirty feet before he was convinced that the woman was Madame Bonacieux and the man in musketeer's uniform Aramis.

D'Artagnan did not reflect that he had known Madame Bonacieux for just three hours, that she owed him nothing more than a modicum of gratitude for saving her from the men in black, and that she had promised him nothing. He considered himself an outraged, betrayed and ridiculed lover; the blood rushed to his face, anger possessed him and he determined to unravel the mystery.

The couple, noticing they were being followed, redoubled their speed. D'Artagnan sped forward, passed them and then turned round so as to meet them squarely in the lamplight. The musketeer stepped back.

"What do you want, Monsieur?" he asked in a voice and with a foreign accent which immediately proved that D'Artagnan had been mistaken.

"It is not Aramis!" he blurted.

"No, Monsieur, it is not Aramis. By your exclamation, I see you have mistaken me for someone else, and so I excuse you."

"You excuse me?"

"Yes," replied the stranger. "And since you have no business with me, kindly step aside and let me pass."

"You are right, Monsieur, my business is not with you
but with Madame."

"With Madame? But you do not know her."

"I beg your pardon, Monsieur, I know her very well."

"Ah," Madame Bonacieux sighed reproachfully. "I had
your promise as a soldier and your word as a gentleman."

"Please take my arm, Madame," said the stranger, "and
let us go on."

Meanwhile D'Artagnan, dazed, downcast and shocked,
stood his ground. The musketeer advanced two steps and
pushed D'Artagnan aside. D'Artagnan sprang backward
and drew his sword. At the same time, swift as lightning,
the stranger drew his.

"In the name of Heaven, Milord!" cried Madame Bonacieux.

"Milord!" cried D'Artagnan, suddenly enlightened. "Milord! I beg your pardon, Monsieur, but can you possibly be—?"

"My Lord Duke of Buckingham," said Madame Bonacieux in an undertone. "And now you may ruin us all."

"Milord, Madame, I ask a hundred pardons. But I love her, Milord, and I was jealous. You know what it is to love, Milord. Pray forgive me and tell me how I may risk my life to serve Your Grace!"

CHAPTER 6:

Of a Queen, a Haberdasher and a Cardinal

Madame bonacieux and the Duke entered the Louvre without difficulty, for she was known to be a servant of the Queen's household and he wore a musketeer's uniform.

Once inside the courtyard, they followed the wall until they came to a small door in the servants' quarters. It yielded to Madame Bonacieux's pressure and they passed into utter darkness; her hand held the Duke's hand, she tiptoed down passages, grasped a banister, felt for the bottom step and began to walk up a staircase. Then Madame Bonacieux ushered him into a dimly lit room.

"You must wait here, My Lord Duke," she whispered.

She went out by the same door, which she locked from the outside, leaving her companion literally a prisoner.

Alone as he was, Buckingham did not experience an instant of fear. A brave, rash, enterprising man, he had learned that the message from Anne of Austria, on the strength of which he had come to Paris, was a snare; but instead of returning to England, he had warned the Queen that he refused to depart without seeing her.

Left alone in the small boudoir, Buckingham walked toward a mirror; his musketeer's uniform, fitting him perfectly, was most becoming to him. Self-confident, certain that the laws which bound other men could not possibly hamper him, he made straight for whatever goal he had set himself. Thus, having succeeded in approaching the beautiful and haughty Anne of Austria several times, he had won her love by dazzling her.

Suddenly a door concealed in the tapestry opened and a woman appeared. It was the Queen.

Anne of Austria, then twenty-six years of age, was at the height of her beauty. Her bearing was that of a goddess; her eyes, sparkling like emeralds, were of matchless splendor yet filled with sweetness and majesty. Her mouth was small and rosy. Her skin was much admired for its velvety softness; her hands and arms, surprisingly white and delicate of texture, were celebrated by all the poets of the age. And her hair, very blonde in her youth, had turned to a warm chestnut; curled very simply and amply powdered, it framed her face admirably.

The Queen took two steps forward. Buckingham threw himself at her feet; before she could prevent him, he had kissed the hem of her gown.

"My Lord Duke," said the Queen, "you must already know that *I* did not write to you."

"I do. Alas! A madman, I, to dream that snow might melt and marble thaw. But, Madame, a lover believes in love. My journey has not been in vain; at least I have seen you."

"You know very well, My Lord, how and why I am here now. Indifferent to my anguish, you insisted on staying here at the risk of your life and the peril of my honor. My Lord, I am here to tell you we must never meet again."

"Speak on, Madame, speak on! The warmth of Your Majesty's voice defeats the harshness of your words."

"My Lord Duke, you forget I never told you I loved you."

"But Your Majesty never told me that you did *not* love me. Oh, tell me, Madame, where shall you, queen as you are, ever find a love like mine . . . a love which neither time nor absence nor despair can quench. . . .

"I first set eyes upon you, Madame, three years ago, and, ever since, I have loved you nobly and ardently as I did that day. Shall I describe the gown you wore, shall I cite each article of apparel that I remember? Ah, Madame, I have but to close my eyes in order to see you just as you were then, and to open them again in order to find you as you are now, one hundred times more beautiful."

"Do not be rash," the Queen murmured. "Do not feed the flame of a vain passion with such memories."

"By what else shall I live, Madame? Each time I beheld Your Majesty, it was as a new diamond which I enclosed in the casket of my heart. Four times I have seen you, and four only!"

"Remember, My Lord, when you sought to return as ambassador to France, His Majesty himself opposed it."

"That is why France is now about to pay for her king's refusal with a war. Now I may no longer see you, Madame, but I can arrange to have news of me reach you day by day.

"I cannot hope to fight my way to Paris, sword in hand; I know this all too well. But a war, Madame, ends in a peace, a peace requires a negotiator. I shall return to Paris, I shall see you again! Thousands of men, it is true, will lose their lives for my joy, but what matter so but I see Your Majesty?"

"My Lord, you call to your defense arguments that accuse you the more strongly. These proofs of love that you invoke are almost crimes."

"That is because you do not love me, Madame. If you

loved me, how differently you would feel! Madame, I find my happiness in illusion and error; I pray you mercifully to leave them to me. You have told me I was drawn to Paris as into a trap, which may cost me my life—"

"God forbid!" The Queen's terror revealed her interest in Buckingham more clearly than words could do.

"Madame, I must tell you that I dreamed a strange dream!" He smiled, at once melancholy and charming. "Who shall say? I may die soon. I do not mention this, Madame, to frighten you. But your words and the hope you have suggested would prove to be a royal wage for even my life—"

"I too feel strange portents; I too dream dreams; I too, queen though I be, saw a vision. It was you, My Lord, lying wounded on a couch, your blood flowing from your veins. It was but a dream which I confessed to God alone and in my prayers—"

"I ask no more. You love me, Madame."

"I . . . I . . ."

"If you do not love me, then why does God send us the same dreams? You love me, Madame, and you will weep my death."

"Ah, Heaven, give me strength. I beg Your Grace to go. Whether I love you or not I implore you to depart. By your love, pray leave me."

"How beautiful Your Majesty is in this supreme moment! How fervently your servant Buckingham worships you!"

"Go, I beg you."

"Madame, let me beg as a token of your indulgence some object which comes from you, something to prove to me that I am not dreaming, something that you have worn. . . ."

"Will you leave if I give what you ask?"

"I swear it."

"Wait then, wait, My Lord—"

The Queen went back to her apartment, returning almost at once with a small rosewood coffer.

"My Lord, here is a gift by which to remember me."

Buckingham took the casket, fell to one knee and pressed his lips to the Queen's fingertips, then rose.

"If I am still alive within six months," he vowed, "I shall see Your Majesty again though I upset the universe to do so."

Meanwhile, what of Monsieur Bonacieux, that worthy martyr to the political and amorous intrigues of an age when political and amorous intrigues went cheek by jowl?

The officers who had arrested him led him straight to the Bastille. Shuddering with fright, he was marched past a platoon of soldiers who were loading their muskets. Then he was taken down a subterranean gallery where he met with the harshest of physical treatment.

Usually prisoners were questioned in their cells, but Monsieur Bonacieux's presence in jail did not warrant such niceties. Two guards seized him, trundled him across a court, propelled him down a corridor flanked by sentinels, thrust open a door and pushed him into a small room to face a table, a chair and a commissioner. The commissioner suddenly looked up, and asked Monsieur Bonacieux his family name, his given name, his age, his profession and his domicile, to which the accused replied:

"Joseph-Michel Bonacieux; fifty years old; haberdasher (retired)." This settled, the commissioner read Bonacieux a long lecture celebrating the deeds and power of the Cardinal:

"An incomparable minister, hum! The conqueror of previous ministries, hum! A statesman whose acts no sane man, hum! would oppose."

"Monsieur, I beg you to believe I yield to none in admiration for the merit of the Cardinal."

"If that is so, why are you in the Bastille?"

"Why am I here? I simply cannot tell you, Monsieur, because I do not know myself. But certainly I never caused My Lord Cardinal the slightest displeasure!"

"Why do you suppose you are accused of high treason?"

"High treason! Why do *you* suppose a wretched haberdasher who loathes Protestants and abhors Spaniards stands here accused of high treason? Come, Monsieur, how could I possibly be suspected of anything?"

"You have a wife, Monsieur Bonacieux, have you not?"

"Ay, Monsieur," the haberdasher acknowledged. (Here's where my troubles begin, he thought to himself.) "I mean I *had* a wife."

"You *had* a wife? What *do* you mean? Where is she?"

"They took her away, Monsieur."

"So they took her away. Do you know *who* abducted her?"

"I think so."

"Who?"

"By your leave, Monsieur, I would not dare accuse anyone . . . I only have suspicions. . . ."

"Whom do you suspect? Come on, speak out, man!"

This question put Monsieur Bonacieux in a very tight corner. Should he deny or should he confess?

"I suspect a tall, dark man, a great lord, I dare say . . . if I am not wrong, he followed us . . . my wife and me . . . several times. . . ."

At this point, the commissioner gave evidence of a certain anxiety.

"His name?"

"I wouldn't know his name, Monsieur. But if ever I saw him, I could spot him out of a thousand."

"Very well, so much for today," said the commissioner. "Meanwhile, I shall report that you know who abducted your wife."

"I didn't say I knew him. On the contrary. . . ."

"Prisoner dismissed! Take him away. Clap him into the handiest cell you find so but it be secure!"

Though his cell was not too disagreeable, Bonacieux could not sleep a wink. All night long he sat rooted to his stool, trembling at the slightest noise; and, when the first rays of daylight crept into his cell, the dawn seemed to him dismal and funereal. Suddenly the bolts of his door shot back and he gave a terrible start. To his surprise, he saw the commissioner and the clerk of yesterday's interview enter.

"This trouble you are in has become much more serious overnight," the commissioner informed Bonacieux. "I advise you to tell the whole truth."

"But I am ready to tell everything I know. Won't you please question me, Monsieur?"

"Well, in the first place, where is your wife?"

"She was abducted."

"But at five-thirty yesterday afternoon, thanks to your efforts, she escaped."

"My wife? Escaped? Poor, poor woman!"

"You visited your neighbor, Monsieur d'Artagnan, yesterday. You had a long conversation with him."

"Yes, yes, Monsieur, yes, it is true, I confess I acted foolishly in visiting Monsieur d'Artagnan."

"The purpose of your visit?"

"I called to beg him to help me find my wife again."

"How did Monsieur d'Artagnan react to your proposal?"

"Monsieur d'Artagnan promised to help me. Alas, I soon realized that he was betraying me."

"You are attempting to obstruct justice, my good man. Do you deny that Monsieur d'Artagnan agreed to drive away the police officers? Do you deny that he kept your wife in hiding?"

"Monsieur d'Artagnan abducted my wife! Monsieur, what on earth do you mean?"

"Fortunately, Monsieur d'Artagnan is in our hands. We shall at once confront you with him."

"By my faith, I ask for nothing better," cried Bonacieux. "I shall not be sorry to see the face of somebody I know."

"Show Monsieur d'Artagnan in," the commissioner ordered.

The guards admitted Athos.

"Monsieur d'Artagnan," said the commissioner, "will you please state what happened between you and Monsieur here?"

"But Monsieur," Bonacieux objected, "this is not Monsieur d'Artagnan."

"What? This is not Monsieur d'Artagnan? Then what is this gentleman's name?"

"I cannot tell you. I do not know this gentleman."

"You have never seen him?"

"Yes, I have seen him, but I do not know his name."

"Your name, Monsieur," snapped the commissioner.

"Athos," the musketeer replied.

"That is not a man's name," the wretched interrogator protested, losing his head. "Athos is the name of a mountain."

"Athos is nevertheless my name."

"But you said your name was D'Artagnan!"

"*I* said that?"

"Certainly you did."

"No, Monsieur. Somebody asked me was I D'Artagnan; I said: 'Do you really think so?' The guards declared they were positive I *was* D'Artagnan. Who was *I* to contradict them?"

"Monsieur, you are insulting the majesty of the law."

"In no wise, Monsieur."

"You are Monsieur d'Artagnan."

"There, you see, once again I hear I am D'Artagnan."

"Monsieur le Commissaire," Bonacieux interrupted,

"Monsieur d'Artagnan is my lodger and, though he does not pay his rent, I most certainly know him. Monsieur d'Artagnan is a youth barely twenty years old; this gentleman here must be at least thirty. Monsieur d'Artagnan serves in the Guards under Monsieur des Essarts; this gentleman belongs to the Musketeers."

"By Heaven, that's true!" the commissioner gasped. But before he could take action, the door swung open and one of the gatekeepers introduced a messenger who handed the commissioner a letter.

"Oh, poor woman, poor woman!" sighed the commissioner, as he finished reading the message.

"Whom are you talking about? Not my wife, I hope."

"Precisely: your wife. You're in plenty of trouble now!"

"But look here, Monsieur le Commissaire," cried the haberdasher, overcome, "will you be good enough to tell me how I can get into worse trouble because of what my wife may be doing while I languish in prison?"

Led back to the same cell he had occupied the night before, Bonacieux sat as though nailed to his stool, weeping. As he himself had said, he was no soldier. In the evening, at about nine, just as he was preparing to retire, he heard steps echoing ever louder and closer in the corridor. The door of his cell was flung open and the guards appeared. Then an officer, close behind the guards, commanded: "Follow me!"

"O God, O God," cried the wretched haberdasher, "now indeed I am lost."

Moving like an automaton, he followed the familiar corridor, crossed a courtyard, then another large building in front of which stood a carriage, flanked by four guards on horseback.

"Get in," said the officer, hoisting him onto the seat and settling himself on Bonacieux's right. A guard locked the door, and the rolling prison moved off, slow as a hearse.

Through the padlocked windows, the prisoner could see a house here, a pavement there, but, a true Parisian, he recognized each street by its stones, signboards and lampposts. As the carriage approached the spot where prisoners from the Bastille were usually executed, he all but fainted. But the crowd Bonacieux saw was not awaiting a victim; it was contemplating a man who had just been hanged. The carriage stopped for a moment, then pursued its way and finally pulled up before a low square door. Two guards bundled Bonacieux down a corridor, up a stairway, and suddenly by a mechanical process, he found himself in an antechamber. He walked as a somnambulist, dimly perceiving objects as through a mist. Had his life depended upon it, he could have summoned no gesture of apology, no cry for mercy.

Gradually, convinced that his fears were exaggerated, he proceeded to wag his head up and down, right and left. Just then an officer opened a door, said a few words to somebody within, and turning to the haberdasher:

"Are you Bonacieux?"

"Yes, Monsieur l'Officer," Bonacieux stammered, more dead than alive. "At your service, Monsieur."

"Step in here, please," said the officer, effacing himself to allow a startled, silent Bonacieux to enter a room where he sensed that he was expected. It was a large room, set aside from the rest of the mansion and richly tapestried; weapons of all kinds adorned the walls; a fire burned in the grate though it was but late September. A square table stood conspicuously in the middle of the room, covered with books and papers.

A man stood with his back to the fireplace. Of medium size, of proud and haughty mien, he had a noble brow, piercing eyes, and a thin face, its thinness emphasized by a slight mustache and a short tapering beard. Though he was scarcely thirty-six or at most thirty-seven, his hair, mustache and beard were turning gray. He wore no sword but otherwise he looked every inch a soldier.

It was Cardinal Richelieu.

At first glance nothing in his appearance denoted a prince of the Church; only those who knew him could have guessed who he was.

The unhappy haberdasher stood by the door; the man by the fireplace gazed at him piercingly as though to read every circumstance of his past. After a moment of silence, he asked:

"Is this the man Bonacieux?"

"Yes, Monseigneur."

"Good. Give me those papers, please. Now you may go!"

The officer picked up a sheaf of papers from the table, handed them to the gentleman, bowed low and retired.

"You are accused of high treason," the Cardinal said slowly.

"So I have been told, Monseigneur." Bonacieux was careful to address his questioner by the title he had heard the officer use. "But I swear I know nothing of all this."

"You have plotted with your wife," the Cardinal repressed a smile, "and with My Lord Duke of Buckingham."

"No, Monseigneur, but I have heard my wife mention that name."

"Under what circumstances?"

"I heard my wife say that the Cardinal de Richelieu lured the Duke of Buckingham to Paris in order to ruin both him and the Queen."

"Your wife said that?" the Cardinal demanded.

"Yes, Monseigneur. But I told her she was wrong to talk about such things. I said that the Cardinal was incapable—"

"Hold your tongue, fool!"

"That is exactly what my wife said, Monseigneur."

"Do you know who abducted your wife?"

"No, Monseigneur."

"Your wife escaped. Do you know that?"

"I learned it in prison, Monseigneur. I was told of it by Monsieur le Commissaire, a most kindly and understanding gentleman."

Again the Cardinal repressed a smile. "Then you are ignorant of what has happened to your wife since her flight?"

"Ay, Monseigneur."

"We shall find out, you may be sure. No one can conceal anything from the Cardinal. The Cardinal knows everything."

"In that case, Monseigneur, do you think the Cardinal would kindly tell me what has happened to my wife?"

"He may and he may not. When you went to call for your wife at the Louvre, did you always take her straight home?"

"Almost never. She always had to do some shopping. I usually left her at the draper's."

"Did you accompany your wife into his house?"

"Never, Monseigneur. I used to wait at the door."

"Would you recognize the door of this house?"

"Certainly."

"Where exactly is it?"

"Number 25 Rue de Vaugirard."

"Excellent!" the Cardinal commented. Then he took up a silver bell, rang it and addressed the officer who appeared immediately.

"Find out if Rochefort is here," he whispered. "If so, send him in at once."

"The Comte de Rochefort is here and craves immediate audience with Your Eminence."

Five seconds later, the door opened, a person entered—

"That's the man!" Bonacieux cried.

"The man?"

"That's the man who abducted my wife."

His Eminence again shook the silver bell. The officer re-appeared.

"Hand this fellow over to the guards. I shall want him presently."

"No, no, Monseigneur, it is *not* the man who abducted my wife. I made a mistake. This gentleman here is a re-spectable man. . . ."

"Take away this idiot," the Cardinal said curtly. Once again Bonacieux found an officer picking him up bodily and conveying him forcibly to a pair of guards.

The gentleman whose entrance caused Bonacieux's dismissal watched his exit impatiently. As soon as the door closed, he turned to the Cardinal.

"They saw each other," Rochefort whispered.

"You mean—?"

"The Queen . . . the Duke . . ."

"Where?" asked the Cardinal.

"At the Louvre."

"Are you sure?"

"Certain, Monsieur le Cardinal."

In answer to the Cardinal's further questions, Rochefort explained what had happened. The Queen was with her ladies-in-waiting in her bedroom when a servant presented Her Majesty with a handkerchief from her laundress, whereupon Her Majesty turned very pale and asked her ladies to await her for ten minutes. She left through the door of her alcove.

The Queen, Rochefort reported, was away from her bed-chamber for three-quarters of an hour, returned, picked up a small rosewood casket stamped with her coat of arms and went away again. This time she was not gone long, but she came back without the casket.

"What was in this casket?"

"The diamond studs His Majesty gave the Queen. During the course of the day, the Lady of the Queen's Wardrobe looked for this casket, seemed worried not to find it and finally asked the Queen about it—"

"And the Queen—?"

"The Queen blushed. She explained embarrassedly that, having broken one of the studs the day before, she had sent it to her goldsmith to be repaired."

"Find out if the repairs were made."

"I have already done so, Your Eminence."

"And the goldsmith—?"

". . . knows absolutely nothing about the matter."

"Good, good, Rochefort, all is not lost! Perhaps, indeed, everything is for the best. Meanwhile, do you know where the Duke of Buckingham is hiding?"

"No, Monseigneur."

"I happen to *know*."

"*You*, Monseigneur?"

"Yes. Or at least I have shrewd suspicions. At 25 Rue de Vaugirard."

"Does Your Eminence wish me to have him arrested?"

"Too late. Both will have fled by now."

"We should at least make sure of this."

"Well, take ten of my guardsmen and search the house thoroughly."

"I shall go instantly, Monseigneur."

Left alone, the Cardinal reflected for an instant, then rang the bell a third time. The same officer reappeared.

"Bring the prisoner in again," the Cardinal ordered.

Monsieur Bonacieux was introduced afresh and, at a sign from the Cardinal, the officer withdrew.

"You have deceived me," the Cardinal said sternly.

"I? I deceive Your Eminence!"

"When your wife went to the Rue de Vaugirard, she was not calling on a draper."

"What was she up to then, dear Heaven?"

Of a
Queen, a
Haberdasher
and a
Cardinal
103

"She was taking messages to the Duke of Buckingham."

"Yes," cried Bonacieux, recalling what he could of these errands. "Your Eminence is right. Several times I told my wife it was surprising to find a draper living in such a house, without a sign at the door. But she always laughed at me. Ah, Monseigneur," the haberdasher threw himself at the statesman's feet, "how truly you are the great Cardinal, the man of genius whom all the world reveres."

Petty as was his triumph over so base a creature as Bonacieux, the Cardinal savored it gratefully. Then, almost immediately, inspired anew, he smiled ever so fleetingly and offered the haberdasher his hand.

"Come, rise, friend, you are a worthy man."

"The Cardinal has touched my hand! The great man has called me his friend!"

"As you have been unjustly suspected, you shall be rewarded. Here, take this purse; it has one hundred pistoles in it. And pardon me for misjudging you."

"*I* pardon *you*, Monseigneur!" Bonacieux hesitated to take the purse, fearing that the Cardinal was jesting. "You cannot mean that!"

"My dear Monsieur Bonacieux, take this purse and let there be no hard feelings between us."

"Hard feelings? No, Monseigneur, I am delighted—"

"Au revoir, Monsieur Bonacieux." The Cardinal motioned him out. "Farewell."

Bonacieux retreated, bowing. When he reached the antechamber, the Cardinal heard him shouting at the top of his lungs:

"Long live the Cardinal!"

This vociferous manifestation of the haberdasher's enthusiasm brought another fleeting smile to the Cardinal's lips.

A few moments later, Rochefort returned. He announced that a foreign gentleman had spent five days at 25 Rue de

Vaugirard. "What are Your Eminence's orders?" he concluded.

"The strictest silence about what has happened; let the Queen believe herself perfectly secure."

"What has Your Eminence done with the haberdasher, Bonacieux?"

"All that could be done with such a man. From now on he will spy on his wife night and day."

Richelieu sat down, penned a letter, stamped it with his private seal, and rang a bell. The orderly officer entered for the fourth time.

"Send for Vitray," the Cardinal ordered. "Tell him he is to go on a journey."

An instant later, Vitray, booted and spurred, entered.

"Vitray," said His Eminence, "you are to leave immediately for London. You will deliver this letter to Milady. Here is an order for two hundred pistoles."

The messenger bowed and retired without a word.

The letter read:

MILADY:

You are instructed to go to the next public ceremony that His Grace the Duke of Buckingham may attend. He will wear on his doublet twelve diamond studs; you will approach him and cut off two of them.

You are to inform me as soon as you have these studs in your possession.

Of a
Queen, a
Haberdasher
and a
Cardinal
105

CHAPTER 7:

The Chancellor Steps In

NEXT day, Athos being still absent, D'Artagnan and Porthos reported his disappearance to Monsieur de Tréville. Tréville repaired instantly to the highest police magistrate; the officer in command of the district was summoned and some time later reported that Athos was in prison. He had refused to speak up because he wished to allow D'Artagnan the time necessary to carry out his plans. This interval assured, Athos boldly declared his own name, expressing some surprise that his identity had been confounded with that of D'Artagnan. He added that he knew neither Monsieur nor Madame Bonacieux . . . that he had never spoken to either . . . that he was involved in these idle proceedings only because he had called on his friend Monsieur d'Artagnan at ten o'clock . . . and that he had previously dined at Monsieur de Tréville's until shortly before ten.

Now men of the long robe are at all times eager to be revenged upon men of the long sword; but the firm and direct statement Athos presented took the magistrate somewhat aback, and the name of Tréville was indeed impressive.

Athos was then sent to the Cardinal, but unfortunately the Cardinal was closeted with the King at the Louvre. At precisely that time, Tréville arrived to call upon the King.

It was common gossip that the King was violently prejudiced against the Queen and, worse, violently jealous of her. Louis XIII had started toward the Queen's apartment, his features set in that mute, pale indignation which when it broke out drove this monarch to commit the most pitiless cruelties. And yet, so far, the Cardinal had not breathed a word about My Lord Duke of Buckingham.

At exactly this point Monsieur de Tréville entered, cool, polite and impeccably clad. Realizing from the Cardinal's presence and the King's sullen rage what had occurred, Tréville felt very much as Samson must have felt among the Philistines. Louis XIII had his hand on the doorknob when Tréville entered. The King swung round.

"Your arrival is timely, Monsieur," he said testily. "I have just learned some pretty things about your musketeers."

"Sire," Tréville countered coolly, "*I* have some pretty things to tell Your Majesty about his men of law."

"Pray explain," the King commanded haughtily.

"I have the honor to inform Your Majesty," Tréville continued coolly as ever, "that a party of commissioners, investigators and policemen took it upon themselves to enter the house of one of my musketeers. They dared arrest him without warrant, led him away through the streets and tossed him into prison. I say without warrant, Sire, because they refused to show me any order; and when I say one of *my* musketeers, I should more properly say one of *your* musketeers. Your Majesty recalls him favorably; his name is Athos."

"Athos?" the King repeated mechanically.

"If Your Majesty recalls," Tréville insisted, "Monsieur

Athos is the musketeer who had the misfortune to wound Monsieur de Cahusac." Tréville paused a moment, then, turning to the Cardinal: "By the way, Monsieur le Cardinal, I trust Monsieur de Cahusac has recovered."

"Quite, thank you," the Cardinal replied, biting his lips.

"May it please Your Majesty, here are the facts. Monsieur Athos had gone to call upon one of his friends who was out. The friend is a young Gascon in Your Majesty's Guards. Athos had barely made himself comfortable at his friend's when a motley crew of bailiffs laid siege to the house, broke down several doors—"

The Cardinal made a sign to the King, as if to say: "That was on account of the matter I just mentioned."

"We know all about *that!*" the King retorted. "It was all done in our service."

"Then it was also in Your Majesty's service that one of my musketeers, an innocent man, was seized and paraded through the streets to serve as the laughingstock of an insolent rabble? This gentleman, I may add," Monsieur de Tréville's voice rose ever so slightly, "has shed his blood at least a dozen times on behalf of Your Majesty and he is ready to do so again."

"Monsieur de Tréville has failed to mention an important fact, Sire," the Cardinal commented drily. "One hour previously, this innocent musketeer and paragon of gallantry, his sword in hand, struck down four commissioners who had been sent personally by myself to inquire into a matter of the highest importance."

"I defy Your Eminence to prove that!" cried Monsieur de Tréville. "Exactly one hour previously, Monsieur Athos dined at my board with the Duc de la Trémouille, the Comte de Châlus and myself."

The King glanced quizzically at the Cardinal.

"Official reports do not lie," the Cardinal said meaningfully.

Tréville broke in. "Is the written testimony of a man of law to be compared to the word of honor of a soldier?" he demanded.

"Come, come, Tréville, hush!"

But Tréville persisted:

"If the Cardinal entertains the slightest suspicion against one of my musketeers, the justice of the Cardinal is famed enough for me to demand an inquiry of my own."

"If I am not mistaken," the Cardinal observed impassively, "a Gascon friend of this musketeer's lives in the house which my police raided."

"Your Eminence means Monsieur d'Artagnan?"

"Do you not suspect this young man of giving bad counsel to—"

"To Monsieur Athos, a man double his age?" Tréville asked wonderingly; and, before the Cardinal could reply, "No, Monseigneur, I do not suspect anything of the kind. Besides, Monsieur d'Artagnan also spent the evening with me."

"Well, well!" the Cardinal exclaimed. "Everybody seems to have spent the evening with you."

"Does His Eminence venture to doubt my word?" Tréville asked hotly.

"Heaven forbid!" the Cardinal said piously. "But tell me, at what time was he at your house?"

"I can tell Your Eminence *that* quite positively. Just as he arrived I happened to notice that it was half-past nine by the clock though I had thought it was later."

"And at what time did he leave your house?"

"At ten—three quarters of an hour after the event."

The Cardinal, who did not question Tréville's integrity, felt victory slipping through his fingers. Here was a mystery he must solve.

"After all, Monsieur," he went on, "Athos was certainly picked up at D'Artagnan's house."

"Is a musketeer in my company forbidden to fraternize with a guardsman?"

"Yes, when they meet in a house that is suspect."

"Quite so, Tréville," the King remarked. "The house is under suspicion. Perhaps you did not know it?"

"Indeed, Sire, I did not. Of course some part of the house may bear investigation but not Monsieur d'Artagnan's apartment. That, I can swear to! If I can believe what the young man says, Sire, Your Majesty has no more devoted servant and the Cardinal no more profound admirer."

The King asked: "Is this the youth who wounded De Jussac in that unfortunate fight near the Carmelite convent?"

"Yes, Sire," Tréville put in quickly. "And he wounded Bernajoux the day after."

"Come, what shall we decide?" the King asked.

"That concerns Your Majesty more than myself," the Cardinal replied. "I maintain that he is guilty."

"And I deny it!" Tréville retorted. "But His Majesty has judges, and those judges will decide."

"Agreed!" said the King. "Let us refer the matter to the judges. It is their business to judge and judge they shall!"

"And yet," Tréville commented, "in these sorry times, it seems a pity that the noblest of men must be subjected to obloquy and persecution. The Army will resent it, I am sure. Are your soldiers varlets that the police may molest them for alleged misdemeanors?"

"Misdemeanors!" The King scowled. "What do *you* know about *them*, Monsieur? Stick to your musketeers and do not annoy us with such statements. What a pother about one musketeer! By Heaven, I shall arrest ten of them, fifty, a hundred, the whole company!"

"So long as the musketeers are victims of your suspicion, Sire, the musketeers are guilty. Therefore, I am prepared to resign my captaincy. Having accused my musketeers, the

Cardinal will, I am sure, proceed to accuse me. Accordingly I prefer to constitute myself a prisoner with Monsieur Athos."

The King, fearing a public scandal, suggested: "If the Cardinal had not certain personal motives—?"

"Excuse me, Sire," the Cardinal interrupted. "The moment Your Majesty considers me prejudiced, I beg to withdraw."

"Come now, Tréville," the King urged, "will you swear by my father that Monsieur Athos was at your house during the event and that he had no hand in it?"

"By your glorious father and by yourself whom I love and revere above all else in the world, I swear it!"

"Pray reflect, Sire," the Cardinal coaxed, "if we release the prisoner, we shall never discover the truth."

"Monsieur Athos will be at hand," Tréville retorted, "ready to testify whenever the gownsmen care to question him."

"Of course, he will not desert," the King agreed, "and he can always be found. Moreover—" here the King lowered his voice and glanced beseechingly at the Cardinal, "let us give them apparent security. It is good policy to do so."

"Order it as you will, Sire; you possess the right of pardon."

"The right of pardon is applicable only to the guilty," Tréville demurred, eager to have the last word, "and my musketeer is innocent."

"He is now in jail?"

"Yes, Sire, held incommunicado, in solitary confinement."

"Confound it!" murmured the King. "What must we do?"

"Sign the order for his release, Sire. That will be the end of it," the Cardinal proposed. "I believe with Your Majesty that Monsieur de Tréville's guarantee is more than sufficient."

Tréville bowed respectfully, with a joy not unmixed with fear; he would have preferred stubborn resistance on the part of the Cardinal to this sudden compliance. The King signed the order for release; Tréville accepted it with alacrity. Just as he was leaving, the Cardinal gave him a friendly smile and said to the King:

"A perfect harmony reigns between the commanding officer of your Musketeers, Sire, and his soldiers. That reflects honor upon all concerned."

Monsieur de Tréville had good reason to mistrust the Cardinal and to sense that all was not finished yet. Scarcely had he closed the door than the Cardinal said to the King:

"Now that we are alone again, Sire, let us converse seriously, if it please Your Majesty." He paused a moment, then added significantly, "Sire, Buckingham has been in Paris five days; he left Paris this morning."

To describe the impression these few words made upon Louis XIII is impossible. The King flushed, then paled; the Cardinal knew at once that his cause had recovered all the ground it had lost.

"My Lord Buckingham in Paris! What brought him here?"

"Doubtless he came to plot with Your Majesty's enemies."

"No, he came to plot against my honor."

"Surely not, Sire. Her Majesty is far too discreet to risk such a scandal. And she loves Your Majesty too dearly."

"Woman is a weak vessel, alas!"

"Nevertheless, Sire, I still maintain that the Duke of Buckingham came to Paris on a political errand."

"And *I*, Monsieur le Cardinal, insist that he came for other reasons. If the Queen is disloyal, she shall rue it."

"This morning Madame de Lannoy told me that two nights ago the Queen had sat up till a very late hour, that the following morning she had wept a great deal, and that she had spent most of that day writing."

"Ah, she has been writing to him," the King said angrily. "Monsieur le Cardinal, I *must* have the papers of the Queen!"

"But how can we seize them, Sire? Obviously neither Your Majesty nor I can undertake to do so. The august spouse of Your Majesty is Anne of Austria, Queen of France, one of the mightiest princesses on earth."

"She is all the more guilty for that very reason, Monseigneur; the more she has forgotten the exalted position she occupies, the lower she has fallen. There is a certain La Porte in her household, is there not?"

"Ay, Your Majesty, I confess I believe him to be the mainspring of all this business."

"Then you agree with me that the Queen is betraying me?"

"I repeat, Sire, I believe that the Queen is plotting against the power of her King, but I do not say she is plotting against his honor."

"I tell you she is guilty on both counts. Her Majesty does not love me, she loves another, she loves the infamous Buckingham! Why did you not have him arrested while he was in Paris?"

"Arrest the Duke of Buckingham? Arrest the Prime Minister of England? How can you think of it, Sire? Then, suppose Your Majesty's suspicions proved justified, what a desperate scandal!"

"But all the while he was in Paris, you kept your eye on him?"

"Yes, Sire."

"You are sure he did not meet the Queen?"

"I believe the Queen too loyal to you to have done so."

"But they corresponded. It was to *him* the Queen wrote all day yesterday. I must have those letters."

"I beg Your Majesty to observe—"

"Are you too betraying me, Monseigneur? Why do you constantly oppose my will?"

"Sire," the Cardinal sighed, "I believed I had proved myself above suspicion."

"Monsieur le Cardinal, you heard me: I will have those letters."

"There is but one way—"

"What is that?"

"Chancellor Séguier, Keeper of the Seals, might be entrusted with this task; it rests entirely within the competence of his post."

"Let him be sent for instantly."

"Your Majesty's orders shall be executed, but—"

"But what?"

"But the Queen may perhaps refuse to obey."

"To obey my orders?"

"Yes, if she does not know these orders come from the King."

"Well then, to dispel any doubts she might have on that matter, I shall go tell her myself."

"I beg you to remember, Sire, that I have done all in my power to prevent a misunderstanding between Her Majesty—"

"Good, good. Now, pray send for the Keeper of the Seals; I go to call upon the Queen."

With which the King departed.

The Queen was surrounded by her ladies-in-waiting. In one corner sat the Spanish Lady of the Bedchamber, Doña Estefana, who had followed the Queen from Madrid. Madame de Guéménée was reading aloud and everyone was listening attentively save the Queen, who had suggested this reading. While pretending to listen, Her Majesty pursued the thread of her own thoughts.

These thoughts, though intent upon love, were tinged with melancholy. The Queen was recalling how she was deprived of her husband's confidence . . . how relentlessly the Cardinal's hatred dogged her footsteps . . . how Richelieu had never forgiven her for repulsing a more tender sentiment on his part . . . how Anne herself had seen her most devoted followers struck down on every side. . . . Truly, she was like those unfortunates who are damned with a fatal gift . . . she brought ruin to everything she touched. . . .

Suddenly the door opened and the King loomed before her. Madame de Guéménée stopped dead in the middle of a sentence and dropped the book on her lap. The ladies all rose.

As for the King, he strode rudely past the ladies and stopped squarely in front of the Queen.

"Madame," he said hoarsely, "you are about to receive a visit from the chancellor, who will communicate to you certain matters with which I have charged him."

The unhappy Queen paled.

"But why this visit, Sire? What can the chancellor tell me that Your Majesty cannot himself tell me?"

For answer, the King turned on his heel just as Monsieur Séguier, Chancellor and Keeper of the Seals, appeared.

Séguier was by nature the drollest of men. He owed his success to the fact that a canon of Notre Dame, who had once served the Cardinal, had referred him to Richelieu as a completely reliable man. The Cardinal trusted him and found no cause to regret it.

"Monsieur," the Queen asked, "what brings you here?"

"Madame, I am here in the name of the King. My purpose, in all honor and with all respect due to Your Majesty, is to make a thorough examination of Your Majesty's papers."

"What, Monsieur? A search? This is an outrage!"

"I most humbly implore Your Majesty's pardon. In this instance I am but the instrument of the King."

"Very well, then; pray search my effects. Estefana, give Monsieur the keys to my drawers and my desk."

For form's sake the chancellor inspected these, but the Queen would not have entrusted so important a letter to drawer or desk. It was his duty now to search the person of the Queen herself. He therefore stepped forward and with the most embarrassed and perplexed air imaginable, ventured:

"Madame, His Majesty is convinced that Your Majesty has written a certain letter. This letter is neither in your desk nor in your cabinets. But it must be somewhere."

The Queen drew herself up to her full height.

"Do you dare lay hands upon your Queen?" she demanded.

"Madame, whatever His Majesty commands, I am in duty bound to accomplish."

"I see!" The Queen looked down scornfully at the chancellor. "It is true I wrote a letter. The letter in question is — here!" And she pressed a beautiful, tapering hand against her bosom.

"I must beg Your Majesty to give me that letter."

"I shall give it to none but the King, Monsieur."

"Madame, had His Majesty desired to receive the letter in person, he would himself have asked you for it. But, I repeat, it is *I* who am charged with requesting it of you and if you do not give it up —"

"What! What do you mean?"

"I mean, Madame, I am authorized to search for the suspicious paper even on Your Majesty's person."

"I will not tolerate it!" The Queen shuddered at this offense to her dignity. Was she, a daughter of imperial blood, to submit to such humiliation? "I would rather die!"

Séguier made a deep bow. It was quite evident that he did not intend to draw back a single step; he had his mission to accomplish and accomplish it he would. Tears of rage welled up in the Queen's eyes.

Determined to obey the King's instructions, Séguier stretched out his hand toward the Queen. The Queen took a step backwards; she turned white as a sheet. Her left hand clutching the edge of a table for support, with her right she drew a paper from her bosom and handed it to the chancellor.

"Here is the letter, Monsieur," she said in a tremulous, choking voice. "Pray take it and deliver me of your odious presence."

Without pausing to examine the letter, Séguier bore it forthwith to the King, who took it with anxious hand, looked for the address, which was missing, turned very pale and opened it slowly. Then, seeing by the first words that it was addressed to the King of Spain, he read it rapidly.

The letter contained a complete plan of attack against the Cardinal. The Queen invited her brother and the Emperor of Austria to threaten war against France unless the Cardinal was dismissed.

The Cardinal then took the letter, read it attentively once, then reread it. "This should convince Your Majesty to what lengths my enemies go," he opined. "Frankly, were I in Your Majesty's place, I should yield to such powerful pressure."

"What, Monseigneur? What?"

"I mean, Sire, that my health is sinking under this burden of unceasing labor and endless strife. I doubt very much whether I can possibly undergo the fatigues of the siege of La Rochelle. I honestly think Your Majesty would do well to appoint some professional soldier to conduct the campaign rather than myself who am a churchman."

"Monsieur le Cardinal, I understand you perfectly. You have my promise that I shall punish all those mentioned in this letter, including the Queen herself."

"Were the Queen to betray Your Majesty's honor, I would urge you to grant no mercy. Here, happily, that is not the question, for you have just acquired fresh proof of the Queen's innocence."

"True, Monseigneur, you were right on that score as usual. Nevertheless the Queen has incurred my displeasure—"

"It is you, Sire, who have now incurred hers. I must say Your Majesty treated her with considerable severity—"

"So shall I always treat my enemies and yours, Monseigneur, however exalted their positions and whatever perils befall me in so doing."

"*I* am the victim of the Queen's enmity, not you, Sire. To Your Majesty, she is a devoted wife. Pray allow me to intercede with Your Majesty on her behalf."

"Let her humble herself then and come to me first."

"On the contrary, Sire, deign to set the example. Your Majesty might do well to find some means of giving the Queen pleasure."

"For instance?"

"For instance, a ball. Your Majesty knows how fond the Queen is of dancing. I am certain the Queen's resentment will melt before an attention of that sort."

"We shall see, Cardinal, we shall see," the King answered. Perhaps the Cardinal was right; perhaps a reconciliation was in order.

"Sire, leave severity to your ministers, clemency is the royal virtue. Exercise it and you will find yourself the happier for it."

The clock struck eleven, the Cardinal rose, bowed low and begged leave to retire, not without imploring his master to compose his royal and marital difficulties.

On the morrow the Queen, after the seizure of her letter, expected serious trouble or at least sullen and acrimonious reproach. To her amazement the King called upon her and seemed to be making overtures for a reconciliation. His Majesty actually announced his intention of giving a ball in the near future.

A ball was so rare a thing in the Queen's life that, as the Cardinal had divined, the mere mention of such gaiety scattered the last traces of resentment from her features, if not from her heart. When she inquired eagerly what day the ball was to take place the King replied that he would have to consult the Cardinal. Indeed, day after day the King consulted His Eminence and day after day His Eminence found some pretext or other to temporize. Time passed and Her Majesty was left in suspense for ten days.

But the Cardinal's period of suspense was not to last longer. Forty-eight hours before he communicated with the King, His Eminence had received a missive from London which read:

I have them but I cannot leave London for want of money. Pray send me five hundred pistoles and within four or five days of receipt I shall be in Paris.

The day the Cardinal received this note, His Majesty asked the usual question; the Cardinal, counting on his fingers, mused:

"She says she will arrive within four or five days of receipt . . . it will take four or five days to get the money to her . . . it will take her four or five days to return . . . eight days minimum, ten days average, twelve at the outside, allowing for contrary winds, accidents and the frailty of woman. . . ."

"Come, Monsieur le Cardinal, when is the ball to be?"

"Today is the twentieth of September, Sire. The aldermen of the city are giving their ball on October third. A most auspicious date, it suits our purpose perfectly, for Your Majesty will not appear to have gone out of your way to be favoring the Queen. And," the Cardinal added in a casual, urbane tone, "pray remember to tell Her Majesty the day before the ball—that is, October second—that you should be pleased to see how the diamond studs you gave her become her. As you know, she has never worn them in public."

The King was somewhat surprised at the Cardinal's referring to the diamond studs. What mystery lay under that insistence?

His Majesty proceeded to the Queen's apartment and as usual uttered fresh threats against her henchmen and henchwomen. Anne of Austria bowed her head in silence and allowed the torrent to flow on, hoping it would eventually spend itself.

"Madame," the King said, "there will soon be a ball at the Hôtel de ville. In order to honor our worthy aldermen, I propose that you appear in ceremonial costume; I am particularly eager that you wear the diamond studs which I gave you on your birthday."

His words were terrible indeed. Anne of Austria blanched, leaned on the console for support and looked up in silent horror. His Majesty kept his eyes riveted on that slender, admirable hand, now bloodless and as though of wax.

"You will appear at this ball, Madame?"

"Yes."

"With those studs, Madame?"

"Yes."

"Then we agree," he said abruptly. "That was all I had to say, Madame."

"But what day will the ball take place?"

"Oh, very shortly, Madame," he replied. "As a matter of

fact, I have forgotten the exact date. I shall ask the Cardinal."

The Queen curtsied less out of etiquette than because her knees were giving way under her. The King went away delighted.

"I am lost, lost," the Queen murmured. "The Cardinal

knows everything; the King is but his tool. But the King will learn the truth soon enough. Oh, what ever shall I do!"

She knelt upon a cushion and prayed, her head bowed, her arms trembling. Her plight was desperate. More closely watched than ever, she understood that one of her ladies-in-waiting or maidservants had betrayed her. But who was the culprit? Contemplating the impending catastrophe and her helplessness, she burst into sobs.

"Can I help Your Majesty?" A voice filled with gentleness and pity intruded upon the Queen's misery. "Can I help?"

The Queen turned sharply round. There was no mistaking the expression of sympathy in that voice. Here was a friend in time of need. As she looked up, Madame Bonacieux stepped into the Queen's apartment. She had been busy sorting gowns and linen in one of the closets when the King entered; now, timidly, she ventured forth.

The Queen gasped at this intrusion; in her dismay she did not immediately recognize La Porte's protégée.

"You have nothing to fear, Madame," said the young servant. "I am Your Majesty's servant, body and soul. I think I can find a way to help you."

"*You?* Great Heavens, *you!* Can I trust in *you?*"

Madame Bonacieux fell to her knees.

"Madame," she vowed, "I swear upon my soul that I am ready to die for Your Majesty." That cry of loyalty sprang from her innermost heart; its fervor and sincerity were unmistakable. "Ay, Madame, I swear that no one is more devoted to Your Majesty than I am. These studs the King requests of you—you gave them to the Duke of Buckingham, did you not? They were in a little rosewood box which he took away with him. Am I mistaken?"

"Ah, no, no," the Queen moaned.

"We must get those studs back, Madame."

"Of course, my child! But how? What to do? How to go about it?"

"Someone must be sent to the Duke."

"But who? Who? Whom can I trust?"

"Have faith in me, Madame; I shall find the messenger, I promise you."

"But I shall have to write a message!"

"Yes, of course, Madame. Two words in Your Majesty's writing and your own seal will suffice."

"But two words might bring about my arrest, divorce and exile!"

"I promise I can have your message delivered safely to the Duke."

"So I must place my life, my honor and my reputation in your hands?"

"Ay, Madame, you must. I know I can save you."

"But how?"

"Madame, my husband is a good, honest man; he will do anything I wish. And he will deliver Your Majesty's letter to the address she desires, without even knowing it is from Your Majesty!"

Fervidly the Queen grasped the young woman's hands and looked deep into her eyes. Convinced of her servant's sincerity, the Queen embraced Madame Bonacieux.

"Do it," she vowed, "and you will save the life and honor of your Queen."

"Then give me that letter at once, Madame. Time presses."

The Queen went to her desk, wrote two short lines and sealed her message with her private seal.

"We are forgetting one very important thing," she said.

"What is that, Madame?"

"Money."

"Your Majesty must not worry about all this. We shall find some way—"

"The truth is that I have no money," the Queen confessed. "But wait!" She picked up her jewel case. "Here," she said breathlessly, "here is a ring of great value; sell it and let your husband leave for London at once."

"You shall be obeyed within an hour, Madame."

Ten minutes later, Madame Bonacieux was at home. She had not seen her husband since his liberation. She was therefore unaware of his change of feeling toward the Cardinal; nor did she know that this change had been intensified by two or more visits from the Comte de Rochefort.

Madame Bonacieux found her husband alone. The unhappy man was with utmost difficulty restoring some order in his house. The furniture was completely destroyed and the closets were empty.

Immediately upon his return, the worthy haberdasher had notified his wife that he was safe at home. She had replied promising that the earliest moment she could steal from her duties would be devoted to paying him a visit.

Madame Bonacieux had married Monsieur Bonacieux at the age of eighteen; she had always lived among her husband's friends, people hardly capable of inspiring a young woman whose heart and soul were above her social position. D'Artagnan was of gentle birth; he was handsome, young and adventurous; he spoke of love as a man who loved and was eager to be loved in return. In all this there was certainly enough to turn a head only twenty-three years old, and Madame Bonacieux had just reached that happy age.

However, Monsieur Bonacieux manifested genuine delight as he advanced toward his wife with open arms. Madame Bonacieux raised her head, presenting her brow to his kiss. "Let us talk a little," she suggested. "I have something of the greatest importance to tell you."

"I too would like to discuss several matters with you. First, can you explain your abduction?"

"That is not important just now."

"Well then, do you want to discuss my stay in prison?"

"I heard of it the day you were arrested," Madame Bonacieux explained. "But I knew you were guilty of no crime or intrigue, so I attached no more importance to your arrest than it warranted. Let us forget your captivity and return to the matter that brings me here."

"What?" The haberdasher was wounded to the quick.

"Are you not here to see a husband from whom you have been separated for a week?"

"Yes, that first! But there is also something else—something on which our fortunes depend—"

"Our fortunes will change considerably from now on, Madame Bonacieux."

"Indeed, yes! Especially if you follow the instructions I am about to give you. There is a good deed to be done, Monsieur, and a great deal of money to be made into the bargain."

Madame Bonacieux knew that by talking of money she was attacking his weakest spot. But a man who had once spoken to Cardinal Richelieu (if only for ten minutes) was no longer the same man.

"Yes, about a thousand pistoles," she went on.

"What is to be done?"

"You must set out immediately. I shall give you a paper which you must not part with on any account whatever. You are to deliver that paper into the proper hands."

"And where am I to go?"

"To London."

"I go to London! Look here, you are joking!"

"An illustrious personage is sending you, an illustrious person awaits you. The reward will exceed your expectations."

"More intrigues, always intrigues!" Bonacieux grumbled. "Thank you, I have had my fill of them. His Eminence the Cardinal has enlightened me on that score!"

"The Cardinal? You saw the Cardinal?"

"He sent for me," the haberdasher answered proudly.

"He ill-treated you? He threatened you?"

"He gave me his hand and called me his friend. I am a friend of the great Cardinal."

"Of the great Cardinal!"

"Do you perchance deny him that title, Madame?"

"I deny him nothing. But there are powers superior to his which do not depend on the whim of an individual or of an event."

"I am sorry, Madame, but I recognize no power other than that of the great man I serve."

"So you are a cardinalist, Monsieur?" she exclaimed. "You serve the party that mistreats your wife and insults your Queen!"

"Private interests are of no import against the interest of all," Bonacieux observed sententiously. "I am for those who support the State."

"The State?" Madame Bonacieux shrugged her shoulders. "Be satisfied with living as a plain, straightforward bourgeois; turn to that side which holds out the greatest advantages."

"Well, well!" Bonacieux slapped a plump round bag which jingled at his touch, "what do you say to this, Madame Preacher?"

"Where does that money come from? From the Cardinal?"

"From him and from my friend the Comte de Rochefort."

"The Comte de Rochefort! Why, it was he who carried me off!"

"That is quite possible, Madame."

"And you accept money from that man?"

"Why not? I suppose you were carried off for political reasons."

"They carried me off to make me betray my mistress."

"Madame, your mistress is a perfidious Spaniard. What the Cardinal has done, was well done."

"Monsieur, I knew you for a coward, a miser and an idiot. But I never supposed you were infamous."

Bonacieux, who had never seen his wife angry, retreated before this outburst of conjugal wrath.

"But what on earth do you want me to do?" he asked. "Tell me!"

"I want you to leave instantly, Monsieur, and carry out the mission with which I have deigned to charge you. If you do this, I shall forgive and forget everything, and—" she held out her hand to him— "I will give you my love again."

Bonacieux was a coward and a miser but he loved his wife. He was touched. Madame Bonacieux saw he was hesitating.

"Well, have you made up your mind?" she asked.

"No, Madame Bonacieux," the haberdasher decided at last. "No, no, no, I positively refuse. Intrigues terrify me. No, I shan't go; decidedly not!"

"So you are scared, are you? Well, if you do not leave immediately, I shall have you arrested by order of the Queen and clapped into that Bastille you dread so much."

Bonacieux carefully weighed the respective angers of Queen and Cardinal; the latter easily won the day.

"You have me arrested by order of the Queen," he threatened, "and I shall appeal to His Eminence."

"Well, I give up my idea! Let us say no more about it."

Bonacieux now recalled somewhat belatedly that Rochefort had admonished him to discover his wife's secrets.

"You might at least tell me what you expected me to do in London?" he suggested.

"There is no point in your knowing," she answered, with instinctive mistrust. "It was a trifling matter."

But the more she excused herself, the more important he believed her secret to be. He therefore decided to hasten to Rochefort to tell him that the Queen was seeking a messenger to send to London.

"Pray forgive me if I must leave you now, dear Madame Bonacieux," he said unctuously. "I shall be back soon, and, if you wait, I will escort you to the Louvre."

"Thank you, Monsieur, I shall return to the Louvre alone."

"As you please, Madame Bonacieux. Shall I see you soon again?"

"Probably. Next week, I hope, my duties will afford me a little liberty."

"We shall meet shortly then?"

"Yes, in a few days."

Bonacieux kissed his wife's hand and set off hurriedly.

"Well, well!" Madame Bonacieux mused as soon as her husband had shut the street door and she was alone. "Poor idiot! Alas, Monsieur Bonacieux, I never did love you much; now, I hate you and you shall pay for it."

Suddenly, hearing a rap at the ceiling, she raised her head. Through the plaster, she heard a voice from the floor above. A man was saying:

"Dear Madame Bonacieux, please open the side door; I shall come downstairs at once."

CHAPTER 8:

On Her Majesty's Service

Pᴀssɪɴɢ through the side door, D'Artagnan announced:

"Forgive me, Madame, if I say so, but your husband is a sorry specimen."

"You heard our conversation?" she asked.

"Every word. First, I discovered that your husband is a simpleton and a fool. Secondly, I gathered that you are in distress, which pleases me beyond words because I can serve you. Third, I realized that to do so I am willing to risk all the fires of Hell. Fourth, I learned that the Queen needs a brave, devoted man to go to London. That is why I am here."

"What pledge can you offer?" she asked timidly. "This mission is a weighty one."

"My pledge will be the love I bear you. You have but to command; I am at your orders."

The young woman paused, wondering whether she dared confide in so young a man. "You are but a boy!" she whispered.

"Monsieur de Tréville will vouch for me! Ask Tréville

whether I can be trusted with so urgent, precious and terrible a secret!"

"But my secret does not belong to me. I am not at liberty to divulge it," she objected.

"You were about to divulge it to Monsieur Bonacieux."

"Ay, Monsieur, just as a woman leaves a letter in the hollow of a tree or pins a note on a pigeon's wing or fastens a message under the collar of a dog."

"Yet you must know I love you."

"So you say."

"I am an honorable man."

"I believe it."

"Then use me . . . let me help you . . . put me to the test!"

As Madame Bonacieux looked at him, her last doubt vanished. There was such ardor in his eyes and such conviction in his voice that she could not but trust him.

"I yield to your protestations and I accept your assurances," she said. "But, God be my witness, I swear that if you betray me I shall kill myself."

"Madame, for my part, I can only swear that, if I die before carrying out your orders, your secret will go with me to the grave."

Madame Bonacieux told him all that worried her now and all that had worried her when they met near the Louvre the night he had challenged her mysterious escort. D'Artagnan was radiant with joy and pride; the woman he loved had confided her deepest, purest secret!

"I go," he vowed, "I go at once!"

"How can you go? What of your captain and your regiment?"

"Constance, you are right; I must get a furlough immediately. I shall call on Monsieur de Tréville this very evening and request him to obtain leave for me from his brother-in-law, Monsieur des Essarts."

"But there is something else," she said hesitantly. "Perhaps you have no money?"

"*Perhaps* is an exaggeration!"

Madame Bonacieux opened a wardrobe; out of it she drew the bag which her husband had been fondling so lovingly half an hour earlier. "In that case, here! Take this!"

"The Cardinal's money!" D'Artagnan roared with laughter. "How entertaining to save the Queen with His Eminence's money!"

"You are a most charming and witty young man; believe me, Her Majesty will not prove ungrateful."

"I need no reward," D'Artagnan protested. "I love you and you allow me to tell you so; that in itself is more happiness than ever I dared hope."

"Hush!"

"What is the matter?"

"Voices—in the street—"

"Voices?"

"My husband's voice—I recognize it—"

"Quick! Come upstairs with me," D'Artagnan urged. "In my rooms you will be as safe as in a church."

Cautiously he unbolted the door and, light as shadows, the pair slipped out into the alley and mounted the stairway to his apartment. Once there, for greater safety, the young man barricaded the door. They moved to the window and through a slit in the shutter espied Monsieur Bonacieux talking to a cloaked figure. At the sight of this man, D'Artagnan leaped up and, half-drawing his sword, sprang toward the door.

It was the man of Meung!

"What are you doing! You will ruin us both!"

"But I have sworn to kill that man!"

"Your life is now devoted to a nobler cause; from this moment on, it is not yours to risk. In the Queen's name, I

forbid you to face any danger other than that of your journey."

"And in your own name, you order nothing?"

"In my own name," she replied with great emotion, "I
beg you to listen. I think they are talking about me."

D'Artagnan returned to the window and listened carefully. Meanwhile Monsieur Bonacieux had opened the
front door and, seeing his apartment empty, had rejoined
the cloaked man.

"She's gone," he announced. "Probably back to the
Louvre."

"You're sure she had no suspicions?"

"No," Bonacieux replied self-confidently. "She is too
superficial a woman for that."

"Is the young guardsman at home?"

"I don't think so. His shutters are closed; I see no light."

"Then let us go to your rooms. We shall be safer there
than in the doorway."

"Oh dear," said Madame Bonacieux, "now we can't hear
them!"

"Nonsense, we shall hear all the better." Removing four
of the floor boards, D'Artagnan carefully uncovered the
aperture he had made, went down on his knees, and motioned to Madame Bonacieux to stoop too. Shoulder to
shoulder, they crouched listening.

"You're sure there is no one?"the stranger was asking.

"I will answer for it."

"And you think your wife—"

"She has gone back to the Louvre!"

"She spoke to no one but yourself?"

"I am sure of it."

"That point is important, you understand?"

"Then the news I brought you has some value?"

"Great value, my dear Bonacieux, great value! You are
quite sure your wife mentioned no one by name?"

"No. She only said she wished me to go to London to serve the interests of some illustrious person."

"The traitor," Madame Bonacieux murmured.

"Silence!" D'Artagnan warned, pressing her hand.

"Never mind," the stranger went on. "You were a ninny not to pretend to accept the commission. The Cardinal would probably have given you letters of nobility."

"All is not lost, Monsieur, my wife adores me and there is still time."

"The dolt," murmured Madame Bonacieux.

"Silence!" D'Artagnan warned again, pressing her hand still more firmly.

"What do you mean, 'there is still time'?" the stranger challenged Bonacieux.

"I shall go to the Louvre, I shall tell my wife I accept, I shall get the letter."

"Well, be off then, quickly. I will return soon to learn the result of your errand."

"The swine!" said Madame Bonacieux, overcome by her husband's infamy.

"Silence!" D'Artagnan repeated, crushing her hand as in a vise.

A sudden terrible howling interrupted their whispers. Downstairs, Monsieur Bonacieux had just discovered the disappearance of his money bag and was crying, "Help! Thieves! I've been robbed!"

"Oh, the idiot!" Madame Bonacieux wailed, "he will rouse the whole neighborhood!"

Bonacieux kept howling for a long time, then ran out. But as such cries were frequent in the neighborhood, they attracted no attention.

"Now that he's gone, it is your turn to go!" Madame Bonacieux told D'Artagnan. "Courage, my friend, but, above all, caution! Remember you owe yourself to the Queen."

"To her and to you, darling Constance," D'Artagnan said passionately. "Rest easy, my love, I shall return worthy of Her Majesty's gratitude."

D'Artagnan went straight to the Tréville mansion, and was shown directly to Tréville's study. Five minutes later Monsieur de Tréville joined him. One glance at the young Gascon's radiant expression told the captain that something new was afoot.

"You asked for me, young man?"

"Yes, Monsieur, I did. You will forgive me for disturbing you when you learn the importance of my errand. Monsieur, the Queen's honor, perhaps her very life, are at stake!"

"What!" Tréville looked about him to make sure they were quite alone. "What do you mean?"

"I mean chance has put me in possession of a secret—"

"—which I hope, young man, you will guard with your very life—"

"—but which I must confide to you, Monsieur. You alone

can help me accomplish the mission I have just received from Her Majesty."

"Did the Queen permit you to divulge this secret?"

"No, Monsieur, I have been pledged to the deepest silence."

"Keep your secret, young man, and tell me what you wish."

"I beg you to ask Monsieur des Essarts to grant me a two-week furlough."

"When?"

"This very night."

"You mean to leave Paris?"

"On a mission."

"Can you tell me where?"

"To London."

"Is anyone seeking to prevent you from reaching your destination?"

"The Cardinal would, I believe, give the world to stop me."

"You are going alone?"

"Quite alone."

"Believe me," Tréville said earnestly, "in undertakings of this kind the chances are about four to one against. There should be four of you!"

"Well, Monsieur, three of your musketeers are dear friends of mine: Athos, P—"

"Yes, I know. Can you pledge them to secrecy?"

"We four are as blood brothers, Monsieur. You need but tell them you trust me, they will take me at my word."

"I can give each of them a two-week furlough, no more. Athos is bothered by his wound, let him go to the waters at Forges; Porthos and Aramis may well accompany the invalid. Their orders will serve to prove that I authorize the journey."

D'Artagnan made out his application; Tréville, receiving it, assured him that his furlough and those of his friends would be in their hands by two o'clock in the morning.

"May I ask you, Monsieur, to send mine in care of Athos?" D'Artagnan requested. "I think it highly unwise to go home."

"Very good. Farewell and bon voyage!" Tréville paused. "By the by, have you any money?"

D'Artagnan turned, tapping the Bonacieux bag which was in his pocket.

As D'Artagnan bowed, Tréville offered his hand, which D'Artagnan shook gratefully.

His first visit was to Aramis, whom he had not called on since that evening on the bridge when he mistook Buckingham for him. Aramis was awake but gloomy and pensive. They discussed matters of current interest. Suddenly there was a knock at the door; a lackey wearing the Tréville livery loomed in the doorway.

"What is this?" Aramis asked.

"The leave of absence Monsieur requested."

"I requested no leave of absence, my good man. There must be some mistake!"

"Hush, Aramis, and be thankful for small mercies," D'Artagnan said royally.

"Do you mind telling me what all this means?" Aramis asked meekly after the lackey had bowed himself out.

"It means a fortnight's leave," D'Artagnan explained. "Fall in and follow me."

"How can I leave Paris without know—"

"—without knowing what has become of *her*, eh?"

"Who?"

"The lady who was here . . . the lady of the embroidered handkerchief."

Aramis turned deathly pale. "Who told you there was a lady here?"

"I saw her."

"Look here, D'Artagnan, as long as you know so much, can you tell me what has happened to her?"

"I dare say she went back to Tours."

"But why did she leave town without telling me?"

"She was afraid of being arrested."

"Why has she not written?"

"For fear of compromising you."

"So long as you are sure she has left Paris," Aramis said, "nothing keeps me here. I am ready to follow you. Where are we off to?"

"First we must see Athos. If you want to come along, do make haste; time is short. And alert Bazin!"

Aramis summoned Bazin, his valet, gave him the necessary instructions and:

"Off we go," he said, picking up his cloak, his sword and his three pistols. "You have spoken of this lady to no one?"

"To no one on earth."

"Thank Heavens!"

They found Athos with his orders in one hand and Tréville's letter in the other.

"Can you explain the meaning of this leave and this letter?" Athos asked in astonishment, then proceeded to read:

My dear Athos,

As I know your health absolutely requires it, I am perfectly willing for you to take a fortnight's rest.

Go to the spa at Forges, then, or to any other spa that you prefer, profit by the waters and come back thoroughly fit.

Cordially yours,

De Tréville

"That letter and that leave," D'Artagnan explained, "mean that you must follow me, Athos."

"On the King's service?"

"King's or Queen's. Are we not servants of both?"

Just then Porthos came in.

"Look here, friends," he said, "here is a queer thing for you! Since when are furloughs granted to musketeers without their being requested?"

"Since the day musketeers have friends to ask for leaves on their behalf," D'Artagnan explained. "We are leaving for London, gentlemen."

"But to go to London we must have money," Porthos objected, "and I haven't a sou."

"Nor I," said Aramis.

"Nor I," said Athos.

"I have," D'Artagnan said triumphantly. "This bag contains three hundred pistoles. Let us each take seventy-five; that is enough to get us to London and back. Besides, don't worry, all of us will not reach London."

"Is this a campaign we are undertaking?"

"A most dangerous one, I warn you."

"Well, if we're risking our lives," Porthos complained, "I would like to know in what cause."

"I agree with Porthos," said Aramis.

"Does the King usually give you his reasons in matters of this sort? No. He tells you gaily: 'Gentlemen, there is fighting in Flanders, or in Gascony. Go fight there!' And off you go! Why do you go? You do not even bother to think why!"

"D'Artagnan is right," Athos declared. "Here are our three furloughs from Tréville and here are three hundred pistoles from Heaven knows where. So let us go get ourselves killed wherever we are told to. D'Artagnan, I am ready to follow you."

"I too," Porthos assured the Gascon. "You may count on me," Aramis chimed in. "When do we go?" Athos asked.

"Immediately; we have not a minute to lose."

Pandemonium broke loose as the young men summoned their lackeys.

"Ho, Grimaud, my boots, properly polished!" Athos cried.

"Planchet, home at once to furbish my equipment!" D'Artagnan commanded.

"Mousqueton, I will give you five minutes to get my gear in shape!" Porthos said in lordly fashion.

"Bazin, you know what to do," Aramis counseled.

When the lackeys had gone, Porthos asked, "What is our plan of campaign? Point one: where are we bound for?"

"Calais," said D'Artagnan. "That is the shortest route to London."

"No one has asked me for my advice," Porthos said, "but I will volunteer it. A party of four, setting out together, would attract too much attention. I therefore suggest that D'Artagnan give each of us his instructions. I am willing to go by the Boulogne road to blaze the trail; Athos can leave two hours later on the Amiens road, Aramis can follow us along the Noyon road, and D'Artagnan can do as he sees fit."

"The plan suggested by Porthos seems to me unfeasible," D'Artagnan commented, "although I am myself at a loss to tell you what to do. I have a sealed letter to deliver." And he tapped his breast. "If I am killed," he went on, "one of you must take it and ride on; if *he* is killed, a third will take his place, and so on. One thing alone matters: the letter must reach its destination."

"Bravo, D'Artagnan, I agree!" said Athos. "We must be logical about all this. Four men, each on his own, are too easily destroyed; four men, shoulder to shoulder, form a troop."

"Let us leave within a half hour," said D'Artagnan.

At two in the morning our four adventurers left Paris. So long as it was night, they exchanged no word, but with the first light of dawn their tongues were loosened and with the sun their gaiety revived.

All went well as far as Chantilly. Eager for breakfast, they alighted at an inn. The lackeys were told to be ready to set off again immediately.

Our friends entered the common room and sat down. A gentleman who had just arrived was breakfasting at the same table. He started talking about the weather, the travelers answered, he drank their healths, and they returned the politeness.

But just as their horses were ready and our friends rose, the stranger proposed to Porthos that they drink to the Cardinal. Porthos replied that he would like nothing better if the stranger would, in turn, drink to the King. The stranger countered that he recognized no other king but His Eminence. Porthos called him a drunkard; the stranger drew his sword.

"You were foolish," said Athos, "but never mind. Kill the man and join us as soon as you can."

And the travelers continued on their way.

At Beauvais they stopped to give their horses a breathing spell and to wait for Porthos. After two hours, Porthos having failed to arrive or to forward news, they resumed their journey.

A league from Beauvais, at a place where the road narrowed between two high banks, they came upon a dozen men who seemed to be busy digging holes to deepen the muddy ruts.

Aramis, fearing to soil his boots in this artificial trench, cursed them roundly. Athos sought to restrain him but it was too late. The workmen started to jeer at the travelers; at their insolence even Athos lost his head and urged his horse against one of them.

At this the workmen retreated as far as the ditch, from which each produced a hidden musket. The result was that our seven travelers were literally riddled with bullets. Aramis received one which pierced his shoulder; Mousqueton, another which embedded itself in the fleshy parts which prolong the small of the back. Only Mousqueton fell from his horse.

"This is an ambush," said D'Artagnan. "Don't waste a shot! Let us be off!"

Aramis, wounded though he was, seized his horse's mane and was borne off headlong with the rest. Mousqueton's horse, rejoining the group, galloped on in formation, riderless.

"That will give us a remount," said Athos.

"I would prefer a hat," D'Artagnan remarked. "Mine was carried away by a bullet. How very fortunate that I did not carry my letter in it."

They galloped on for another two hours at top speed though their horses began to give signs of failing.

Hoping to avoid trouble, the cavalcade had chosen side roads but at Crèvecoeur Aramis declared he could go no farther. So they left him at an inn with Bazin who, to be frank, was more of a nuisance than a help in a skirmish, and they started off again, hoping to sleep at Amiens.

"Confound it!" Athos cried to D'Artagnan, as they raced off, the cavalcade reduced to themselves and their valets, "I vow I won't play into their hands again; no one will make me open my mouth or draw my sword till we reach Calais!"

"Let us make no vows; let us gallop if our horses can manage it!"

The quartet reached Amiens at midnight and alighted at the *Sign of the Golden Lily.*

The host looked like the most honest man on earth; he begged to lodge the masters each in a comfortable room, but unfortunately these charming rooms were at opposite ends of the inn. D'Artagnan and Athos refused. The host protested that he had no other rooms worthy of Their Excellencies, to which they replied that they would sleep on mattresses in the public chamber. They had just arranged their bedding and barricaded the door from within when there was a knock at the courtyard shutter. They asked who was there and recognized the voices of Planchet and Grimaud.

"Grimaud can take care of the horses," Planchet volunteered, "and if you gentlemen are willing, I shall sleep across the doorway."

Planchet climbed in through the window and settled himself across the door; Grimaud went off to lock himself in the stable, promising that he and the four horses would be ready by five o'clock in the morning.

At four o'clock in the morning they heard a terrible riot in the stables. Grimaud had sought to awaken the stableboys; they had turned upon him and beaten him severely. Athos and D'Artagnan saw the poor lad lying senseless on the ground, his head split. Some ostler had struck him from behind with the handle of a pitchfork.

Athos went downstairs to pay the bill while D'Artagnan and Planchet waited for him at the street door. The host's office was in a low-ceilinged back room to which Athos was requested to go. Entering without the least mistrust, he found the host alone, seated at his desk, one of the drawers of which was half open. Athos took two pistoles from his pocket to pay the bill; the host accepted the coin and then, having turned it over in his hands several times, suddenly shouted that it was counterfeit.

"I shall have you and your confederate arrested as coiners!" he cried.

At the same instant four men, armed to the teeth, entered by side doors and fell upon Athos.

"I'm trapped!" Athos yelled at the top of his lungs. "Run, D'Artagnan! Spur, Spur!" And he fired two pistols.

D'Artagnan and Planchet needed no further invitation. Unfastening their horses from the gatepost, they leaped upon them, buried their spurs in their flanks and set off at full gallop.

"Do you know how Athos fared?" D'Artagnan asked of Planchet as they raced on.

"Monsieur, I saw a man fall at each of his shots. As I glanced through the glass door, I caught sight of him using his sword to advantage."

At a hundred paces from the gates of Calais D'Artagnan's horse sank under him; the blood flowed from his nose and eyes and nothing could be done to get him up again. Planchet's horse refused to budge. Congratulating themselves on being so close to the city, they abandoned their mounts and ran toward the port. On the way Planchet drew his master's attention to a gentleman and his lackey who were some fifty paces ahead. The gentleman was bustling about authoritatively, asking here and there whether he could find passage to England immediately.

"Nothing easier," said the skipper of a vessel about to sail, "but we had orders this morning to allow no one to sail without express permission from the Cardinal."

"I have that permission," the gentleman said.

"Monsieur must have it certified by the Governor of the Port," said the skipper. "When that is done, please give me first choice. I've a fine vessel and a crack crew."

"Where shall I find the Governor?"

"About three-quarters of a mile out of town. Look, Monsieur, you can see his house from here—over there, at the foot of that little hill—that slate roof . . ."

"Thank you," said the gentleman and, with his lackey, he made for the Governor's house, D'Artagnan and Planchet following at an interval of five hundred paces. No sooner outside the city than D'Artagnan quickened his pace, overtaking the gentleman just as he was entering a little wood.

"Monsieur," he said, "you appear to be in a vast hurry."

"I could not be more pressed for time, Monsieur."

"I am distressed to hear that, Monsieur, for I too am pressed for time and I was about to ask a favor of you."

"What favor, pray?"

"I want your movement orders. I have none and need some."

"You are jesting, I presume."

"I never jest."

"Let me pass!" the other insisted.

"You shall not pass!"

"My dear young man, I shall blow your brains out. Ho, Lubin! my pistols!"

"Planchet, *you* handle the lackey, *I* shall manage the master."

Emboldened by his earlier adventures, Planchet sprang upon Lubin and soon had him flattened out, Planchet's bony knee pinning Lubin's narrow chest to the ground.

"Carry on, Monsieur," Planchet called. "My man is accounted for."

The gentleman drew his sword and sprang upon D'Artagnan but he met more than he had bargained for. Within three seconds D'Artagnan pinked him thrice, dedicating each thrust as he dealt it: "One for Athos!" he cried. "One for Porthos!" and at the last, "One for Aramis!"

At the third thrust the gentleman fell like a log. D'Artagnan stretched out his hand to search for his victim's travel orders when the wounded man, who had not relinquished his sword, pinked D'Artagnan in the chest, crying:

"And one for you!"

"And one for me!" D'Artagnan cried in a fury, nailing him to the earth with a fourth thrust.

This time the gentleman fainted. D'Artagnan plucked the order from the pocket into which he had seen the gentleman stuff it. It was in the name of the Comte de Vardes.

Lubin kept howling for help, but D'Artagnan gagged

him with his handkerchief and bound him to a tree. They drew the Comte de Vardes' body close to him.

"Now to the Governor's!" said D'Artagnan briskly.

"But you are wounded, Monsieur!"

"Oh, that's nothing. A mere scratch."

They soon reached the worthy official's country house; the Comte de Vardes was announced; D'Artagnan entered.

"You have an order signed by the Cardinal?" the Governor asked.

"Of course, Monsieur. I am one of the Cardinal's most faithful servants."

"Apparently His Eminence is anxious to prevent someone from crossing to England."

"Yes, Monsieur, one D'Artagnan, a Gascon gentleman."

"Do you know him personally?"

"Intimately, Monsieur."

"Pray describe him to me, then."

"Nothing could be simpler," D'Artagnan assured him. And he proceeded to furnish the most minute description of the Comte de Vardes.

"Is he accompanied by anyone?"

"Yes, by a valet named Lubin."

"We will keep a sharp lookout for them," the Governor promised as he signed the order, "and if ever we lay hands on them, His Eminence may be sure they will be returned to Paris under heavy guard."

The Gascon bowed to the Governor, thanked him and took his leave. Once out of doors, master and lackey set off at top speed. Taking a long detour, they skirted the wood, entering the town by another gate. As they reached the harbor, they found the vessel still ready to sail and the skipper awaiting them alongside.

"Well?" he asked as D'Artagnan appeared.

"Here is my pass, signed and countersigned."

"And the other gentleman?"

"He will not leave today," D'Artagnan explained. "But never mind: I will pay for both of us."

"In that case we shall set sail at once."

"The sooner the better," D'Artagnan agreed, leaping into the rowboat, Planchet behind him.

At daybreak, the vessel was a few leagues off the English coast; the breeze had been slight all night and the sailing slow. By ten o'clock the craft dropped anchor in Dover harbor. Half an hour later D'Artagnan set foot on English soil crying, "Here I am at last!"

But that was not all, they must get to London. In England the post was well organized and post horses readily available. D'Artagnan and Planchet took advantage of this and, preceded by a postilion, they reached the capital within four hours.

D'Artagnan did not know London and he could not speak one word of English, but he wrote the name of Buckingham on a piece of paper and everyone to whom he showed it pointed out the way to the Duke's mansion.

The Duke was at Windsor, hunting with the King. D'Artagnan asked for the Duke's confidential valet, Patrick, who spoke perfect French. He explained that he had come from Paris on a matter of life and death and that he must speak to his master immediately.

At Windsor Castle they inquired for the Duke and were told that the King and Buckingham were in the marshes two or three leagues distant. As they reached the place twenty minutes later, Patrick recognized his master's voice, calling his falcon back to him.

"Whom am I to announce to His Grace?" Patrick asked.

"The young man who, one evening, challenged His Grace when His Grace and a lady were bound for the Louvre."

"A somewhat peculiar introduction, Monsieur, if I may say so."

"You will find it as good as any other."

Buckingham recalled the incident at once. Recognizing the uniform of the Guards, he rode straight up to D'Artagnan. Patrick kept discreetly in the background. At once, Buckingham, reining in his horse, cast all discretion to the winds. Voicing all his fear and love: "Has any harm befallen Her Majesty?" he asked.

"I think not, Milord. Nevertheless, I believe Her Majesty to be in great danger from which Your Grace alone can save her."

"I? God help me, I would be only too happy to be of service to the Queen. Speak, man, speak up!"

"Pray read this letter, Milord."

"A letter from whom?"

"From Her Majesty, I think."

"From Her Majesty!" Buckingham repeated, turning so pale that D'Artagnan feared he was about to faint. His hands trembling, he broke the seal.

"Why is this letter ripped here?" Buckingham asked, his finger on a portion of the letter where the paper was pierced through.

"I had not noticed that, Milord," D'Artagnan said. "The Comte de Vardes made that hole when his sword pinked my chest."

"Are you wounded?" Buckingham asked, unfolding the letter.

"Nothing serious, Milord, a mere scratch."

"Great Heavens, what have I read?" Buckingham cried aghast. Then, imperiously: "Stay here, Patrick, or rather find the King wherever he is and tell His Majesty that I beseech him to excuse me but that a matter of the utmost importance calls me to London." Turning to D'Artagnan: "Come, Monsieur, come!" he ordered.

And both set off toward the capital at full gallop.

CHAPTER 9:

The Rendezvous

Along the way the Duke drew from D'Artagnan not all that had happened but what D'Artagnan himself knew. What surprised him most was that the Cardinal, so vitally interested in preventing the youth from reaching England, had been powerless to intercept him. Listening to D'Artagnan's plain, matter-of-fact account, the Duke looked at the Gascon from time to time in wonder, as if he could not understand how so much prudence, courage and devotion could belong to a man who looked barely twenty.

The horses went like the wind and in no time at all they reached London. Entering the courtyard of his mansion, Buckingham dismounted without bothering about his steed, tossed the reins over its neck and rushed to the front steps.

The Duke walked so fast that D'Artagnan had some trouble in keeping up with him. They passed through several apartments; presently they reached a bedroom which was at once a miracle of taste and splendor. In the alcove of this room was a door cut through a tapestry; the Duke opened it with a small gold key which he wore on a chain of the same metal around his neck.

"Come in, my friend, come in," Buckingham invited, "and if you are so fortunate as to be admitted to Her Majesty's presence, pray tell her what you have seen."

D'Artagnan followed the Duke into a small chapel tapestried with Persian silk and gold brocade and brilliantly lighted by a great number of wax tapers. Above a kind of altar and beneath a blue velvet canopy, surmounted by red and white plumes, was a life-size portrait of Anne of Austria, so faithful that D'Artagnan uttered an exclamation of surprise. Beneath the portrait was the casket which held the diamond studs. The Duke opened it and drew out a large bow of blue ribbon sparkling with diamonds.

"Here," he said, "here are these precious diamonds with which I had vowed to be buried. The Queen gave them to me, the Queen requires their return. So be it. Her will be done."

Slowly, one after the other, he kissed the beloved studs with which he must reluctantly part. Suddenly he uttered a terrible cry.

"What is it, Milord?" D'Artagnan exclaimed anxiously.

Buckingham winced; he was shaking like a leaf.

"Milord, what—?"

"All is lost!"

"But—?"

"Two of the studs are missing. There are only ten here!"

"If they were stolen—if Milord suspects anyone—perhaps that person still has them—"

"Wait, wait!" cried the Duke. "The only time I wore these studs was at a ball a week ago. Lady Clark, with whom I once had a falling out, stood beside me quite a long time as we made up our differences. Yes, that's it! That woman is an agent of the Cardinal's."

"Then he has agents all over the world?"

"Yes, yes, everywhere." Buckingham gnashed his teeth
with rage. "He is a terrible enemy." There was a long silence. Then, passionately: "Tell me, when is this ball in
Paris to take place?"

"Next Monday."

"Next Monday. Five days from now. Ah, we have time
and time aplenty!" Flinging open the door: "Patrick!" he
called, "Patrick, send for my jeweler and my secretary!"

The promptness with which the servant withdrew bore
eloquent testimony to his discretion and obedience. The
secretary was the first to appear, because he lived in the
ducal mansion. He found Buckingham seated at a table in
his bedroom, writing orders in his own hand.

"Jackson," said the Duke, "you will call upon the Lord
Chancellor immediately and inform him that I commit
these orders to him for execution. I wish them to be issued
forthwith."

The secretary glanced at the orders and smiled. "Is My
Lord Chancellor to forward a reply to the King if His Majesty should happen to inquire why no vessel of his is to
leave any British port?"

Buckingham drew a deep breath. "Should His Majesty
so inquire, the Lord Chancellor is to reply that I am determined on war and that this measure is my first act of hos-
tility against France."

The secretary bowed and retired.

"Well, we are safe on that score," Buckingham said jauntily. "I have just clapped an embargo on all vessels at present in His Majesty's ports."

D'Artagnan stared with stupefaction at this man who,
invested with unlimited power by his sovereign, was thus
abusing the royal confidence to serve his own interests.
D'Artagnan's expression was so candid that Buckingham
could not fail to read his thoughts. He smiled.

"Yes, yes!" he said impetuously, "Anne of Austria is my

true Queen. At one word from her, I would betray my country and my sovereign. She asked me not to send the Protestants of La Rochelle the aid I had promised them; I have not done so. I broke my word, but what of that?"

D'Artagnan mused on the mysterious and tenuous threads upon which the destinies of great nations and the lives of mere men are sometimes hung. He was lost in these thoughts when the goldsmith entered.

O'Reilly, master of his guild, was an Irishman. Among the most skilled workmen of Europe, he earned five thousand pounds a year from Buckingham's custom alone.

"Come in here, O'Reilly, come in!" Buckingham led the goldsmith into his chapel. "Look at these studs and tell me what they are worth apiece."

"Fifteen hundred pounds apiece, and beauties they be, M'Lud," O'Reilly said pontifically.

"How soon can you make two studs to match these ten?"

"In a week, Your Grace."

"O'Reilly, I will give you three thousand pounds for each of the two studs if I can have them by the day after tomorrow."

"M'Lud, have them you shall!"

"You are worth your weight in gold, Master Goldsmith, but that is not all. These studs must not be entrusted to anybody; the work must be done here, under this roof."

O'Reilly knew the Duke; he realized that any objection would be futile and he made up his mind then and there.

"May I let my wife know, please, M'Lud?"

"Certainly. You may even see her, my dear O'Reilly. Your captivity will be a mild one, rest assured."

Having settled this matter, Buckingham turned his attention to D'Artagnan.

"Now, my young friend," he said affably, "all England is yours. What can I do for you?"

"Thank you, Milord, all I need is sleep!"

While D'Artagnan slept, an ordinance was published in London forbidding the departure of all vessels bound for France. Public opinion viewed this act as a declaration of war between the two kingdoms. Two days later, the new studs were finished, their luster and workmanship so perfect that not even an expert dealer could have distinguished them from the others. The Duke summoned D'Artagnan.

"Here are the studs you came to fetch," he said. "I trust you will report that I have done all that was humanly possible."

"Milord need have no qualms on that score," D'Artagnan assured him. "I shall tell what I have seen." Buckingham nodded. "But Your Grace has not given me the casket," D'Artagnan said in surprise.

"The casket would only be an encumbrance, my friend." Buckingham sighed. "Besides, I treasure it, for it is all I have left of the Queen's. You will tell Her Majesty that I am keeping it."

"I shall deliver your message word for word, Milord."

"And now," Buckingham resumed, looking earnestly at the young man, "how can I ever repay my debt to you?"

D'Artagnan blushed; obviously the Duke was trying to get him to accept some gift. But the idea that the blood of his comrades and his own were to be paid for with English gold was strangely repugnant.

"Let us understand each other, Milord," he said courteously. "I am in the service of the King and Queen of France. Your Grace sees therefore under what auspices I have come here. What is more, I might perhaps never have undertaken all this had I not wished to please someone who is my lady, just as the Queen is yours."

The Duke smiled. "Yes, I see! Indeed, I dare say I know the lady you refer to. It is—"

"I have not mentioned her name, Milord—"

"True, Monsieur. My gratitude for your devotion belongs to that lady—who shall remain nameless."

"Exactly, Milord. At this moment, with war looming between our countries, I confess I can see nothing in Your Grace but an Englishman, hence an enemy. Nevertheless, nothing will prevent me from carrying out my mission in every detail."

"We Englishmen say: 'Proud as a Scot,' " Buckingham murmured.

"We Frenchmen say: 'Proud as a Gascon,' " D'Artagnan replied, bowing. "The Gascons are the Scots of France."

"Come now, you cannot leave like this. Where are you off to? How will you get away?"

"That's true. I had forgotten that England was an island and you were its king."

"Upon my soul! You Frenchmen are cocksure! Go to the port, ask for the brig *Sund,* and give the captain this letter. He will convey you to the harbor of Saint-Valéry. It is used by fishermen only. When you land there, go to a mean-looking little inn on the waterfront. You can't mistake it, it is the only such place. There you will ask for the host and say: *Forward!* That is the password. He will give you a fully saddled horse and tell you what road you are to take. In this way you will find four relays on your route. If you will give your Paris address at each relay, the four horses will follow you there. These horses are equipped for campaigning. Proud though you are, you will not refuse to accept one for yourself and one for each of your companions. Remember that they will serve you to make war against us."

"Milord, I accept with pleasure!" D'Artagnan bowed low. "Please God, we shall make good use of your gift."

"Now, your hand, young man. Perhaps we shall meet soon on the field of battle. Meanwhile, we part good friends, I trust."

D'Artagnan bowed again and hastened to the port.

Opposite the Tower of London, he found the *Sund* and gave the captain his letter; the captain had it certified by the Governor of the Port and they set sail at once.

Fifty vessels were waiting to leave as soon as the prohibition was lifted. As the *Sund* passed close alongside one of them, D'Artagnan fancied he saw a familiar figure—the woman of Meung, the woman whom the stranger had called Milady and whom our Gascon had thought so beautiful. But thanks to the swift tide and to the brisk wind, the *Sund* passed so quickly that he caught little more than a glimpse of her.

Next day he landed at Saint-Valéry and easily identified the inn Buckingham had mentioned. There he found the host and whispered: *"Forward!"* The host immediately led up a horse, already saddled, and asked D'Artagnan if he needed anything else.

"I want to know the route I am to take."

The landlord told him, adding, "At Neufchâtel, at the *Sign of the Golden Harrow*, give the innkeeper the password and you will find a horse, ready saddled, just as you did here."

Four hours later at Neufchâtel, D'Artagnan found a fully saddled mount waiting for him. He was about to transfer the pistols from one saddle to the other when he noticed that his new mount was already furnished with similar ones.

"Your address in Paris?"

"Royal Guards, Monsieur des Essarts, Commanding Officer. What route am I to take?"

"The Rouen road, but do not go through the city. At the hamlet of Ecouis, you will find an inn, only one. Don't judge it by appearances; there you will find a horse as good as this one."

"Same password?"

"Exactly."

D'Artagnan waved his hand and made off at full speed. At Ecouis the same scene was repeated: a host equally obliging . . . a fresh, fully equipped horse . . . a request for his Paris address . . . a statement of the same . . . a wave of the hand and a cloud of dust as he galloped off toward Pontoise. . . .

Here he changed horses for the last time and at nine o'clock galloped into the courtyard of the Tréville mansion. He had covered nearly sixty leagues in twelve hours.

On the morrow all Paris was agog with talk of the ball which the aldermen were to give in honor of the King and Queen. For the past week feverish preparations for this important occasion had made the city hall hum with activity. The city carpenters erected scaffolds to seat the ladies invited. The city grocers had furnished the reception rooms with two hundred white waxen torches, a piece of luxury unheard of at that period. No fewer than twenty violinists were to play, at double their usual wage on condition, rumor said, that they played the night through.

At ten o'clock in the morning Monsieur de la Coste, ensign in the King's Guards, followed by two officers and several archers of the Corps of Guards, called upon the City Registrar, to demand the keys of all doors, rooms and offices in the building.

At eleven o'clock a captain of the guards appeared with fifty archers who immediately took up their stations at the posts assigned them.

At three o'clock, two companies of guards reported, one French, the other Swiss. At six in the evening the guests began to arrive. Fast as they entered, they were ushered to their seats on the scaffolding in the great hall. At nine o'clock Madame la Première Présidente, wife of the Chief Magistrate, swept into the City Hall. Next to the Queen she was the most important personage of the ball. She was received by the notables of the city and shown to a loge immediately opposite the one the Queen was to occupy.

At ten o'clock, the King's collation, consisting of preserves, confitures and other sweetmeats, was prepared in a little chamber and placed in front of the silver service of the City, which was guarded by four archers. At midnight loud cries and vociferous cheers rose from the street, marking the King's progress as he passed through the city along thoroughfares illumined with colored lanterns.

Aldermen and city councilors, wearing their broadcloth robes and preceded by six sergeants, each of whom bore a torch, advanced to attend upon the King. Meeting His Majesty on the steps, they stopped while the Provost of the Merchants made the official speech of welcome. His Majesty, in full dress, was accompanied by His Royal Highness, the Duc d'Orleans (his brother), by the Grand Prior, in all the splendor of his ecclesiastical robes, by the Duc de Longueville, Governor of Normandy, and by a host of other dignitaries.

No one in the crowd failed to notice that the King looked glum and preoccupied.

A dressing room had been prepared for the King and another for his brother with masquerade dress in each; the same had been done for the Queen and the wife of the Chief Magistrate.

Half an hour later loud cheers were heard, proclaiming the Queen's arrival; aldermen and councilors, as before, followed the sergeants to the steps of the city hall where they repeated the ceremony of welcome.

The Queen entered the great hall. To the public she too, like the King, looked sad and, above all, fatigued. Just as she arrived, the curtains of a small gallery, which had until then remained closed, were suddenly parted to reveal, for an instant, the pale face of the Cardinal. His eyes, piercing bright, were fastened upon those of the Queen; and as he noted that she was not wearing the diamond studs, a smile of fierce, cruel joy passed over his lips.

Suddenly the King appeared at one of the doors of the hall with the Cardinal. His Majesty wore no masquerade dress and the ribbons of his doublet were scarcely tied. The Cardinal was dressed as a Spanish Cavalier. His Majesty made his way through the crowd and bowed to the Queen.

"Well, Madame, pray why are you not wearing your diamond studs?" he asked.

The Queen, looking around her, descried the Cardinal in the background, smiling diabolically.

"Sire," she replied in faltering tones, "I feared something might happen to them in such a throng."

"There you were wrong, Madame! If I presented them to you it was because I wished you to wear them."

The King's voice trembled with anger. The bystanders, wide-eyed and completely bewildered, stood aside, wondering what could be the matter.

"I can easily send for them, Sire," the Queen offered.

"Pray do so, Madame, pray do so as quickly as possible. The ballet is to begin within an hour."

There was a buzz of chatter. Surprise and confusion filled the hall; everyone had noticed that something was awry between King and Queen, but both had spoken so low that the bystanders had discreetly stepped aside. The violins began to play at their loudest but nobody listened.

The King was the first to emerge from his dressing room, clad in a becoming hunting costume. He was followed by his brother and other nobles, similarly appareled.

The Cardinal drew near the King and handed him a tiny casket. Opening it, the King found two diamond studs.

"What does this mean?" he asked in astonishment.

"Nothing, Sire! But if the Queen wears her studs, I beg you to count them. Should you find that the Queen wears but ten, Sire, pray ask Her Majesty who could have stolen the two that are here?"

The King looked blankly at the Cardinal and was about to ask him something when suddenly a cry of admiration rose up on all sides. It was the Queen, making her entrance. If His Majesty appeared to be the first gentleman of the realm, the Queen was undoubtedly the most beautiful woman in all France. Her riding habit suited her marvelously well, setting off her figure to excellent advantage. She wore a beaver hat with blue feathers, a tight-waisted jacket of pearl-gray velvet fastened with diamond clasps, and a skirt of blue satin embroidered with silver. On her left shoulder sparkled the diamond studs, on a bow of the same color as her plumes and her skirt.

The King trembled with joy, the Cardinal with anger, but they were still too far from the Queen to count the studs. Her Majesty was wearing them, to be sure, but were there ten or twelve?

At that moment the violins gave the signal for the ball to open. The King advanced toward the Chief Magistrate's wife, who was to be his partner; his brother advanced toward the Queen. They took their places and the ballet began.

When it was finished, each gentleman led his lady back to her place; but the King, availing himself of his privilege to leave his lady where she stood, advanced eagerly toward the Queen.

"I thank you, Madame, for deferring to my wishes," he said graciously, "but I believe two of your studs are missing. I am bringing them back to you."

Whereupon he handed the Queen the two studs the Cardinal had given him.

"What, Sire!" cried the Queen, feigning surprise, "you are giving me two more! Then I shall have fourteen in all!"

The King, at last in a position to count, could scarcely believe his eyes. Turning aside sulkily, he summoned the Cardinal and, sternly:

"Well, Monsieur le Cardinal," he asked, "what does this mean?"

"It means, Sire, that I wished to present Her Majesty with those two studs but, not venturing to present them myself, I adopted this means of doing so."

The Queen flashed him a smile which for all its brilliant graciousness yet proved that she was not duped by this ingenious piece of gallantry.

As for D'Artagnan, having witnessed the Queen's triumph over the cardinal, he was about to go home when he felt a light touch on his shoulder. Turning around, he saw a young woman who beckoned him to follow her. This young woman wore a black velvet mask, but despite this precaution, he recognized the alert, sprightly and shapely Madame Bonacieux.

The evening before, they had barely exchanged a few words in the quarters of Germain, the porter. So eager was D'Artagnan, what with the objects and message he brought, and so eager was Madame Bonacieux to communicate both to the Queen, that they tarried but a few moments. Tonight, however, D'Artagnan hoped for better, moved as he was by both love and curiosity. As he followed her on and on through corridors that became more and more deserted, he sought to stop the young woman, and look into her eyes if only for an instant. But, quick and elusive as a bird, she always slipped through his hands. Finally Madame Bonacieux opened a door and ushered him into a small antechamber that was completely dark. There again she bade him be silent. Then she opened an inner door concealed by a tapestry, a brilliant light spread through the room, she disappeared, and all was darkness again.

D'Artagnan stood there waiting in the shadows. Now,

sounds came from the next room quite clearly. D'Artagnan actually caught a few words of conversation.

Although he did not know the Queen, he soon distinguished her voice from the others, first by a slight foreign accent, then by that tone of domination natural to sovereigns. He heard the voice approach, then withdraw from the door. Then the knob turned and the door opened stealthily. D'Artagnan even saw the shadow of a person who, walking up and down, occasionally intercepted the light.

At length a hand and arm of wondrous form and whiteness appeared through the tapestry. D'Artagnan, under-

standing that this was his recompense, fell to his knees, grasped the outstretched hand and respectfully pressed it to his lips. Before he realized what had happened, the hand was withdrawn and, as he looked down, blinking, at his own hand, he saw and felt an object in his palm, a hard, bright object which he recognized as a ring.

The sound of voices in the next room gradually diminished, the echo of departing footsteps reached him, and the door to the corridor suddenly opened. Madame Bonacieux entered briskly.

"You, at last!" cried D'Artagnan.

"Hush!" she commanded, pressing her hand on his lips. "Not a sound! You must go away at once just as you came."

"But when shall I see you again? When? And where?"

"You will find a note from me waiting at your home. Begone now, I implore you; it is three o'clock in the morning. Begone and God bless you!"

D'Artagnan ran home immediately.

"There's a letter for you, Monsieur," Planchet told him, "but it's very odd. I had the key to your apartment, yet when I came back, there was the letter in your bedroom!"

D'Artagnan tore open the letter. It was from Madame Bonacieux and ran as follows:

Great thanks are due you and await your presence so that they may be given you. Pray come this evening at about ten o'clock to Saint-Cloud and wait opposite the lodge that stands beside the mansion of Monsieur d'Estrées.

C. B.

D'Artagnan read the note over and over; then he kissed it and held it up before him, gazing avidly at the lines traced by the hand of his beautiful sweetheart. After much ado he went to bed and fell into a deep sleep crowned with golden dreams.

Rising at seven o'clock in the morning, he summoned Planchet, who at his second call opened the door, his countenance still dark with anxiety.

"Planchet, I shall probably be gone all day," D'Artagnan announced. "Your time is your own until seven o'clock this evening. At seven be ready with two horses."

"So we are in for it again, Monsieur? Where will their bullets pepper us—in the head or in the back?"

"You will take along your musketoon and a pair of pistols."

"I knew it . . . I was certain . . . that letter . . ."

"Cheer up, lad, don't be afraid! We are off on a little jaunt!"

"I shall be ready, Monsieur, at seven sharp. But I thought Monsieur had only one horse in the stables at the Guards' barracks."

"There may be only one now; by this evening there will be four."

At the front door he found Monsieur Bonacieux, who greeted him so warmly that he felt compelled to pass the time of day with him. The conversation quite naturally revolved upon the unhappy man's imprisonment. Monsieur Bonacieux, unaware that D'Artagnan had overheard his conversation with the man of Meung, described all the tortures he had undergone in the Bastille, and its amenities (bolts, cranks, screws, racks, scourges, thumbscrews and wheels) and its wickets, dungeons, loopholes and gratings.

D'Artagnan listened with exemplary politeness and when Bonacieux was done, inquired, "What about Madame Bonacieux? Did you find out who abducted her?"

"Ah, Monsieur, they took good care not to tell me that, and my wife has sworn to me by all that's sacred that she does not know. But you yourself, Monsieur?" he continued in the most genial tone. "What have *you* been up to these last few days?"

"My friends and I took a little trip."

"Did you go far from Paris?"

"Heavens, no, only forty leagues or so. We took Monsieur Athos to Forges for a cure. My friends stayed on there."

"But *you* came back, eh?" the haberdasher asked in the most roguish and jocular tone. "I dare say some pretty lady has been awaiting you here with the utmost impatience."

D'Artagnan roared with laughter.

"Undoubtedly Monsieur will be rewarded for his diligence," Bonacieux hazarded.

"Well, this evening will come soon, thank Heaven! Probably you are looking forward to it as impatiently as I am. Are you expecting Madame Bonacieux tonight?"

"Madame Bonacieux is not at liberty this evening," the haberdasher said gravely.

"So much the worse for you, my dear host. As for me, when I am happy, I wish the whole world to be so. But apparently that is impossible!"

And D'Artagnan strode off, roaring with laughter over a joke he thought he alone could appreciate.

"Have a good time!" Bonacieux growled in a sepulchral tone.

D'Artagnan left for Monsieur de Tréville's in order to substantiate the vague report he had submitted on his fleeting visit the night before.

He found Tréville highly elated. The King and Queen had been charming to him at the ball. It is true the Cardinal was particularly sullen and at one o'clock, pleading illness, had left the ball.

"And now, my young friend," Tréville lowered his voice and glanced carefully around, making sure they were quite alone, "now let us talk about you. Obviously your happy return has something to do with the King's joy, the Queen's triumph and the Cardinal's confusion. You will have to be very cautious indeed."

"What have I to fear, Monsieur, so long as I enjoy the favor of Their Majesties?"

"You have everything to fear, believe me!"

"Do you think the Cardinal knows as much as you, Monsieur? Do you think he suspects I have been to London?"

"Great Heavens, were you in London? Was that where you found that beautiful diamond I see on your finger? Take care, my dear D'Artagnan, a gift from an enemy is not particularly profitable."

"This diamond does not come from an enemy, Monsieur," D'Artagnan explained. "It comes from the Queen. Her Majesty gave it to me personally."

"How did this happen?"

"It happened while I was kissing Her Majesty's hand—"

"You kissed the Queen's hand!" Tréville looked at D'Artagnan more closely.

"Her Majesty did me the honor to grant me this signal favor."

"In the presence of witnesses? How rash of her, how terribly rash!"

"No, Monsieur, do not worry, no one saw the Queen!"

And D'Artagnan related every circumstance of the night before.

"Look here, young man, let me give you a piece of advice, sound advice, the advice of a friend—"

"I would be much honored, Monsieur."

"Well, go to the nearest jeweler and sell him that diamond for whatever he will give you."

"I, sell this ring—? I, sell a ring which comes to me from my Queen! Never!"

Nevertheless, Tréville's solemn warning worried the Gascon.

"Confound it, Monsieur, what am I to do?"

"Be constantly and steadfastly on your guard. The Cardinal has a long memory and a long reach."

"But what can he do, Monsieur?"

"Good Heavens, how can I tell? His Eminence has all the devil's calendar of tricks at his command. The best you can possibly hope for is to be arrested."

"Even His Eminence would not dare to arrest a soldier in His Majesty's service!"

"Did they hesitate about arresting Athos?" Monsieur de Tréville sighed. "Advice is cheap, but I beg you to take that of a man who has been at Court for thirty years. Suspect everyone: your friend, your brother, your sweetheart—especially your sweetheart!"

D'Artagnan blushed, and asked, "My sweetheart? Why should I suspect her more than anyone else, Monsieur?"

"Because the Cardinal uses the ladies to the best advantage; they are his most efficient agents. By the way, what of your three comrades?"

"Well, Monsieur, I lost them by the wayside: Porthos at Chantilly with a duel on his hands . . . Aramis at Crèvecoeur with a bullet in his shoulder . . . and Athos at Amiens accused of counterfeiting."

Monsieur de Tréville pointed out that these three instances were proof of the Cardinal's long reach.

"Were I you, I would very quietly take the road to Picardy and make inquiries about the fate of my comrades who, I dare say, richly deserve that courtesy."

"Monsieur, your advice is excellent and I promise to set out tomorrow."

"Tomorrow? Why not this evening?"

"This evening, sir, I am unavoidably detained in town."

"Come, lad, away with you this evening."

"Impossible, Monsieur."

"You have pledged your word to spend the evening in town?"

"Yes, Monsieur."

"Do you need any money?"

"I still have fifty pistoles. That should certainly serve my needs."

"And your friends?"

"I doubt whether they need money, Monsieur. Each of us had seventy-five pistoles when we left town."

"Well, good luck to you, lad."

"Thank you, Monsieur."

D'Artagnan left Tréville, more than ever touched by his paternal solicitude for the men under him, his musketeers, the crack soldiers of the Army. He had a busy evening before him. He must visit Athos, Porthos and Aramis in turn. He did so, to discover that none of them had reported home; their lackeys, too, were absent, and there was no news of masters or servants. Passing by the Guards' barracks, he looked into the stables. Three of the four horses Lord Buckingham had given him were already in their stalls. Planchet, much impressed, had groomed down two of them.

"Monsieur, how glad I am to see you!"

"Why, Planchet?"

"Do you trust Bonacieux, Monsieur?"

"As I would the plague."

"Well, Monsieur, this is what happened," he explained. "While you were talking to Monsieur Bonacieux, I watched him. I didn't hear a word you said, but I saw him fidgeting about and I swear he turned pale and blushed and looked very uncomfortable—"

"Indeed?"

"Pray listen, Monsieur. So soon as you turned the corner of the street, Bonacieux picked up his hat, closed the door and ran down the street."

"Right, Planchet, the man is a suspicious character.

Never mind though; we will pay no rent until we thrash all this out."

At nine o'clock D'Artagnan again stopped at the barracks of the Royal Guards. Planchet awaited him, fully armed. The fourth horse had arrived. D'Artagnan made sure that Planchet had his musketoon and one pistol, both primed; he himself slipped two pistols in his holsters and they rode off.

So long as they were in the city, Planchet kept at a respectful distance; but as the road loomed up before them, ever darker and more deserted, he kept inching up closer. D'Artagnan could not but notice that his lackey was uneasy.

"Well, well, Planchet, what is the matter?"

Planchet, sighing, returned to his besetting idea. "Monsieur," he said, "there is something about Bonacieux—something evil in his eyebrows and something downright vicious in the play of his lips—"

"Why mention Bonacieux now?"

"Monsieur, a man thinks as he must, not as he will."

"That is because you are a coward."

"Monsieur, prudence is a virtue."

"And you are very virtuous, eh?"

"Look, Monsieur, there to the left. Don't you see a musket gleaming? Let us duck quickly—"

"Are you frightened, Planchet?"

"Not in the least, Monsieur. But I beg leave to observe that it is turning very cold and likely to turn colder . . . that cold brings on chills . . . that chills cause rheumatism . . . and that a lackey with rheumatism is worse than useless."

"Very well, Planchet, if you feel cold, you can go into one of those huts there."

D'Artagnan dismounted, tossed his steed's bridle to Planchet and muffling himself snugly in his coat, vanished into the darkness, bound for Saint-Cloud. There, he turned behind the château, found a tiny lane, and in a few minutes reached the lodge beside the mansion of Monsieur d'Estrées.

It was very bleak and stood in a very lonely spot. On one side the outer wall of the mansion loomed high above the lane; on the other a tall hedge screened off a small garden at the end of which stood a shabby hut. All was silence, an eerie silence that made him feel a hundred leagues from the capital. He glanced carefully about him, then leaned against the hedge, staring across the garden and beyond the lodge at the dense fog that swathed the mysterious immensity of Paris. Faintly, out of the shadowy void, he could distinguish a few lights.

Dismal though the prospect was, D'Artagnan found everything to his taste; dark though the night, his thoughts were roseate and opaque, they glimmered diaphanous through the shadows. Presently the chimes of the church of Saint-Cloud boomed the hour of ten. At the last stroke, his heart racing within him, he stared up at the lodge, all the windows of which were shuttered save one on the first floor. D'Artagnan waited blithely for a half hour, staring up at one part of the ceiling, which was clearly visible, admiring its gilded moldings, and speculating how lavish the apartment might be. The belfry of Saint-Cloud sounded the half hour.

This time, quite unconsciously, D'Artagnan shuddered. Perhaps he was beginning to feel the cold and mistook a wholly physical sensation for a mental impression. Somewhat uneasy at the silence and loneliness, he returned to his post. Eleven o'clock struck.

Now he thought fearfully that something might have happened to Madame Bonacieux. Nervously he clapped his hands three times, but there was no answer, not even an echo. He approached the wall and attempted to scale it but he could obtain no hold on it and broke several fingernails in the effort. Looking about at a loss, he saw the trees again, shimmering in the light from the room above; perhaps by climbing the tallest of them he could look into the room. The tree offered no difficulty. In a few moments his keen gaze enjoyed an unobstructed view into the lodge.

Straining his eyes to gaze through a perfectly transparent window, D'Artagnan was horrified at what he beheld. The mild, subdued light of the lamp, shining steadfastly, revealed a scene of frightful disorder. One window was broken . . . the door to the room had been forced and, smashed in, hung limply on its swollen hinges . . . a table, obviously set for supper, lay overturned, its four legs gaping . . . the floor was strewn with fragments of glass and crushed fruits . . . . There could be no doubt of it, the room had witnessed a violent, desperate struggle. D'Artagnan even thought he detected shreds of clothing amid this grotesque disorder and traces of blood on tablecloth and curtains.

Aghast, D'Artagnan climbed down from his point of vantage, his heart thumping against his ribs. The soft light still glimmered across the cold dark shadows. Looking about him, D'Artagnan noticed that the ground underfoot seemed to have been trampled upon. There were marks of carriage wheels, of horses' hoofs and of men's footsteps. Obviously a carriage had driven in from the direction of Paris and, describing a circle, driven off again toward the city. Or vice versa.

Pursuing his investigations, D'Artagnan suddenly came upon a glove. It lay close to the wall . . . a woman's glove undoubtedly . . . and torn . . . its palm muddy, the top immaculate . . . but a glove which had been wrenched off a lady's hand in a violent tussle . . .

As the impact of his discoveries made itself felt, an icier and more abundant sweat broke in large beads over D'Artagnan's forehead. A terrible anguish gripped him, his heart was oppressed, his breath came short and fast. Striving for self-control, he told himself that this lodge had nothing to do with Madame Bonacieux . . . that his Constance had specified he was to stand opposite the lodge, not to enter it . . . that her duties might conceivably have kept her in Paris . . . And yet he realized this was but wishful thinking.

A savage rage swept over him as, losing all sense of reality, he ran down the lane as though the devil himself were at his heels. Time passed and he ran on, this way and that. Then he ran back to the château, hoping against hope that some new development in his absence might have shed light on the mystery.

The lane was still deserted; the same calm, soft light still shone from the window. In despair he looked about him and once again saw the dark, silent hut at the end of the garden.

To his first frantic knocking there was no reply. He stood quite still for a moment, his heart heavy as lead. A deathly silence reigned over the tumble-down dwelling. He kept knocking with a sort of blind fury.

Presently, fancying he heard a slight noise within, he stopped knocking and pleaded to be admitted. At length an old worm-eaten shutter swung ajar on creaky hinges but was slammed shut as soon as the rays of a wretched lamp in one corner of the hovel had lighted up D'Artagnan's sword belt, the pommel of his sword and the butts of the pistols in his holsters. D'Artagnan managed to catch a glimpse of an old man's face.

"In the name of Heaven, listen to me," D'Artagnan begged. "I have been waiting for someone who has not come; I am dying of anxiety. Has any mishap occurred here? Speak, I implore you!"

Slowly the window swung open again and the same face

appeared again, looking even paler than before. D'Artagnan told his story simply and accurately without mentioning any names.

The old man listened to him attentively with an occasional nod of approval. When D'Artagnan had finished he shook his head with a rueful air that presaged nothing good.

"So you saw something, eh?" D'Artagnan tossed the old man a pistole. "Tell me what you saw and I give you my word as a gentleman that I shall not repeat one syllable of it."

The old man read such suffering and such sincerity in D'Artagnan's expression that he motioned to him to listen, and said in a low voice:

"It was just about nine o'clock. I heard a noise in the lane and wondered what it could be. As I went to my door I could see somebody at the gate in the hedge, trying to get in. Three men stood by the gate. Over there in the shadows stood a carriage with two horses. A groom, a few paces away, held three saddle horses which doubtless belonged to my three visitors.

"'Well, gentlemen,' I cried, 'what can I do for you?'

"'Have you a ladder?' one of the gentlemen asked me. From his tone and air, I judged him to be the leader of the group.

"'Ay, Monsieur, the ladder I use when I pick my fruit.'

"'Lend it to us and then go back to your house again. Here is a crown for your trouble. And remember this! If you breathe one word of what you see or hear, you are a dead man.'

"I shut the hedge gate behind them and went back into the house but I passed out again through the back door. From there I could see everything without being spotted.

"The three men drew the carriage up quietly and a little man got out, a fat, short, elderly man with graying hair and dressed in mean black clothes. He climbed the ladder very carefully, glanced slyly into the room, came down as quietly as he had gone up, and told the others:

" 'She's there, all right!'

"Then the man who had spoken to me went to the lodge, drew a key from his pocket and opened the door; then he went in, closed the door behind him and disappeared; then I saw the two others climbing the ladder. The little old man stayed by the door of the carriage; the coachman tended the carriage horses, and the lackey held the saddle horses.

"All at once, a hullabaloo broke loose in the lodge, like the screaming and howling of a thousand devils. A lady rushed to the window and opened it as if to jump out; but when she saw two men on the ladder, she ran back into the room. They immediately climbed in, more quickly than I can tell you, Monsieur.

"Then I saw no more, but I can tell you this: there was a smashing of furniture such as I hope never to hear again. The lady cried for help, but what could I do, old as I am, Monsieur, and against six men? The lady's cries grew fainter and fainter. Then two men came down the ladder with the lady in their arms. They carried her into the carriage, the little old man got in too, and slammed the door shut.

"There you have the story, Monsieur. After that the only thing I heard was yourself knocking and the only thing I saw were your weapons shining in the dark."

Overcome by the horror of this story, D'Artagnan stood stock-still, gaping, while all the demons of jealousy and anger rioted in his heart.

"Can you tell me anything about the ringleader?" D'Artagnan asked.

"You want me to tell you what he looked like? Well, Monsieur, he was a tall, dark, spare man with a swarthy complexion, black moustaches and eyes as black as the ace of spades. He looked like a nobleman."

"That's the man!" D'Artagnan gasped. "Once again and forever, my demon, the man of Meung." He wrung his hands, then, more calmly: "What about the other man?" he asked.

"Which one do you mean?"

"The little oldish one."

"Oh, he was no nobleman, Monsieur, I can vouch for that. Besides he did not wear a sword and the others ordered him about every which way."

"Some lackey, I dare say," D'Artagnan murmured.

With a heavy heart D'Artagnan retraced his steps toward the ferry, a prey to the most sanguine sentiments one moment and to the bitterest the next. Doubt, grief and despair made a battleground of his heart.

"Ah, if only my friends were with me!" he exclaimed. "Athos, Porthos, Aramis, you would give me some hope of finding her. But who knows what on earth has become of you?"

CHAPTER 10:

Of Porthos and Aramis

D'ARTAGNAN did not go straight home. Instead he stopped off to call on Monsieur de Tréville, who listened patiently to his young protégé's story.

"This all reeks of the Cardinal," he commented. "You must leave Paris as soon as possible just as I told you last night. For my part I shall see the Queen."

Encouraged by Tréville's attitude, D'Artagnan resolved to follow his advice immediately. But first he must go home where Planchet no doubt would now be waiting. There was Monsieur Bonacieux too.

D'Artagnan found his landlord on the doorstep, clad in morning dress and staring up at the sky. The fellow's complexion was yellow and sickly with that pallor which indicates an excess of bile in the blood. D'Artagnan perceived something particularly crafty and perfidious in his wrinkled features.

Repelled by Bonacieux's unpleasing exterior, our Gascon intended to pass by without speaking, but Monsieur Bonacieux accosted him as he had done the day before.

"Well, young man!" he declared with mock joviality, "we seem to have made quite a night of it, eh? Home at seven in the morning, I see!"

"No one can hold *that* against *you,* Monsieur Bonacieux."

Bonacieux turned pale and smiled wryly.

"What a gay blade you are, Monsieur; you *will* have your joke, won't you? But what the deuce were you up to last night?" He stared at D'Artagnan's boots. "Very muddy, eh? Dirty work at the crossroads?"

Suddenly D'Artagnan thought: a fat, short, elderly man with graying hair and dressed in mean black clothes . . . a man who was no nobleman for he wore no sword . . . a man whom the others ordered every which way . . . a lackey, no doubt . . . Bonacieux himself!

"Come, my good man, you're joking! If my boots could do with a sponging, your shoes and stockings could do with a brush! Have you been gadding about too, my dear landlord?"

"No, no, no, Monsieur, I went out to Saint-Mandé to find out about a servant."

To D'Artagnan the fact that Bonacieux cited Saint-Mandé was eminently suspicious, for Saint-Mandé was east of Paris, Saint-Cloud, west. Bonacieux's guile offered D'Artagnan a glimmer of consolation, the first he had experienced. If the haberdasher knew where his wife was, somewhere and somehow he might be persuaded by forcible means to divulge his secret.

"My dear landlord, do you mind if I do not stand on ceremony with you?" D'Artagnan inquired.

"Of course, go ahead, Monsieur."

"I'm parched with thirst. May I go drink a glass of water in your kitchen? After all, as neighbor to neighbor—"

And without awaiting his landlord's permission, he went quickly into the house. As he passed through the apartment a rapid glance at the bed told him that no one had slept in it.

"Many, many thanks, Monsieur Bonacieux," D'Artagnan said as he drained his glass. "Now I shall go up to my place and have Planchet brush my boots. When he is done I will send him down to you to look after your shoes and stockings if you like. One good turn deserves another."

At the top of the stairs D'Artagnan found Planchet plunged in abject confusion.

"Ah, Monsieur," the lackey wailed, "I was wondering when you would come home."

"What is the matter?"

"I will give you a hundred guesses, Monsieur. Imagine who called on you while you were away?"

"Well, who? Speak up, man."

"The Captain of the Cardinal's Guards."

"Did he come to arrest me?"

"He told me he came at the express command of His Eminence to offer you His Eminence's compliments and beg you to proceed with him to wait upon His Eminence. He whispered: 'Tell your master that His Eminence is very well disposed toward him.'"

The Captain of the Cardinal's Guards had then asked Planchet where his master had gone. The lackey had volunteered the information that D'Artagnan had set off for Troyes in Champagne.

"Planchet, my friend, you are worth your weight in gold!" D'Artagnan said, chuckling. Then briskly: "We are leaving town in a quarter of an hour," he announced.

"Heaven bless me, I was on the point of giving Monsieur just that advice," the lackey said, slapping his hip.

"You said I had gone to Champagne; we will therefore set off in the opposite direction. Remember, I should like to find out what has happened to Athos, Porthos and Aramis. So pack up and off we go!"

D'Artagnan sauntered off to the Guards' barracks. Ten minutes later his lackey arrived, bearing his portmanteau.

"Capital!" D'Artagnan exclaimed. "Now saddle the horses."

"Does Monsieur think we shall travel faster with three extra horses?" Planchet's expression was a picture of shrewdness.

"No, my witty friend," D'Artagnan replied, "but if we have five horses the three musketeers can ride home, provided we find them alive."

The two travelers arrived at Chantilly without mishap and repaired to the inn where they had put up on their previous journey. D'Artagnan dismounted, left his lackey to attend the horses and entered a small private room, ordering the best wine and heartiest meal the house could afford.

The Royal Guards were known to be recruited from among the noblest gentlemen of the realm, and, flanked by a lackey and three extra horses—magnificent nags they were, too—D'Artagnan cut a considerable swath. The landlord, therefore, served him in person, and D'Artagnan, observing this attention, ordered him to bring two glasses.

"By my faith, my dear host," he paused a moment to fill both glasses, "I hate to drink alone; you shall therefore join me."

"Monsieur does me much honor, but if I am not mistaken I have had the honor of seeing you before."

"That is very likely. As a matter of fact, I was last here some ten or twelve days ago, with some friends of mine, some musketeers."

"Really, Monsieur!"

"Yes. One of them, a somewhat stout gentleman, had a slight argument with a man totally unknown to any of us."

"Monsieur is doubtless referring to Monsieur Porthos?"

"Exactly; he was traveling with us. Come, my dear host, tell me frankly. Has anything untoward befallen him?"

"Monsieur Porthos did us the honor of remaining here, Monsieur. Indeed, I must confess that we are somewhat worried about certain expenses, Monsieur."

"Well, if he has run up a bill, my dear landlord, he is certainly in a position to pay his score!"

"Monsieur's words are a solace to my soul!" The host sighed. "You see, we advanced considerable cash to Monsieur Porthos, and this very morning the surgeon swore that if Monsieur didn't pay him he would hold me responsible."

"Monsieur Porthos is wounded, then?"

"That I cannot tell!"

"Tell me, may I see Monsieur Porthos?"

"Certainly, Monsieur. Just take the stairs, walk up one flight and knock at the door of Number One. But be sure to say who you are. Otherwise Monsieur Porthos might mistake you for one of my staff. Heaven help us, he might lose his temper and spit you like a fowl or blow your brains out."

"What on earth have you done to him?"

"We simply asked him for money, Monsieur."

"Don't you realize that when Monsieur Porthos is out of funds, any reference to money is apt to anger him?"

"We thought so, too, Monsieur. Maybe we chose the wrong moment to approach Monsieur Porthos. At any rate, he flew into a towering rage and committed us to all the devils of Hades. To be sure, he had been gambling the night before."

"Gambling, eh? And with whom?"

"Good Heavens, Monsieur, how can I tell?"

"And I suppose poor Porthos lost all his money!"

"Not only his money, Monsieur, but even his horse." The landlord proceeded to unfold his tale of woe. Having gone to inform Monsieur Porthos that his horse was being taken away, he was greeted with a volley of oaths for his pains. He soon realized no money was forthcoming; he had therefore hoped that Monsieur Porthos would at least condescend to honor a rival inn with his patronage. But no, Monsieur Porthos replied that the Grand Saint-Martin was very comfortable and that he intended to remain there.

"Is Mousqueton here too?"

"Ay, Monsieur! Five days after you left, the lackey returned, somewhat the worse for wear. Still, that lackey is considerably nimbler and spryer than his master. He commandeers things right and left. Instead of waiting for us to refuse him something, he goes ahead and pinches it!"

"Porthos will pay you."

The landlord cleared his throat and heaved a sigh of doubt. "I trust he will pay the surgeon too," he said.

"So he *was* wounded, eh?"

"Well, Monsieur, Porthos boasted about riddling the stranger like a sieve, but it was the stranger who pinked him. It was soon over. Before Monsieur Porthos could say *knife,* the stranger put three inches of steel in his chest. When the gentleman insisted on knowing whom he had bested, he apologized for having mistaken Monsieur Porthos for a certain Monsieur d'Artagnan, and rode away."

"Good. I know what I wanted to know."

With which D'Artagnan nodded to the host and climbed the stairs, leaving the good man somewhat more cheerful. At the top of the stairs, he saw a monstrously conspicuous door, with, over the panel, a gigantic sign traced in black ink reading: Number One. D'Artagnan, knocking, was summoned to enter. He was greeted with a hilarious spectacle.

Porthos lay back in bed in sumptuous comfort. He was playing cards with Mousqueton. A spit loaded with partridges was turning gaily before the fire. At either side of the spacious chimney piece, on twin andirons, stood two chafing dishes over which two boiling stewpans exhaled

the most fragrant odor of fricassee of hare—and a fish stew
with prevailing flavors of wine, onions and herbs.

Seeing his friend, Porthos cried out with joy.

"D'Artagnan! You! By Heaven, you are welcome, my
dear fellow. Forgive me for not rising to greet you." Then
with a certain degree of embarrassment, Porthos added,
"Have you heard about me?"

"No! Tell me all about yourself, Porthos."

"Ah, it's a sorry story," Porthos sighed. "You left me here
fighting against a stranger and guess what happened! I
tripped on a stone and sprained my knee."

"What dreadful luck!"

"I was terribly bored here. And I had the seventy-five
pistoles you lent me. So I gambled with a gentleman who
happened to be staying here overnight. I lost both the
money and my horse! But enough of my woes, my dear
D'Artagnan, tell me about yourself."

"Oh, I've been very well. But your landlord, my dear
Porthos," D'Artagnan pointed to the full saucepans and
empty bottles, "your landlord seems to be doing his
share, eh?"

"The host is doing an indifferent job, my friend, his treatment of us has been only so-so. Four days ago he had the
cheek to present his bill and I had to toss both him and the
document out of my apartment. This made me a victor of
sorts and a conqueror, if you like; but a prisoner, too."

D'Artagnan laughed jovially as he asked, "Don't you
sally forth occasionally, my friend?" And once again he
surveyed the fragrant saucepans.

"Not I, alas," Porthos vouchsafed. "As you see, my
wretched knee nails me to my bed. But Mousqueton does
an occasional job of foraging and so we do not lack for pro-
visions."

Mousqueton stared modestly at the ground.

"It's no trick, Monsieur," he said, "all you need is to be nimble and spry. I happen to have been brought up in the country, and my father in his leisure moments used to do a bit of poaching now and again—"

"Tell me about it," D'Artagnan urged.

"It was father who taught me how to lay a snare and to ground a line. He was a past master, Monsieur, and I an apt pupil. So you can understand that when I found our shabby host serving us up lumps of meat fit only for clodhoppers, I decided to do something about our delicate stomachs. Monsieur Porthos and I are not used to eating poorly! So I went back to poaching, Monsieur. As I strolled in the woods I set a snare here and there in the runs; and as I reclined on the banks bordering the royal waters, I slipped a line or two into the fishponds. Wherefore, praise Heaven! we lack for no partridge or hare or carp or eel, as Monsieur will presently witness."

"But the wine, Mousqueton? Does your host furnish it?"

"Well, Monsieur, yes, he does and no, he doesn't. Our host has a very respectably stocked cellar but he insists on wearing the keys on his person. But fortunately the cellar boasts a loophole; I cast a lasso through this loophole and, as I know where the best wines stand, I direct my lasso in that quarter."

Mousqueton bowed modestly, adding:

"Perhaps Monsieur would care to sample one of our bottles and tell us quite frankly what he thinks of our wares. . . ."

As D'Artagnan, having settled Porthos' debt to the inn, journeyed onward, a profound melancholy weighed heavily upon his heart. He thought of the young and pretty Madame Bonacieux; and his sorrow rose from his fear that some misfortune had befallen the poor woman.

Now nothing makes time pass more quickly and shortens a journey more effectively than thoughts which absorb the thinker's every faculty. D'Artagnan covered the eight leagues between Chantilly and Crèvecoeur at whatever gait his horse chose to adopt. Of what he had seen on the road, he remembered nothing. It was not until he glimpsed the inn where he had left Aramis that he collected himself and, shaking his head, brought his horse up to the door at a trot.

This time it was no host but a hostess who greeted him.

"My dear Madame," D'Artagnan asked before dismounting, "could you tell me what has happened to a friend of mine, whom we were obliged to leave here about twelve days ago?"

"Does Monsieur mean a handsome young man? Twenty-three or twenty-four years old? A gentle, pleasant-spoken and very well built young man?"

"Your description fits him like a glove. What's more, he was wounded in the shoulder."

"He's still here, Monsieur."

D'Artagnan leaped off his horse, and tossed the reins to Planchet.

"Madame," he cried, "where is my dear Aramis?"

"Begging your pardon, Monsieur, I doubt whether he can see you just now."

"How so?"

"Monsieur, he is with the priest of Montdidier and the Superior of the Jesuits of Amiens. He has decided to take up Holy Orders."

"Ah, yes, I had forgotten he was but a musketeer *pro tem.*"

"Well, Monsieur has only to take the right-hand staircase off the courtyard and knock at Number Five on the second floor."

Following her instructions, D'Artagnan found Bazin mounting guard. The valet, stationed in the corridor, barred all entrance the more intrepidly because after years of trial he now found himself within sight of the goal he had so steadfastly dreamed of. Ever since he could remember, poor Bazin had hoped to serve a churchman and, year after year, he had been longing for the day when Aramis would at last exchange the uniform for the cassock. In his present frame of mind, then, Bazin could not have imagined anything more unwelcome than D'Artagnan's arrival, but D'Artagnan simply moved him aside with one hand and with the other turned the handle of the door to Room Number Five.

He found Aramis clad in a black gown, his head surmounted by a sort of round, flat, black headdress not unlike a skull cap. The musketeer was seated at an oblong table covered with scrolls of paper and huge volumes in folio. At his right sat the Superior of the Jesuits; at his left the priest of Montdidier.

Hearing the door open, Aramis looked up and recognized his friend. But to D'Artagnan's immense surprise, his appearance seemed to make but a slight impression on Aramis.

"Good day to you, my dear D'Artagnan," Aramis said with utter calm, "believe me, I am happy to see you."

"And I too," D'Artagnan assured him, "although I am not

yet quite certain that this is Aramis. I feared I had mistaken your room and walked in upon some churchman. Then when I saw these two Fathers by your side I suddenly thought you were dangerously ill. Perhaps I am disturbing you, my dear Aramis?"

"You are not disturbing me," Aramis assured D'Artagnan. "On the contrary, my dear friend, I vow I am delighted that you have come back from your travels safe and sound. This gentleman is a friend of mine," Aramis explained unctuously to the two clerics. "He has just escaped considerable danger."

"Praise God!" and "God be praised, Monsieur!" the ecclesiastics intoned, bowing in unison.

"Your arrival is most timely, my dear D'Artagnan," Aramis continued smoothly. "By taking part in our discussion you can perhaps shed some light of your own upon the subject we were discussing. Monsieur the Superior of the Jesuits at Amiens, and Monsieur the priest of Montdidier, and I are arguing about certain theological problems which have long fascinated us."

"The opinion of a man of the sword can carry no weight," D'Artagnan protested, somewhat uneasy at the turn the conversation was taking. "Surely the learning of these gentlemen can settle all your doubts?"

Again the two men in black bowed in unison.

"Not at all, my dear D'Artagnan, I know your opinion will be much appreciated," Aramis pursued in honeyed tones. "Here is the point: I am presenting a thesis which the Superior believes ought to be very dogmatic and didactic."

"You are presenting a thesis?"

"Of course he is," the Jesuit replied. "For the examination preceding ordination, a thesis is always requisite."

"Ordination!" D'Artagnan echoed, flabbergasted, for he

still could not bring himself to believe that Aramis was about to become a priest.

Aramis sat back in his armchair, looked down at his hand, as white and as dimpled a hand as the fairest woman might boast; then he dropped his arm so that the blood might flow down to his fingertips. "Well, D'Artagnan, just as I told you, the Superior would wish my thesis to be thoroughly dogmatic, whereas I would prefer it to be thoroughly idealistic." With exquisite tact he added urbanely, "I need scarcely translate Latin for you because you know Latin." And he launched into what was just so much gibberish to D'Artagnan.

"Work slowly and diligently," the priest counseled at last, when Aramis ceased his harangue. "I am sure we are leaving you in the best possible frame of mind."

"Yes, the ground of the Lord is richly sown," said the Jesuit.

"Farewell, my son," said the priest. "I shall come back tomorrow."

"Farewell until tomorrow, my young friend," said the Jesuit. "You give promise of becoming a light of the Church; God grant that this light prove to be a consuming fire."

The two men in black rose stiffly, bowed ceremoniously to Aramis and D'Artagnan, and moved toward the door. Bazin, who had been standing by, overhearing the entire discussion with pious jubilation, sped forward toward them, and ushered the clerics out with much respectful consideration.

Left alone at last, the two friends were lost in an embarrassed silence. Presently Aramis broke the ice.

"As you see," he volunteered, "I have reverted to my original ideas. My plans of retirement were formed long since, as you know."

"Granted, my dear Aramis, but pray spare me theologics; you must surely have had enough of them for one day. Also I happen to have had no food since ten o'clock this morning and I confess I am extremely hungry."

"We will dine shortly, my friend. We are having spinach, to which we will add eggs."

"It scarcely sounds like succulent fare, my dear Aramis, but I will put up with it for the sake of your company."

D'Artagnan then questioned Aramis about his intention to take up Holy Orders. His friend replied that he was not about to enter the Church but rather to re-enter it. Surely D'Artagnan must know this.

"I?" D'Artagnan asked in amazement. "I know nothing whatever about it, Aramis."

"Well, I had been at the seminary ever since the age of nine and I was within three days of my twentieth birthday. One evening, as I was visiting friends whose home I frequented with much pleasure, an officer who was jealous of me chanced to enter suddenly without being announced. That evening I had just read my verses to the lady of the house, who was leaning over my shoulder and reading them a second time. When I left, the officer followed me out.

" 'Monsieur l'Abbé,' he said, 'do you care for canings?'

" 'I cannot say, Monsieur,' I replied, 'no one has ever dared give me one.'

" 'Well, then, listen to me, Monsieur l'Abbé: if you ever return to the house where I met you this evening, I shall give you a sound drubbing.'

"Now I am a gentleman born and I am hot-blooded, as you may have noticed, my dear D'Artagnan. Accordingly I informed my superiors that I did not feel sufficiently prepared to be ordained, and at my request the ceremony was postponed for a year. I promptly sought out the best fencing master in Paris and arranged to take lessons from him every day for a whole year. Then on the first anniversary of the day I was insulted, I hung my cassock on a peg, assumed the costume of a cavalier and attended a ball given by a lady of my acquaintance which I knew my man was to attend. He was there as I had expected. I went up to him as he was singing a love song. I interrupted him in the middle of the second verse.

" 'Monsieur,' I asked, 'do you still object to my returning to a certain house and do you still intend to cane me if I choose to disobey you?'

"He looked at me with considerable astonishment and said:

" 'Ah, yes, yes, yes, I remember now. Well, what do you want of me?'

" 'I would like you to take a little turn with me outside immediately, if you please!'

" 'Come along then,' the officer said. 'As for you, ladies, pray do not disturb yourselves. Just allow me enough time to kill this gentleman and I will return to finish our song.'

"We went out. I took him to exactly the same spot where a year before, hour for hour, he had insulted me. We drew our swords and I killed him."

"You did!" D'Artagnan exclaimed.

"The matter obviously created some scandal," Aramis continued, "and I had perforce to renounce the cassock, temporarily at least. Athos and Porthos both prevailed upon me to solicit the uniform of a musketeer. My request was granted and here I am now. But you can see why I want to return to the Church."

"But why today rather than yesterday or tomorrow, Aramis?"

"This wound has come as a warning from Heaven."

"Your wound! Nonsense! I swear it is not your wound

that is causing you the greatest pain at this moment!"

"What should it be then?" asked Aramis, blushing.

"Another wound, Aramis, the wound in your heart, a deeper and bloodier wound inflicted by a woman."

"Dust am I and to dust I return," Aramis said with increasing melancholy. "Life is replete with humiliations and sorrows; all the threads that bind it to happiness break one by one in the hollow of a man's hand." Aramis passed from dejection to a certain bitterness. "My dear D'Artagnan," he begged, "believe me, if you have any wounds, then make sure to conceal them."

"And so you are renouncing the world forever, eh? Your decision is irrevocable and the die is cast."

"Forever and ever. The world is but a sepulcher, no more, no less."

"Well, then, let us drop the subject," D'Artagnan proposed. "I am perfectly willing to burn this letter I have here."

"A letter?"

"A letter I picked up at your lodgings."

"What in the world—?"

"Confound it, I think I must have lost that letter," D'Artagnan said maliciously as he pretended to search for it. "But no matter! Happily the world is a sepulcher, men are but shadows, and love is a lure."

"D'Artagnan, D'Artagnan, please! You are killing me! Put me out of my misery!"

"Well, here is the letter at last!" D'Artagnan said blithely. "I don't know how I could have misplaced it."

Aramis sprang up, seized the letter and proceeded to read or rather to devour it, his face radiant.

"Oh, thank you, D'Artagnan, thank you!" Aramis cried in a delirium of joy. "She was forced to return to Tours, she loves me still! Come, my dear friend, let me embrace you. I am overwhelmed with sheer, rapturous happiness."

In their animal exuberance the pair began to dance around a venerable volume of Saint Chrysostom, which presently fell to the floor. At that moment Bazin entered with omelette and spinach.

"Away with you, wretch!" Aramis shouted. "Go back where you came from. And for Heaven's sake, remove those ghastly greens and those putrid eggs instantly! Order a well-larded hare, a fat capon, and a leg of mutton rich with garlic!"

CHAPTER 11:

Of Athos and His Wife

Next morning when D'Artagnan called on Aramis he found his friend staring out of the window.

"What a princely joy to ride on such steeds!" said Aramis.

"Well, my dear Aramis, that joy will be yours, for one of them belongs to you."

"Either stop joking this early in the morning, my friend, or tell me, which horse is mine?"

"Whichever of the three you choose, Aramis; I myself have no preference."

"What about that sumptuous equipment?" Aramis inquired skeptically. "I suppose it is also mine?"

"Of course!"

"I choose the one that ginger-headed stableboy over there is pacing."

"It is yours for the asking, Aramis."

"Praise Heaven, I could ride that horse with thirty bullets inside me. Ho, Bazin, come here at once!" A dull and dispirited Bazin shuffled in. "Polish up my sword, prepare my hat, brush my cloak, and load my—"

"Your last order is unnecessary," D'Artagnan broke in. "There are loaded pistols in the holsters." Basin sighed. "Come, Bazin, do not take things amiss. People may gain the Kingdom of Heaven under all sorts of conditions! Paradise is not reserved exclusively for clerics."

"Alas, Monsieur," Bazin sighed, with tears in his eyes. "My master might have become a bishop or even a cardinal."

As they reached the stables Aramis became more alert. When his horse was led up: "Hold my stirrups, Bazin," he commanded and sprang into the saddle with his usual agility and grace. But after a series of vaults and curvets, the noble animal had bested his noble master and Aramis, grown very pale, swayed in the saddle. With Bazin's help D'Artagnan carried Aramis back to his chamber.

"You were too weak and it is better so," he told his friend. "Be sure to take good care of yourself. I will go alone in search of Athos."

Whereupon they parted and D'Artagnan trotted off along the road to Amiens. Several problems assailed him. How was he to find Athos, if find him he could? And in what state? He had left his friend in a very critical condition. Athos might very easily have been killed. Here was a gloomy prospect but one he must face.

Of D'Artagnan's friends, Athos was the eldest and therefore the most remote from him, apparently, in tastes and interests. Yet of his friends it was Athos he preferred.

D'Artagnan admired the man's noble bearing, his unmistakable distinction. He admired the occasional flashes of grandeur which burst from out the modest shadows in which he usually chose to remain; he admired the unfailing serenity and equanimity which made of Athos the best of companions; he admired his somewhat mordant gaiety, which was always both gentle and wise; he admired his courage, which might have seemed rash, had it not sprung from the rarest self-control; and finally, he admired Athos most because he felt drawn toward him more through respect than through friendship.

Like all the great nobles of that period, Athos rode, fenced and shot to perfection. What is more, his education had been so little neglected that even with regard to scholastic studies, he could afford to smile at the scraps of Latin which Aramis served up and which Porthos pretended to understand. Best of all in him was his unassailable honor in an age when soldiers compromised so easily with their religion and consciences. And yet, Athos in his hours of potation—and they were not infrequent—would lose all trace of his brilliance and lapse into melancholy.

Wine could not be held primarily responsible for his dejection. On the contrary, he drank only in order to combat it—alas! in vain. Gambling was not responsible for his melancholy state, either. Athos gambling remained impassive, winner or loser. One night at the Musketeers Club he won six thousand pistoles, then promptly lost all his winnings, then mortgaged his gold-embroidered dress belt and then recouped all without turning a hair. Finally, his depression did not spring, as so often happens with the English, from the climate; Athos was gloomier than ever toward the finest season of the year, during the months of June and July.

The mystery which surrounded him served to heighten people's interest in this man who had never revealed anything about himself, however insidiously he had been questioned.

"Alas!" D'Artagnan said. "Poor Athos may well be dead at this moment, and dead by my fault! It was I who dragged him into this business."

"There's something else, too," Planchet replied. "We must remember that we probably owe our lives to him, Monsieur."

The lackey's comment redoubled D'Artagnan's eagerness to ascertain what fate had befallen Athos. By about noon they drew up before the accursed inn. The host advanced, bowing, to meet him.

"Do you recognize me?" D'Artagnan asked sharply.

"No, Monsieur, I have not that honor," the host replied very humbly.

"Well, let me refresh your memory. About a fortnight ago, you had the audacity to accuse a gentleman of passing counterfeit money. What has become of this gentleman?"

"This is what happened, Monsieur," the landlord said tremulously. "I will tell you all, for you are the gentleman who left when I had that unfortunate difference with the gentleman you mentioned."

"I am listening."

"I was warned by the authorities that a notorious counterfeiter would arrive at my inn with several companions disguised as guards or musketeers."

"Go on, go on!" D'Artagnan urged impatiently.

"The authorities sent me a reinforcement of six men and, acting upon their strict orders, I took all measures necessary to secure the persons of the alleged coiners."

"Again!" D'Artagnan exclaimed, his blood boiling at the ugly word.

"Forgive me for mentioning such things, Monsieur, but they form my excuse. The authorities had terrified me and you know that an innkeeper must keep in with the authorities."

"But where is the gentleman? What has happened to him? Is he dead? Is he alive?"

"Patience, Monsieur, I am coming to that. You know what happened and your precipitate departure seemed to substantiate what occurred. The gentleman, your friend, defended himself desperately. Unfortunately for him, through some silly misunderstanding, his valet had quarreled with the six officers, who were disguised as stable-boys—"

"Ah, you scoundrel, all of you were in the plot."

"Oh no, Monsieur, there was no plot at all."

"For Heaven's sake," D'Artagnan shouted. "Tell me what happened to Athos."

"Well, Monsieur, he fought against at least five men, after having put two out of commission with his pistols. Then, retreating as he fought, he locked himself in my cellar."

"I see," D'Artagnan said wryly. "You decided to make him your prisoner."

"Our prisoner, Monsieur! No, no! He imprisoned himself. For my part, Monsieur, as soon as I came to my senses, I called upon the Governor, told him all that had happened and asked him what to do with the prisoner. But the Governor was flabbergasted; it seems I had made a mistake, Monsieur. I had helped arrest an innocent gentleman while the coiners escaped. So I betook myself straightway to the cellar to set the gentleman free. But Heaven preserve us, Monsieur, he would not leave the cellar, he said, except upon his own conditions.

" 'First,' the gentleman said, 'I want my valet sent down here fully armed.'

"We hastened to comply with this order and had the valet carried down to the cellar, wounded though he was. Then his master, having admitted him, barricaded the door again, and ordered us to stay where we belonged."

"But where is he, where is Athos?"

"In the cellar, Monsieur."

"What, you wretch! You have been keeping him in the cellar all this time?"

"Merciful Heaven, no, Monsieur! *I* keep *him* in *my* cellar? Oh, you have no idea of what he is up to! He insisted on staying there. We pass him down some bread at the end of a pitchfork every day through a vent; but, wellaway! it is not bread and meat that he absorbs most. Once I tried to go down with two of my servants, but he flew into a towering rage. I heard the gentleman priming his pistols and the lackey cocking the musketoon."

D'Artagnan laughed uncontrollably at the landlord's woebegone expression.

"What has happened since?" he asked.

"Since then, begging your pardon, we have been leading the most miserable existence imaginable. All our supplies are in that cellar; our choicest wines in bottles, other wines in casks, our beer, our spices, our bacon, our sausages! As we are not permitted to go down there, we are compelled to refuse food and drink to our clients. Our inn is losing customers and money every day. Another week with your friend in the cellar and I shall be a ruined man."

D'Artagnan heard an uproar rising from the cellar and, preceded by the host, who wrung his hands, and followed by Planchet, he headed toward the theater of operations.

Two English gentlemen who had just arrived and who had called for food and drink were exasperated. They had ridden hard and long and were dying of hunger and thirst.

"But this is an outrage!" one of them cried in excellent French, though with a foreign accent.

"How dare this lunatic prevent these good people from getting their own wine out of their own cellar!" the other demanded.

"Let us break in!"

"Yes, and if he gets too wild, we'll kill the fellow!"

"Just one moment, gentlemen," D'Artagnan cautioned, drawing his pistols from his belt. "Nobody is to be killed, if you please!"

"Come on, gentlemen, try to get in!" Athos challenged calmly from the other side of the door.

There was a moment of silence, after which the Englishmen determined not to give in. Their pride was at stake, and to withdraw would be humiliating. The angrier of the pair went down the six steps leading to the cellar door and kicked it furiously.

"Planchet," D'Artagnan ordered, cocking his pistols, "I will handle the one up here, you answer for the one kicking at the door."

"D'Artagnan!" cried Athos cavernously from the lower darkness. "It is D'Artagnan, I think."

The Englishmen had drawn their swords, but they found themselves caught between two fires.

"Take cover, D'Artagnan," Athos warned crisply. "I am about to fire!"

But D'Artagnan knew better. Here was a case for common sense and D'Artagnan's common sense never abandoned him.

"Gentlemen," he shouted, "pray think what you are about! My lackey and I have three shots apiece and the cellar can produce as many. Allow me to settle your problem, gentlemen, and my own. Presently you shall have all you want to drink, I assure you."

"If there's any wine left," Athos jeered.

A cold sweat broke over the landlord's face and, judging by his wriggling, doubtless trickled down his spine.

"There must be plenty down there," D'Artagnan said. "Never you worry, landlord, two men cannot have drunk your cellar dry. Gentlemen, sheathe your swords if you will."

Whereupon, setting the example, D'Artagnan replaced his pistols in their holsters, and turning to Planchet, motioned to him to uncock his musketoon.

"And now, Milords, go back to your apartment; I warrant that in ten minutes you shall have all the wine you want."

The Englishmen bowed in appreciation and withdrew.

"We're alone now," D'Artagnan called. "Open up, Athos!"

A great sound of shuffling, a creaking of logs and a groaning of beams ensued, as the beleaguered Athos in person dismantled his bastions and counterscarps. A few seconds later the broken door parted and Athos poked his pallid face between the split panels to survey the situation. They embraced heartily. Then as D'Artagnan sought to drag his friend from his damp quarters he realized that Athos was reeling and tottering.

"Were you wounded?" he asked anxiously.

"No, no, no, no, no, my dear fellow, I'm tipsy."

D'Artagnan burst into peals of laughter that changed the landlord's chills into a burning fever. Suddenly Grimaud appeared behind his master, his musketoon on his shoulder, soaked front and back in a fatty liquid that the innkeeper recognized as his choicest olive oil.

In single file, Athos, D'Artagnan, Grimaud, the innkeeper and his wife proceeded across the public room and went upstairs to the best apartment in the inn, commandeered by D'Artagnan. Mine host and his wife hurried to the cellar, armed with lamps, to take a rapid inventory of their stock. Finding their own property accessible at long last, they faced a hideous spectacle.

Beyond the barricade which Athos had shattered there were great puddles of olive oil here and deep pools of wine there, over which swam a flotsam and jetsam which, on closer scrutiny, turned out to be the bones of hams and sausages consumed.

In the cellar a species of fury followed upon amazement and rage. The host, seizing a spit, rushed to the room our friends occupied.

"Wine ho, landlord!" Athos ordered as the innkeeper made his appearance.

"Wine!" the landlord bawled, unable to believe his ears. "Why, you have already drunk more than one hundred pistoles worth of it."

"You have only yourself to blame."

"But I have lost all the oil in my cellar."

"Oil is a sovereign balm for wounds, landlord. My poor lackey Grimaud used it to treat the wounds you inflicted upon him."

"My sausages are all eaten up."

"I daresay there are plenty of rats in your cellar."

"You shall pay for all this," the innkeeper cried in exasperation.

"Oh, you fool," Athos rose to his feet, swayed and then subsided. Presently he continued, "We are not the devils we seem, my good man. Come, stand and let us talk all this over quietly."

The landlord approached gingerly.

"Listen, my good man," Athos said, "while I recall what happened. As I was about to settle my score, I laid down my purse on the table. Where is the money?"

"I deposited it at the City Registrar's."

"Very well, produce my purse and you can keep the money that was in it."

"Surely Monsieur knows that the authorities never relinquish anything they lay their hands on."

"Well, my good friend, all that is *your* problem!"

"Monsieur's horse is in the stable," the landlord put in eagerly.

"How much is that horse worth?" D'Artagnan asked.

"Fifty pistoles at most," the landlord answered shrewdly.

"It is worth eighty," D'Artagnan insisted. "Keep it, host, and let us forget the whole matter."

"What!" Athos objected. "You are selling *my* horse?"

"Athos, I have brought you another horse instead."

"And a magnificent animal it is, too, Monsieur!" the landlord commented.

"Very good," Athos drawled. "Now that I have a younger and handsomer mount, keep the old one, landlord, and fetch us up some wine."

"And don't forget to take up four bottles of the same to the two English gentlemen," D'Artagnan ordered.

"Now that we are alone, my dear D'Artagnan," Athos said as soon as the door closed, "what about Porthos and Aramis?"

And when D'Artagnan had told him: "Your news is good," Athos said as he filled his glass and D'Artagnan's. "But you, my friend, you look anything but happy."

"Ah, my dear Athos, I am the unhappiest of us all!"

"You unhappy! Come, how are *you* unhappy? Tell me."

D'Artagnan related his adventure with Madame Bonacieux as Athos listened in complete silence. Then, when D'Artagnan was done: "All these things are but trifles," Athos commented.

"I know that is your favorite expression, Athos; you dismiss the most harrowing events as mere trifles. That comes very ill from you who have never been in love."

Athos, who had been staring down at the table, suddenly drew himself up. His dull vacant eyes lighted up for an instant, then turned listless and glassy as before.

"True," he admitted quietly, "true! I have never been in love."

"Philosopher as you are, remote from our human sentimentalities, pray instruct and sustain me," said D'Artagnan. "I want to know why love's course never runs smoothly."

"I wonder what you would say if I were to tell you a real love story?"

"Tell me your story, Athos, please."

Athos collected himself and as he did so D'Artagnan perceived that he grew pale apace.

"One of my friends," Athos began, then with a melancholy smile he interrupted his story: "Please observe this happened to one of my friends, not to me—" and, resuming: "One of my friends, a count in my native province—Berry, that is—a man nobly born, once fell in love. He was twenty-five, the girl sixteen and beautiful beyond description. She lived in a small straggling township with her brother, who was a priest. Nobody knew where they came from, but seeing how beautiful she was and how pious her brother, nobody ever inquired. My friend, the hero of this tale, was lord of the country. He married her, fool, idiot, imbecile that he was!"

"How so, if he loved her?"

"Patience, D'Artagnan, and you shall see!" Athos gulped down the contents of half his glass. "My friend took her to his château and made her the first lady of the province."

"What happened then?" D'Artagnan asked.

"One day my friend was out hunting in the woods with his wife." Athos lowered his voice and spoke very rapidly. "She fell from her horse and fainted. The count rushed to help her and, as she had difficulty in breathing, he slashed her bodice with his dagger, baring her throat and shoulders." Suddenly Athos burst into shrill, forced peals of laughter. "And guess what he found on her right shoulder?" he concluded.

"How could I know? Tell me, if you will."

"A fleur-de-lis," said Athos, "yes, a fleur-de-lis. She had been branded by the Royal Executioner." And Athos drained his glass at one gulp.

D'Artagnan gasped. "And what did your friend do?"

"He was a great nobleman, D'Artagnan; he enjoyed the right of both petty and superior justice in his own domain. He tied her hands behind her back, and hanged her to a tree."

"Great Heavens, Athos, a murder!"

"Exactly: a murder, no less!" Athos turned pale as a corpse. "That cured me of beautiful, poetical and loving

women!" he wound up. "May God grant you the same en-
lightenment but less painfully! Come, let us drink up."

"So the comtesse is dead?" D'Artagnan stammered.

"Of course, dead as a doornail."

"What about her brother?" D'Artagnan asked timidly.

"Oh, I made inquiries about him in order to have him
hanged too, but he had left his curacy just the day before.
I never found him."

"What a ghastly tale!" D'Artagnan exclaimed.

"Come, try some of this ham, D'Artagnan; it is deli-
cious," Athos said. "What a pity there were not four more
such hams in the cellar; then I might have downed fifty
bottles more!"

The next morning D'Artagnan repaired to his friend's
room, firmly resolved to renew the conversation of the evening before. But he found Athos fully himself again, in
other words, the shrewdest and most impenetrable of men.
After they had exchanged a hearty handshake. the musketeer, anticipating D'Artagnan, broached the matter first.

"I was drunk yesterday, my dear D'Artagnan," he confessed. And he gazed at D'Artagnan with an earnestness
that embarrassed our Gascon. "I remember dimly we spoke
of people being hanged. The hanging of people is my particular nightmare, the obsession of Athos drunk."

"You told me the story of a tall blonde woman who was
very beautiful, who had extraordinary blue eyes and—"

"And who was hanged!"

"Precisely! She was hanged by her husband, who was a
nobleman of your acquaintance."

Changing the subject suddenly, Athos said, "By the way,
I must thank you for the horse you brought me."

"You like it, eh?"

"Heavens, you begin to awaken my regrets."

"Regrets?"

"Yes, but—oh, well, I got up this morning at six o'clock.

As I went into the common room I heard a guest, an Englishman, haggling with a horse dealer over a mount. (His own died yesterday from a stroke.) I drew near and, finding that he was offering a hundred pistoles for a fine burned-chestnut nag: 'Look you, Monsieur,' I said, 'I too have a horse for sale. Do you consider him worth a hundred pistoles?' I asked. 'If so, I will play with you for him.'

" 'Play at what?'

" 'At dice.'

"No sooner said than done.

"I lost the horse," Athos confessed, "but I did win back the saddle." And as D'Artagnan looked somewhat put out: "Are you annoyed?" he asked candidly.

"Yes, I admit I am, Athos."

"Well, my friend, I was bored to death, and anyhow, I swear I do not like English horses."

D'Artagnan looked as glum as ever.

"I am much vexed that you should set such store by horseflesh, my friend, because I am not yet at the end of my story."

"After losing my horse with a throw of nine against ten — rotten luck, eh? — I was inspired to stake yours. A capital idea, don't you think?"

"An idea perhaps, but surely you did not put it into execution?"

"Of course I did! I lost your horse with a throw of seven against the Englishman's eight. Short of one point. You know the saying."

"Athos, I vow you have taken leave of your senses."

"To be frank, D'Artagnan, I lost your horse with all his equipment."

"But this is ghastly!"

"Wait, lad, you have not heard all. We still had that diamond sparkling on your finger."

"Merciful Heavens! I *do* hope you did not mention my diamond!"

"Why not, my friend? With it I might win back our horses and our harnesses and even enough cash to get us home. Well, I mentioned your diamond to the English gentleman who, it appears, had noticed it too."

"Get on, Athos, get on, my friend, I implore you."

"This is what happened: we divided the diamond into ten parts, each worth one hundred pistoles."

"Bah!" D'Artagnan said. "You want to make me lose my Gascon temper."

"No, my friend, I have never been less in a mood for jesting. Here I had been out of circulation for a whole fortnight; I had not seen a human face except Grimaud's, which I know by heart; my sole consolation was our host's wine."

"That was no reason for staking my diamond."

"Do hear me out," Athos replied. "Remember: we had ten parts of the diamond to gamble for, each worth one hundred pistoles. At the thirteenth throw, I had lost everything! Number thirteen has always been fatal; it was on July thirteenth that I—"

"Athos!" cried D'Artagnan, rising angrily from the table. "I—"

"Patience, my friend," Athos counseled. "Mine was a sound plan. That Englishman was an eccentric like many of his race. I saw him conversing with Grimaud two mornings ago; and Grimaud immediately reported back to me that the Milord wished to attach him to his household. What could *I* do, knowing all this, but set up Grimaud as a stake divided into ten parts, each worth one hundred pistoles."

Vexed though he was, D'Artagnan could not help laughing at the comicality of the situation.

"You used Grimaud as a stake?"

"Yes," Athos pursued nonchalantly, "and with the ten parts of Grimaud I won back your diamond."

Somewhat relieved, D'Artagnan gave free rein to his mirth.

"Very funny!" he said. "I haven't heard so amusing a story in years!"

"To cut a long story short, I emerged with your harness and mine and that's where we stand now."

D'Artagnan breathed as though the weight of the entire hostelry had been lifted off his chest.

"My diamond is still safe then?" he asked timidly.

"Safe as houses, my dear fellow. And we still have the harnesses of your nag and mine."

"But of what use can our harnesses be without horses?"

"D'Artagnan, I have an idea about that problem."

"What do you propose, Athos?"

"Luckily, my Englishman and his companion are still here. If I were you, I would stake our harnesses against the horse I lost."

"Would you really do that, Athos?" D'Artagnan asked.

"As I am an honest man, ay; I vow I would."

"But having lost both horses, I am particularly anxious to save the equipment."

"What a pity!" Athos said coldly. "That Englishman's pockets are bulging with money. Come along, lad, try one throw."

Athos went off in search of the Englishman, whom he found in the stables, viewing the harness with a covetous eye. He was able to impose his own conditions: both harnesses against either one horse or one hundred pistoles at the winner's choice. The Englishman and Athos shook hands to seal the bargain.

After the usual courtesies had been exchanged, D'Artagnan took up the dice and, with trembling hand, rolled a trey!

Athos, shocked as he noted how pale his friend turned, said, "Ha, partner, that was a sorry throw!" and, nodding toward the Englishman, "Our adversary will have his horses fully equipped."

Triumphant, the Englishman did not even bother to shake the dice but threw them on the table without looking down.

"Look at *that!*" Athos remarked in his usual calm tones. "There's an extraordinary throw for you. I've only seen it happen four times in my life. A pair of aces losing to a trey!"

The Englishman looked down at the table, incredulous, then surprise loomed large over his features. D'Artagnan, following his glance, was overcome with pleasure.

"So, Monsieur, you have won back your horse!" the Englishman said ruefully.

"I have indeed!"

"One moment, Milord," Athos broke in. "With your permission, I should very much like to have a word with my friend here."

"Pray do, Monsieur."

Athos drew D'Artagnan aside. "Were I you, D'Artagnan, I would take the hundred pistoles. As you know, you staked the harnesses against the horse or one hundred pistoles in cash, at your choice."

"I know that."

"Well, I would take the money."

"And I intend to take the horse."

"You are wrong, D'Artagnan. What on earth can two of us do with but one horse? Remember we need money to get back to Paris."

"But how shall we get back to Paris?"

"Quite easy! We will ride our lackeys' horses. People can always tell by our looks that we are persons of quality."

"So your advice is—?"

"—to take the hundred pistoles, D'Artagnan! With such a sum we can relax a little."

"Relax! I, relax? No, no, Athos! As soon as I reach Paris, I shall go search for the beautiful and unhappy woman I love."

"All right, which do you think will help you most in your quest: one hundred jingling golden coins or a horse? Take the money, my friend, I repeat; take the hundred pistoles."

D'Artagnan needed but one more reason to surrender and this last reason seemed convincing. He therefore acquiesced and chose the hundred pistoles, which the Englishman paid out on the spot.

Departing, D'Artagnan and his friend bestrode the nags of Planchet and Grimaud respectively, the lackeys following afoot in their wake, carrying the saddles on their heads. Reaching Crèvecoeur, from afar they sighted Aramis seated at the window, leaning over the sill in deep melancholy.

"I was meditating upon the celerity with which the goods of this world leave us," Aramis confessed. "My handsome English horse has just vanished amid a cloud of dust; he is a living image of the fragility of earthly things."

"What do you mean?"

"I mean that I have just made a fool's bargain. I got only sixty louis for a horse that, judging by his gait, can cover five leagues an hour at an easy trot."

D'Artagnan and Athos burst out laughing.

"My dear D'Artagnan," Aramis apologized, "pray do not be too angry with me, necessity knows no law. Besides, I am the person most severely punished. Ah, you two fellows are good managers; you ride your lackeys' horses and have your own magnificent mounts led by hand gently and by easy stages."

Just then a market cart drew up before the inn. Grimaud and Planchet emerged, the saddles on their heads. The cart was returning empty to Paris and the two lackeys, in return for their transportation, had agreed to slake the driver's thirst along the road.

"What's this?" Aramis cried as he saw them arrive. "Nothing but saddles? Ho, Bazin, bring my new saddle and carry it along with those Planchet and Grimaud are wearing!"

They chatted a few minutes about their plans; then they set forth to join Porthos. They found him up and about, much less pale than he had been on D'Artagnan's first visit. He was seated at a table which, though he was alone, was set for four. The dinner consisted of meats succulently dressed, of choice wines and of superb fruits.

"Ha!" he exclaimed, rising to greet them. "Your arrival is wonderfully timed, gentlemen; you must dine with me."

D'Artagnan said admiringly, "Unless my eyes mistake me, I see a crisply larded fricandeau and a filet of beef—"

"I am recuperating, I have to build myself up," Porthos explained.

"Was this dinner intended for you alone, Porthos?"

"No, Aramis, I was expecting several gentlemen of the neighborhood who have just sent word to me that they cannot come. You three shall take their places and I shall lose nothing by the exchange. Ho, Mousqueton, bring up some chairs."

After ten minutes of hearty eating, Athos said suddenly, "Do you know what we are eating here?"

"I," said D'Artagnan, "am eating veal stuffed with prawns and marrow."

"I," said Porthos, "am enjoying the best lamb I have tasted in many moons."

"I," said Aramis, "am savoring the most succulent breast of chicken I ever tasted."

"You're all mistaken, gentlemen," Athos announced gravely, "you are eating horseflesh."

"What?— We are eating what?"

Porthos alone made no reply—for he too had sold his horse.

"Ay, Porthos, horseflesh, that's what we're eating, isn't it?" Athos went on. "And the saddle as well, probably."

"No, gentlemen, I kept the harness," Porthos confessed.

"Upon my word," Aramis declared, "we are all alike!"

CHAPTER 12:

Lady Clark

Almost penniless and required to equip themselves for the campaign against the English, our friends found Paris a very sad place. Athos refused to leave home, while Grimaud heaved cavernous sighs. Aramis wrote elegant verse, while Bazin haunted the churches. D'Artagnan worried about Madame Bonacieux, while Planchet contemplated the course of flies across the room. Porthos swaggered about, while Mousqueton collected breadcrusts for future meals. Desolation reigned.

One day D'Artagnan saw Porthos strolling into the church of Saint-Leu and followed him instinctively. The church happened to be very crowded. Porthos walked over to the nearest pillar and leaned against it. D'Artagnan stood near a similar pillar on the opposite side. Porthos was gazing with great admiration at a lady seated close to the choir —a beautiful lady, attended by a young Negro who bore the red velvet cushion upon which she knelt, and by a maidservant.

The beautiful lady made a deep impression on Porthos.

And she made an even deeper impression on D'Artagnan as he recognized in her the lady of Meung, whom his persecutor, the man with the scar, had addressed as Milady.

When the service was over, D'Artagnan followed Milady out of the church, saw her step into her carriage and heard her order the coachman to drive to Saint-Germain. Returning home, he ordered Planchet to saddle two horses, and then he called upon Athos.

When Planchet poked his head meekly through the door to announce to his master that the horses were ready:

"What horses?" Athos demanded.

"Two horses that Monsieur de Tréville puts at my disposal," D'Artagnan explained suavely. "I am off for a jaunt to Saint-Germain."

"What on earth are you going to do at Saint-Germain?"

D'Artagnan told him how he had seen Milady in the church. It was not she, beautiful though she was, whom he sought to find again but his arch-enemy, the man of Meung.

"I see," Athos observed contemptuously. "You are in love with this lady as deeply as you were once in love with Madame Bonacieux."

"Nonsense, Athos!"

"Very well, amuse yourself with Milady, my dear fellow. I wish you the best of luck."

"Come, Athos, why not go for a ride with me through the forest of Saint-Germain?"

"My dear D'Artagnan, I ride when I own a horse. When I have none, I walk."

D'Artagnan and Planchet set off briskly toward Saint-Germain. All along the road the young Gascon reflected about Madame Bonacieux. Although not given to sentimentality, D'Artagnan had been deeply stirred by her beauty and charm and loyalty. Meanwhile he proposed to investigate Milady. She had spoken to the man in the black cloak, therefore she must know him. And D'Artagnan was certain that the man in the black coat had carried off Madame Bonacieux the second time, just as he had carried her off the first.

At Saint-Germain, as he looked for traces of Milady, passing a pretty villa, he fancied he recognized a familiar face.

"Look, Monsieur," Planchet said, "it's poor old Lubin, the lackey of the Comte de Vardes, whose score you settled so nicely at Calais."

"Well, go try to find out if his master is dead."

Planchet dismounted and walked up to Lubin, who, as he had expected, failed to identify him. The two lackeys engaged in friendly conversation while D'Artagnan turned the two horses into a lane behind a thick hedge through which he had a fine view of the villa. Presently he heard the rumble of a carriage approaching and he saw Milady's coach draw up in front of him.

Milady leaned out, her lovely blonde head clearly visible, to give orders to her maid. The maid walked to the terrace where D'Artagnan had first caught sight of Lubin. Suddenly an order from within the house summoned Lubin indoors. The maid then approached Planchet, whom she mistook for Lubin, and handed him a note.

"This is for your master," she said. Then she ran back to the carriage, which drove off.

Planchet twirled the note between his fingers. Then he jumped down from the terrace, ran toward the lane and met D'Artagnan some sixty feet away.

"A note for you, Monsieur," he told D'Artagnan.

D'Artagnan opened the letter and read:

A person who takes more interest in you than she is willing to confess, wishes to know on what day it would suit you to take a walk in the forest of Saint-Germain.

Tomorrow at the Hostelry of the Field of the Cloth of Gold a lackey in black-and-red livery will await your reply.

"Ha, things are warming up considerably!" D'Artagnan exclaimed. "It seems that both Milady and I are anxious about the health of the same person. Tell me, Planchet, how is our good Monsieur de Vardes? Apparently very much alive."

"Indeed, yes, Monsieur, that is, as alive as can be expected, what with the wounds of four neat sword thrusts. Lubin did not recognize me. He told me our adventure from beginning to end."

"Bravo, Planchet, now let us overtake that carriage."

This did not take long; within a few minutes they sighted the carriage drawn up by the roadside, an elegantly dressed cavalier at the door. Milady and the stranger were talking in English. D'Artagnan easily perceived that the beautiful woman was very angry.

The cavalier laughed heartily, which seemed still further to exasperate Milady. D'Artagnan, believing it was high time he intervened, drew up to the door on his side of the carriage and, doffing his hat respectfully, said:

"Madame, may I offer you my services? I notice this gentleman has incurred your displeasure."

Milady turned toward him in great astonishment.

"Monsieur," she replied in excellent French, "I should welcome your protection but for the fact that the person I am quarreling with is my brother."

"Pray excuse me, then, Madame."

The stranger bent low over his horse's head to look through the carriage window.

"What is this simpleton talking about?" he asked in French. "Why doesn't he go about his business?"

D'Artagnan in turn leaned down to look through the carriage window from his side, and: "Simpleton, yourself!" he declared. "I am staying here because such is my good pleasure."

"Home, Basque, at once!" Milady called to the coachman without a word to either cavalier.

The Englishman made a move as if to follow the carriage but D'Artagnan caught at his bridle and stopped him dead, for he had recognized the man who at Amiens had won a horse from Athos and almost a diamond from D'Artagnan.

"Monsieur," D'Artagnan cried, "you seem to be even more of a simpleton than I am. You have forgotten a previous quarrel that we have not yet settled. I trust you have a sword at home, Monsieur."

"I have plenty of such playthings," the Englishman answered haughtily.

"Well then, Monsieur, pray pick out your longest toy and let me see the color of it this evening."

"Where, if you please?"

"Behind the Luxembourg Palace at six. By the by, Monsieur, you doubtless have friends to second you?"

"I have three who will be honored to join us."

"Three? Splendid! I too have three friends who will support me. I might add that three is my lucky number."

"May I ask who you are, Monsieur?"

"I am Monsieur d'Artagnan, a Gascon gentleman, serving in the Royal Guards; my commanding officer is Monsieur des Essarts."

"I am Lord Winter, Baron of Sheffield."

"Your servant, Monsieur le Baron, though your names are hard to remember."

At the appointed hour our friends and their lackeys met the four Englishmen behind the Luxembourg Palace in an enclosure used as grazing ground for goats. Athos gave the herder a coin to insure his withdrawal.

The Englishmen were considerably disturbed by the odd names of their adversaries. When Athos, Porthos and Aramis announced their names, Lord Winter objected.

"But, gentlemen, we do not know who you are. We refuse to fight against persons with such names; they are names of shepherds!"

"As you have guessed, Milord, these are but names we have assumed," Athos explained.

"That makes us the more eager to know your real names."

Athos, drawing his own adversary aside, whispered his real name. Porthos and Aramis followed suit, and three of the four Englishmen were convinced they were not dealing with shepherds.

"Are you ready, gentlemen?" Athos asked and, as friend and foe agreed, "On guard, then!" he cried.

At once eight swords flashed across the rays of the setting sun and the combat began with a fury natural between men who had double reason to be vindictive. Athos fenced calmly and methodically as at a practice bout in a fencing hall. Porthos, sobered by his mishap at Chantilly, sparred with careful strategy, Aramis, Canto III of his latest poem unfinished, hastened to get done with the fighting.

Athos was the first to dispatch his adversary. One thrust sufficed. Porthos was the second to settle his opponent, who fell to the grass with a wound in the thigh. Porthos, picking him up in his arms, carried him back to his coach. Aramis harried his opponent so forcefully that the Englishman, having retreated over fifty paces, took frankly to his heels amid the jeers of the lackeys.

As for D'Artagnan, he first stood purely and simply on the defensive. Eventually he disarmed his opponent with a turn of the wrist. The Englishman, swordless, took a few steps backward, but his foot slipped and he fell to the ground.

"I could kill you, Monsieur," cried the Gascon, "for you are at my mercy. But I prefer to grant you your life for the sake of your sister."

The Englishman rose, embraced D'Artagnan and shook hands all round.

"And now, my friend, if I may call you so," Lord Winter said to D'Artagnan, "I shall present you to my sister, Lady Clark."

D'Artagnan, blushing, made a bow.

Taking leave of him, Lord Winter gave D'Artagnan Milady's address and offered to call for him. D'Artagnan suggested the Englishman stop by for him at eight o'clock; he would be visiting Athos then, and they could conveniently leave from there.

His forthcoming meeting with Milady filled our young Gascon's mind. Recalling the strange circumstances in which she had entered his life, he was convinced that she must be some creature of the Cardinal's, yet he felt invincibly drawn to her by some incomprehensible fascination. He had certain qualms, too. Would Milady recognize him as the man she had encountered at Meung and at Dover? Again, the fact that she must know him to be a friend of Tréville's and therefore devoted body and soul to the King, would necessarily deprive him of some part of his present advantages. However, a man of twenty and born in Gascony does not worry much over such trifles.

First, D'Artagnan went home to dress in the most flamboyant fashion his wardrobe permitted, then he called on Athos.

"What?" Athos protested. "You have just lost a woman whom you considered good, charming, perfect, and here you go running headlong after another."

D'Artagnan felt the truth in the reproach.

"I loved Madame Bonacieux with my heart," he explained. "I love Milady with my head. If I am so eager to be introduced to her, it is mainly because I want to ascertain what part she plays at Court."

Lord Winter arrived punctually. A handsomely appointed carriage waited below and two mettlesome, spanking horses brought them to Milady's in a few minutes.

Lady Clark received D'Artagnan ceremoniously. Her mansion was remarkably sumptuous, and although most English residents had left or were about to leave France because of the war, obviously the general measure which drove the English home did not apply to her.

Presenting D'Artagnan, Lord Winter said, "Sister, here is a young gentleman who held my life in his hands. He refused to take advantage of his victory. Pray thank him, Madame."

Milady frowned slightly, a faint shadow spun cloudlike over her radiant brow, and a most peculiar smile appeared on her lips. Observing these three reactions, D'Artagnan felt something like a shudder pass through him.

"Pray let me welcome you, Monsieur," said Milady in a voice whose singular gentleness belied the symptoms of ill-humor D'Artagnan had just observed.

The Englishman then turned toward them and related the duel in full detail. Milady listened with the greatest attention, but, despite the effort she made to dissimulate, it was clear that this recital vexed her.

The comely maid who had admitted them now came in again and said something in English to Lord Winter. He immediately asked permission of D'Artagnan to retire, excusing himself on the grounds of urgent business.

D'Artagnan shook hands with Lord Winter and returned to Milady. With surprising mobility her features had regained their gracious composure. Only a few little spots of red on her handkerchief betrayed the fact that she had bitten her lips so hard as to draw blood.

The conversation took a more cheerful, livelier turn. Milady appeared to have completely recovered. She explained that Lord Winter was not her brother but her brother-in-law. From Milady's remarks, D'Artagnan sensed that a veil of mystery covered her, but he could not yet see under this veil.

D'Artagnan, profuse in gallant speeches and lavish in protestations of devotion, uttered a good deal of nonsense. Milady, accepting it, smiled benevolently upon the gushing Gascon. When he took leave of her, on the staircase he met the pretty maid who, as she passed him, blushed to the roots of her hair.

Next day he called on Milady again to be received even better than the evening before. She seemed to take a great interest in him. Where did he hail from, she asked, who were his friends, and had he ever thought of entering the Cardinal's service?

For a lad of twenty, D'Artagnan was, as we have seen, extremely prudent. Remembering his suspicions of Milady, he praised the Cardinal to the skies, and assured her that he would certainly have joined the Cardinal's Guards instead of the Royal Guards had he happened to know Monsieur de Cavois as he knew Monsieur de Tréville.

Leaving at the same hour as on the previous evening, D'Artagnan again met Kitty, the attractive maid, in the corridor. She looked at him with an unmistakable expression of admiration, but D'Artagnan, absorbed by thoughts of the mistress, had no eyes for the servant.

Meanwhile D'Artagnan became more infatuated with Milady hour by hour.

One evening when he arrived, he found Milady's maid, Kitty, under the gateway of the mansion. This time pretty Kitty took him gently by the hand.

"Good!" thought D'Artagnan, "her mistress has charged her with some message for me."

"May I have two words with you, Monsieur?"

"Speak, my child, speak. I am listening."

"If Monsieur will follow me?"

"Where you please, my dear child!"

"Then come!"

So Kitty, who had not released his hand, led him up a little dark, winding staircase and, after ascending about fifteen steps, opened a door.

"Come in here, Monsieur. This is my room, it communicates with my mistress's sitting room by that door. But you need not fear. She will not hear what we are saying."

D'Artagnan gazed around him and stared at the door which Kitty said led to Milady's sitting room.

Kitty heaved a deep sigh. "So you love my mistress very dearly, Monsieur?"

"Ay, more than I can say, Kitty."

Kitty breathed another sigh.

"But my mistress does not love Monsieur at all."

"What!" D'Artagnan gasped. Then: "Did she charge you to tell me so?" he asked.

"Oh, no, Monsieur! Out of my regard for you, I resolved to tell you myself."

"I am obliged to you, my dear Kitty."

"What do you think of this?" Kitty demanded, drawing a little note from her pocket.

"Is it for me?" D'Artagnan asked, snatching the letter.

"No, it is for someone else."

"For someone else?"

"Read the address."

D'Artagnan, obeying, read: FOR MONSIEUR LE COMTE DE VARDES.

The memory of the scene at Saint-Germain flashed across the mind of the presumptuous Gascon. In a move as quick as thought he tore open the letter, and he read:

You have not answered my first note. Are you indisposed or have you forgotten the glances you favored me with at the ball? I offer you an opportunity now; do not let it slip through your fingers.

"Poor dear Monsieur d'Artagnan!" Kitty whispered.

"Do you pity me, little one?"

"Ay, truly, with all my heart, for I know what it is to be in love."

"Well then, will you help me to avenge myself on your mistress?"

"And what sort of vengeance would you take?"

"I want to triumph over her and supplant my rival."

"I shall never help you to do that, Monsieur."

"Why not?"

"For two reasons."

"What reasons?"

"First, my mistress will never love you, and my second reason is: in love, each for himself!"

Then only did D'Artagnan recall Kitty's languishing glances, and the deep sighs she could not quite stifle.

"Tell me, Kitty dear," he asked. "This evening—the time I usually spend chatting with your mistress—shall I stay and talk with you instead?"

"Oh, yes," said Kitty, clapping her hands. "Please, please do!"

Time passed quickly, and suddenly Milady's bell rang.
"Heavens!" Kitty cried in alarm. "My mistress is calling
me! Go, please go at once!"

D'Artagnan rose and took his hat as if he intended to
obey; but instead of opening the door leading to the staircase, he whisked open the door of a great closet and locked
himself in from the inside.

D'Artagnan could hear Milady scolding her maid for
some time. Presently she calmed down and the conversation turned on him.

"I have not seen our Gascon tonight," Milady remarked.

"What, Madame, he hasn't come? Can he possibly be
fickle?"

"I hold this gallant in the palm of my hand."

"What will you do with him, Madame?"

"Kitty, that man and I have to settle something he does
not even dream of. Why, he almost ruined my credit with
the Cardinal. Oh, but I will be revenged!"

"I thought Madame loved him."

"*I* love him? I detest him! A ninny who held Lord Winter's life in his hands and did not kill him! I lost an income
of fifteen thousand pounds by it! What is more, I should
long ago have revenged myself on him. But the Cardinal,
I don't know why, requested me to conciliate him."

"But Madame has not conciliated that little woman the
Gascon was so fond of."

"You mean the haberdasher's wife. Pooh! He has already
forgotten she ever existed."

A cold sweat broke out over D'Artagnan's brow.

"That will do," he heard Milady say. "Go back to your
own room and, tomorrow, try again to get me an answer
to the letter I gave you for Monsieur de Vardes."

D'Artagnan heard the door close, and he opened the
closet door.

"Oh, good Heavens!" said Kitty in a low voice. "What is the matter with you? How pale you are!"

"That abominable creature!" murmured D'Artagnan.

"Hush, Monsieur, hush! And please go!" Kitty begged.

Instead, D'Artagnan tried to find out from Kitty what had become of Madame Bonacieux. But the poor girl swore she knew nothing at all about it.

As to the cause which almost made Milady lose her credit with the Cardinal, Kitty was equally ignorant. But in this instance D'Artagnan was better informed than she. Surely it was the affair of the diamond studs that had brought disfavor down upon her head.

But the clearest thing of all was that the hatred, the deep hatred that Milady felt for him, sprang from the fact that he had not killed her brother-in-law.

Next day D'Artagnan returned to Milady's. He found Kitty at the door and learned that Milady had ordered Kitty to come to her at nine o'clock in the morning to take a third letter to the Comte de Vardes.

D'Artagnan made Kitty promise to bring him that letter the following morning.

True to her promise, Kitty called at D'Artagnan's apartment with the letter.

D'Artagnan read:

This is the third time I have written to you to tell you that I love you. Beware that I do not write to you a fourth time to tell you that I detest you.

If you repent for having acted toward me as you have, the young girl who bears this note will tell you how a man of spirit may obtain his pardon.

D'Artagnan flushed and grew pale several times as he read this note.

"Oh! you love her still!" said Kitty, who had not taken her

eyes off the young man's face for an instant. She sighed. D'Artagnan took up a pen and wrote:

MADAME,

Until the present moment I could not believe that your two previous letters were addressed to me, so unworthy did I deem myself of such an honor. Besides, I was so seriously indisposed that I could not have replied to them in any case.

I will come to crave my pardon at eleven o'clock this evening.

From one whom you have rendered the happiest of men,

COMTE DE VARDES

"There," said the young man, sealing the letter and handing it to Kitty, "give this to Milady. It is Monsieur de Vardes' reply."

Poor Kitty suspected the contents of the note. She turned deathly pale. "Please tell me what your note says," she asked.

"Milady will tell you."

"Ah! you do not love me!" Kitty wailed. "I am so unhappy!"

Intent on searching for their outfits, our four friends had agreed to report once a week at about one o'clock, with Athos for host. Their first meeting was on the same day that Kitty had brought D'Artagnan the letter. D'Artagnan found Athos and Aramis plunged in a philosophical discussion. Aramis felt inclined to resume the cassock; Athos, as usual, neither encouraged nor dissuaded him.

After a moment's conversation Mousqueton entered and begged Porthos to return to his lodgings.

Porthos rose, bowed to his friends and followed Mousqueton.

An instant after, Bazin asked for Aramis.

"A man is waiting to see Monsieur at home, a beggar."

"Give him alms, Bazin, and bid him pray for a poor sinner."

"He said, 'If Monsieur Aramis hesitates to come, tell him I am from Tours.'"

"From Tours!" cried Aramis. "A thousand pardons, gentlemen." And, rising in his turn, he too set off hurriedly.

"I wager these fellows have managed their business and are fully equipped," said Athos. "To change the subject: Monsieur de Tréville told me you were visiting those suspect English protégés of the Cardinal. What about it?"

"Well, it is true I visit an Englishwoman, the one I told you about. I have acquired certain knowledge that she is concerned in the abduction of Madame Bonacieux."

"Yes, I understand now," Athos said with a smile. "To find one woman, you are courting another."

CHAPTER 13:

Milady's Secret

THAT evening D'Artagnan called on Milady at about nine. He found her in a delightful mood, but by ten o'clock she seemed restless and fidgety for reasons that D'Artagnan understood perfectly well. When he took his leave, Milady offered him her hand to kiss. As he did so, he realized that the pressure of her fingers was inspired not by coquetry but by gratitude at his departure.

D'Artagnan then made his way alone to the staircase and up to Kitty's little apartment. He had guessed correctly; Milady had received the letter, and had told her servant that, for reasons of State, the Comte de Vardes must not be seen entering or leaving an English household. As the hour of the eleven o'clock meeting with De Vardes approached, Milady called Kitty, had all but one candle extinguished in the sitting room, and ordered Kitty back to her own room with instructions to bring De Vardes to the sitting room as soon as he arrived.

Kitty did not have long to wait. D'Artagnan immediately opened the door leading to Milady's sitting room.

"What is that noise?" Milady demanded.

"It is I," said D'Artagnan in a low voice. He blew out the

lone candle and, in the darkness, whispered, "It is I, the Comte de Vardes."

"Oh, Comte, Comte," Milady said in her softest, warmest tone as she pressed his hand in her own. "How happy I am in the love that your glances and words have expressed whenever we have met. I too love you! Tomorrow, yes, tomorrow I must have some token from you which will prove that you are thinking of me. For my part, lest you be tempted to forget me, pray take this."

Saying which, she slipped a ring from her finger onto D'Artagnan's.

"Oh, keep this ring for love of me. Besides," she added in a voice tremulous with emotion, "by accepting it, you do me a favor greater than you could possibly imagine. Poor angel!" she continued. "That Gascon monster all but slew you, didn't he? Are your wounds still painful?"

D'Artagnan assured her that he was in considerable physical distress.

"Set your mind at rest," Milady murmured. "I myself will avenge you—and cruelly!"

This woman exerted an unaccountable power over D'Artagnan. He hated her with all the bitterness of offended pride; nevertheless all his plans for immediate vengeance had completely vanished.

At length the clock struck the half-hour and it was time for him to go. His only feeling as he left Milady was one of complete confusion.

Next morning D'Artagnan hastened to visit Athos, for he wanted his advice.

"Your Milady," Athos said, "seems to me to be an infamous creature. All the same, you were wrong to deceive her. No matter how you look at it, you have a dangerous enemy on your hands."

As he spoke, Athos looked steadily at the sapphire D'Artagnan wore in place of the Queen's ring.

"I see you are looking at my ring," said the Gascon.

"Yes. It reminds me of a family heirloom. Did you trade your diamond for it?"

"No, it is a gift from Milady. She gave it to me last night."

"Let me have a look at it."

Athos examined it carefully and, growing very pale, tried it on the third finger of his left hand; it fitted as though made to order.

"You know this ring?" D'Artagnan asked.

"I thought I did but I was probably mistaken," Athos replied. Then: "Look," he said sharply, pointing to a scratch on the ring. "What a coincidence!"

Mystified, D'Artagnan inquired if Athos had ever been in possession of Milady's ring.

"I inherited it from my mother," Athos told him, "and Mother inherited it from *her* mother. I told you it was an heirloom."

"And you—hm!—you s-s-old it?" D'Artagnan stammered.

"No," said Athos with an enigmatic smile, "I gave it away."

Athos grasped his hand. "D'Artagnan," he said earnestly, "you know how much you mean to me. I implore you to follow my advice. Give up seeing this woman!"

"You are right, I will have done with her! Honestly, Athos, she terrifies me!"

"Bravo, lad, you will be doing the right thing."

When he arrived home, D'Artagnan found Kitty waiting for him. She declared falteringly that her mistress had despatched her once again to the Comte de Vardes to ask him to meet her again as soon as possible. D'Artagnan penned the following brief missive:

Do not count upon me to meet you again, Madame. Since my convalescence, I have so many affairs to settle that I am obliged to regulate them somewhat. When your turn comes again, I shall have the honor to apprise you. Meanwhile, I kiss your hand and remain,

Your Ladyship's most faithful servant,
DE VARDES

D'Artagnan showed Kitty what he had written. Despite the danger Kitty ran she sped blithely back to Milady's. Milady opened the letter with an expectancy as lively as Kitty's in delivering it; but at the first word she read, she turned livid. Then, furiously, she crushed the paper and, her eyes blazing, demanded, "What is this?"

"The answer to Milady's letter," Kitty replied, shaking like a leaf.

"Impossible," cried Milady. "Impossible! No gentleman would write such a letter to a woman."

That evening Milady gave orders that when D'Artagnan came as usual, he was to be admitted immediately. But he did not come. Next evening Milady was even more impatient; she renewed her order concerning the Gascon, but once again she waited for him in vain.

Wednesday morning, when Kitty stopped in at D'Artagnan's, she was no longer lively as on the two preceding days. D'Artagnan asked the girl what was the matter. For answer she drew a letter from her pocket. It was in Milady's handwriting, only this time it was addressed to D'Artagnan, not to De Vardes. Opening it, he read:

DEAR MONSIEUR D'ARTAGNAN—

It is wrong of you thus to neglect your friends particularly at the moment when you are about to leave them for so long a time.

My brother-in-law and I expected you yesterday and the day before but in vain.

Will it be the same this evening?

Your very grateful
LADY CLARK

As nine o'clock struck, D'Artagnan was at Milady's. She was pale and looked weary. Her eyes especially were worn, either from tears or lack of sleep or fever.

"I feel poorly," she said, "very poorly."

"Then I am surely intruding," he answered. "No doubt you are in need of rest and I will excuse myself."

"No, no! On the contrary, Monsieur d'Artagnan, do stay. Your company will divert me."

Gradually, Milady became communicative. She asked D'Artagnan if he had pledged his love to any lady.

"Alas!" he sighed. "How can you be so cruel as to put such a question to me who from the moment I saw you have breathed solely for *you?*"

"Then you love me?"

"Need I tell you so? Have you not noticed it?"

"Perhaps, who shall tell? But as you know, the prouder a woman's heart is, the more difficult it is to capture."

"Pooh! I am not one to fear difficulties! Nothing frightens me save impossibilities."

"Tell me now," she coaxed, "what would you do to prove this love you boast of?"

"Everything that could be required of me. Command me, I am at your service."

"Everything?"

"Everything!" D'Artagnan promised blithely.

For a moment Milady seemed pensive and undecided; then, as if abruptly coming to a decision: "I have an enemy," she began.

"I cannot believe it."

"I may reckon upon you as an ally?"

D'Artagnan raised his head. "I am at your orders, Madame."

"Are you quite certain?" Milady asked with a lingering doubt.

"Name the scoundrel who has brought tears to your beautiful eyes and I—"

"His name is *my* secret."

"Yet I must know it, Madame."

"His—name—is—"

"De Vardes, I know it!"

"Tell me, tell me, I say, *how* do you know it!"

"I know it because yesterday he displayed a ring of yours. I will avenge you of this wretch," D'Artagnan boasted.

"My brave friend, I cannot thank you enough. And when shall I be avenged?"

"Tomorrow you will be avenged or I shall be dead."

A bell rang, and soon Kitty appeared in the doorway.

"Lord Winter to see you, Milady," she announced.

"Go out this way," Milady ordered D'Artagnan, opening a small secret door, "and come back at eleven. We will then conclude our conversation. Kitty will show you to my sitting room."

D'Artagnan paced round the Place Royale five or six times, turning at every ten steps to look at the light shining through the blinds of Milady's drawing room. At length he heard chimes striking eleven o'clock. He returned to the mansion and rushed up to Kitty's room. Milady, listening for every sound, had heard D'Artagnan enter. She opened the door for him.

"Come in!" she said.

As the door closed behind them, D'Artagnan felt he had attained the sum of all his hopes. It was no longer for his rival's sake that Milady showed him favor; she now seemed to prize him on his own account. Faintly, deep in his heart, a secret voice warned him that she was using him as the tool of her vengeance. But pride, self-conceit and folly silenced the feeble murmur of the voice of reason.

Milady immediately asked him if he had planned exactly how he would bring about a duel with De Vardes on the morrow.

But D'Artagnan foolishly forgot himself and replied that it was too late in the evening to consider duels and sword thrusts.

His cold reception of the only interests which occupied her mind frightened Milady and she began to question him more pressingly. D'Artagnan, who had never given this impossible duel a serious thought, attempted to change the conversation.

"Are you afraid, perhaps, my dear D'Artagnan?" she asked in a shrill scornful voice which rasped strangely.

"You surely cannot think so, dear love. But suppose this poor Comte de Vardes was less guilty than you imagine?"

"At all events, he has deceived me," Milady insisted. "Having deceived me, he deserves death."

"He shall die then, since you condemn him!" D'Artagnan vowed with a firmness that convinced Milady of his unwavering devotion. And she at once gave him a dazzling smile.

"Honestly, I *do* feel sorry for poor De Vardes since you have ceased to love him," said D'Artagnan. "Besides, I alone know that he is far from being deceitful as you think."

"Indeed!" Milady seemed somewhat uneasy. She stared up at him, her gaze growing brighter apace.

"Well, *I* am a man of honor," D'Artagnan declared. "And if my excessive love for you has made me guilty of offending you, you will forgive me?"

"Perhaps!"

"You invited De Vardes to meet you in this very room last Thursday, I believe."

"No, no, that is not true."

"Do not lie to me, my beautiful angel!" He smiled. "That would be useless! The Comte de Vardes of Thursday, and D'Artagnan are one and the same person."

Milady turned to rush from the room. In despair, he caught her by the shoulder and implored her pardon. With a powerful jerk, she strove to shake herself free. This movement tore the cambric at the neck of her gown, and ripped it down one shoulder. On this beautiful, white, exquisitely rounded shoulder D'Artagnan was inexpressibly shocked to see the fleur-de-lis, that indelible flower branded upon criminals by the degrading iron of the Royal Executioner.

"O God!" D'Artagnan gasped.

In the look of terror that swept over his face, Milady read her own denunciation. She turned upon him, no longer a furious woman now, but a wounded panther.

"Ah, wretch! You know my secret! You shall die for it." Darting across the room to an inlaid casket on the table, she seized a small dagger and, wheeling round again, threw herself with one bound upon D'Artagnan.

Now D'Artagnan was a brave man. But he was aghast at her distorted features, her horribly dilated pupils, her livid cheeks. He recoiled as he would have done before the onset of a serpent crawling toward him. As he moved back, his sword came into contact with his cold, clammy hand. Nervously, almost unconsciously, he drew it. Milady, undaunted, attempted to seize the blade with her hands, but D'Artagnan kept it free from her grasp, now holding it leveled at her eyes, now at her breast. This maneuver enabled him to spring through the door leading to Kitty's apartment and slam it shut.

With a strength and violence far beyond those of an ordinary woman, Milady attempted to tear open the door but, finding this impossible, she kept stabbing frantically at it.

"Quick, Kitty, quick!" D'Artagnan whispered behind the locked door. "Help me get out of here! Unless we look sharp, she will have me killed by the servants."

Kitty led him quickly downstairs through the darkness. It was in the nick of time; Milady had already awakened the whole mansion. The porter had not finished drawing the cord to open the street door when Milady screamed from her window:

"Porter! Don't let anyone out!"

D'Artagnan rushed on, too bewildered to worry about what would happen to Kitty. He dashed across half Paris, and stopped only when he reached the sanctuary he hoped Athos might provide for him.

Athos greeted him anxiously. "Are you wounded, my friend?" he asked. "How pale you are!"

"No, but something frightful has just happened to me. Are you alone, Athos?"

"Yes."

"Good! Good!" And D'Artagnan rushed into the musketeer's bedroom.

After closing the door and bolting it so that they would not be disturbed, Athos turned to the Gascon.

"Come, speak. Is the King dead? Have you killed the Cardinal? You seem terribly upset."

"Athos," D'Artagnan said solemnly, "brace yourself to hear an unheard-of, an incredible story."

"Well?" Athos said inquiringly.

"Well," D'Artagnan replied. "Milady is branded. She bears a fleur-de-lis upon her shoulder."

"Ah!" groaned the musketeer.

"Tell me, Athos," D'Artagnan went on, "are you sure *the other woman* is dead?"

"*The other woman?*" Athos mumbled so low that D'Artagnan barely heard him.

"Yes, the woman you told me about one day at Amiens."

Athos groaned again and buried his head in his hands.

"This woman is twenty-six or twenty-eight," D'Artagnan volunteered.

"Blonde, is she not?"

"Yes."

"Light blue eyes of a strange brilliancy with very black eyelids and eyebrows?"

"Yes."

"Tall? Slender? Shapely?"

"Exactly!"

"The fleur-de-lis is small, russet in color, somewhat faded by the application of poultices?"

"The brand is faint, yes, Athos."

"But you said she was English."

"They call her Milady, but she might well be French. After all, Lord Winter is only her brother-in-law. I am very much afraid," D'Artagnan concluded, "that I have invited a terrible vengeance upon both of us!"

"Right you are," said Athos, "with her after me, my life wouldn't be worth a counterfeit sou. Luckily we leave Paris the day after tomorrow, probably for La Rochelle—"

"Athos, there is something horribly mysterious under all this. She is one of the Cardinal's spies, I am certain. You must take the sapphire back, Athos."

"I—I take back that ring? Never!"

"Sell it then," D'Artagnan suggested.

"Sell a jewel my mother bequeathed me!"

"Pawn it! You can probably borrow over a thousand crowns on it."

"What a smart lad you are!" Athos smiled. "I agree, let us pawn the ring, but only on one condition."

"What?"

"Five hundred crowns for you, five hundred for me."

"Absurd, Athos! I don't need a quarter of the sum. Besides, you forget I, too, have a ring."

"A ring to which you apparently attach more value than I do to mine," Athos replied.

They reached D'Artagnan's safely but found Bonacieux posted on the doorstep. The haberdasher stared at D'Artagnan and, with mock affability: "Make haste, my dear lodger," he cried, "there's a very pretty girl waiting for you upstairs and you know women don't like to be kept waiting."

It could only be Kitty. D'Artagnan darted down the alley, took the stairs three at a time, and, on the landing, found her crouching against his door, trembling hysterically.

Before he could say a word: "You swore to protect me," she sobbed. "You swore to save me from her anger, Monsieur!"

They soothed Kitty as best they could and were discussing her future when Aramis entered. Long before they had finished their story, he exhibited a letter from a cousin in the provinces, asking him to find her a maid at once. Kitty would fill the bill perfectly.

"Kitty, before we part, I must ask you something," D'Artagnan said. "Tell me, have you ever heard about a young woman who was carried off one night?"

"Let me see . . . oh, yes!"

"You see, my child, probably it was Madame Bonacieux, the wife of that unspeakable baboon you saw on the doorstep."

"Oh, you remind me of the terror I have been through! Pray Heaven he didn't recognize me!"

"Recognize you? Have you ever seen him before?"

"Certainly. He came to Milady's twice."

"My dear Athos, we are caught in a network of spies," said D'Artagnan. "Go down, Athos, he mistrusts you less than he does me. See if he is still at the door."

Athos went down and returned at once.

"He is gone to report that all the birds are hugging the dovecote."

"Very well then, let us all fly," Aramis proposed. "We can leave Planchet here to bring us news."

"And now, Kitty dear," D'Artagnan said, "you know it is not safe for any of us to be found here. We must separate. We shall meet again in better days."

"Whenever we meet again and wherever it may be," Kitty answered solemnly, "you will find me loving you as deeply as I do today."

That afternoon Athos and D'Artagnan assembled the musketeer's full equipment in barely three hours, thanks to the pledge of the sapphire heirloom.

At four o'clock the four friends met again, Athos playing the host. Suddenly Planchet entered, bringing two letters addressed to D'Artagnan. The first was a small paper, neatly folded, once only, lengthwise; the other was a large square sheet, resplendent with the fearsome arms of His Eminence. At the sight of the little letter, D'Artagnan's heart beat the faster, for he recognized the handwriting. So he took it up first and eagerly read the following:

If you happen to stroll along the road to Chaillot next Thursday evening at seven o'clock, be sure to look carefully into the carriages as they pass. But if you value your life and the lives of those who love you, do not utter a word or make the slightest gesture indicating that you have recognized the woman who is risking everything in order to see you for but an instant.

There was no signature.

"It is obviously a hoax!" said Athos. "Don't go, D'Artagnan."

"And yet the handwriting looks familiar."

"What if we *all* went?" Aramis suggested. "Surely they cannot gobble up three musketeers, one guardsman, four lackeys, four horses, weapons, harness and the rest?"

Athos reminded D'Artagnan of the second letter. "What about *that?*" he challenged. D'Artagnan opened the second letter. It read:

Monsieur d'Artagnan, of the Royal Guards, Des Essarts, Company Commander, is expected at the Palais-Cardinal this evening at eight o'clock.

La Houdinière
Captain of Guards

That evening our four friends made a splendid cavalcade in their new equipment, with four dapper valets behind them. Near the Louvre the four friends met Monsieur de Tréville, who was returning from Saint-Germain. D'Artagnan profited by the circumstance to tell Tréville about the letter with the great red seal and the Cardinal's signet.

A lively canter brought our friends to the Chaillot road by twilight. After they had waited a quarter of an hour, just as night was falling, a carriage appeared, speeding down the Sèvres road. A presentiment told D'Artagnan instantly that this carriage bore the person who had arranged the rendezvous. Suddenly a woman's face appeared at the window, two fingers to her mouth as though to enjoin silence or to blow him a kiss. D'Artagnan uttered a cry of joy. The carriage had passed by, swift as a vision, but the apparition was a woman and the woman was Madame Bonacieux.

The carriage pursued its way at the same swift pace, entered Paris and disappeared. D'Artagnan, dumbfounded, stood rooted to the spot. What was he to think? If it was

Madame Bonacieux and if she was returning to Paris, why this fugitive meeting, why this simple exchange of glances, why this lost kiss? If, on the other hand, it was not Madame Bonacieux—a perfectly plausible conjecture, since his eyes might well have deceived him in the near-darkness—was this not a plot in which his enemies were using for decoy the woman he was known to love?

"They are undoubtedly transferring her from one prison to another," D'Artagnan mused. "But what can they intend to do to the poor girl? And how shall I ever meet her again?"

They heard the half-hour strike from a belfry near by; it was seven-thirty. His friends reminded D'Artagnan that he had a visit to pay, adding significantly that he still had time to change his mind. But at once headstrong and curious, D'Artagnan was determined to go to the Cardinal's palace.

Our friends then returned to the Tréville mansion and enlisted the help of nine musketeers. Athos divided them into three groups, took command of one and assigned the other two respectively to Porthos and Aramis. Each group took its stand in the darkness close to one of the side entrances to the Cardinal's palace. D'Artagnan, for his part, boldly entered through the main gate.

Having reached the antechamber, D'Artagnan presented his letter to the usher on duty, was shown into a vestibule and then passed into the interior of the palace. The usher led him down a corridor, across a vast salon and into a library where he found a man seated at a desk, writing. He heard the usher announce him, then bow his way out silently. D'Artagnan stood on the threshold, waiting.

At first he thought he was up against some magistrate who was looking over some record, prior to questioning him. On closer examination, he saw that the man seated at the desk was the Cardinal!

CHAPTER 14:

The Siege of La Rochelle

The Cardinal's chin rested in the palm of his hand. He looked very intently at the young man. But the Gascon kept a good countenance and stood, hat in hand, awaiting the Cardinal's pleasure.

"You are a certain D'Artagnan from Gascon," the Cardinal observed.

"Ay, Monseigneur."

There was a silence. Then Richelieu continued:

"You set out from Gascony some seven or eight months ago to try your fortune in the capital?"

"Ay, Monseigneur."

"You passed through Meung, where something untoward occurred."

"Monseigneur, this is what happened. I—"

"Never mind, young man." The Cardinal smiled. "You were recommended to Monsieur de Tréville, were you not?"

"Yes, Monseigneur, but in the trouble at Meung—"

"Yes, yes, I know, you lost your letter of recommendation. However, Monsieur de Tréville judged you at a glance and arranged for you to join the Royal Guards—"

"Ay, Monseigneur."

"And you were led to hope that some day or other you might join the Royal Musketeers."

"Monseigneur is perfectly informed," said D'Artagnan, bowing.

"Since then your life has, I believe, been eventful. One day you happened to stroll by the Carmelite convent when it would have been healthier for you to be elsewhere. Another day you and your friends journeyed to Forges, doubtless to take the waters. But they stopped en route, whereas you continued. It is all quite simple—you had business in England."

"Monseigneur, I was going—"

"I may add that on your return you were received by an august personage. I see you wear the keepsake she gave you."

Too late, D'Artagnan twirled his ring inward to conceal the jewel.

"The following day, you were invited to report here but you saw fit to ignore the request."

It was that very evening that Madame Bonacieux had been abducted.

"In short," the Cardinal continued, "having heard nothing of you for some time, I wished to know what you were doing. Besides, you *do* owe me some thanks. You must yourself have noticed how considerately you were treated in all these circumstances."

D'Artagnan bowed respectfully.

"Sit down there in front of me, Monsieur d'Artagnan; you are too well-born to stand listening to me like a lackey." The Cardinal pointed to a chair. "You are a brave man, but I must warn you that here you have powerful enemies. Be very careful, Monsieur, or they will destroy you!"

"Alas, Monseigneur, they can readily do so. But I am young, Monseigneur, my age is that of extravagant optimism."

"Extravagant optimism is pabulum for fools, Monsieur, and you are a man of intelligence. Tell me, what would you say to a commission as ensign in my Guards and to a lieutenancy after the campaign? You accept, do you not?"

D'Artagnan, deeply embarrassed, could but reply, "Ah, Monseigneur!"

"You refuse, then?"

"I serve in His Majesty's Guards, Monseigneur, and I have no reason to be dissatisfied."

"But it seems to me that my Guards are also His Majesty's Guards. Anyone serving in a French corps serves the King."

"Your Eminence misunderstood me."

"You want an excuse to transfer, is that it? Well, here it is. I offer you promotion; the campaign is about to open; opportunity knocks at your door. For yourself personally, you are assured protection in high places." The Cardinal cleared his throat. "I have here a complete file concerning you. Think it over, young man, and make up your mind."

"Your kindness overwhelms me, Monseigneur. But since you permit me to speak frankly—"

"Certainly; speak out—"

"I would presume to say that all my friends serve in either the Royal Musketeers or in the King's Guards; that all my enemies, by an inconceivable quirk of fortune, are in the service of Your Eminence. So that if I accepted your flattering offer, I would be ill-regarded among the King's forces and ill-received among Your Eminence's."

The Cardinal smiled disdainfully.

"Are you so conceited as to believe my offer does not match your merits?" he asked.

"Monseigneur, you are a hundred times too kind to me. The siege of La Rochelle is about to open, Monseigneur. I shall be serving under the eyes of Your Eminence. If I am fortunate enough to perform some brilliant action there, I shall feel I have earned the protection with which Your Eminence honors me."

The Cardinal glanced shrewdly at D'Artagnan with an expression of annoyance, tempered by a certain reluctant esteem.

"Well, well, keep your freedom then, preserve your sympathies, cherish your hatreds—"

"Monseigneur—"

"I wish you no ill, Monsieur." Richelieu looked meaningfully at him, stressing his words. "In the future," he said, "if some mischance should happen to befall you, remember that it was *I* who sought *you* out and that I did what I could to forestall a catastrophe."

These final words, conveying the grim doubt they did, dismayed D'Artagnan more than any threat could have done.

All next day was spent in preparations for departure. D'Artagnan paid Monsieur de Tréville a farewell call. At the time, the separation of the musketeers and the guards was supposed to be but a temporary measure, since the King was holding his Parliament that very day and proposing to leave on the morrow.

That night all the comrades of Monsieur des Essarts' guards and of Monsieur de Tréville's musketeers convened to affirm their long-standing friendship. As may be imagined, the night proved a boisterous and riotous one.

At the first peals of reveille, the friends parted company, the musketeers hastening to the Tréville mansion, the guards to Monsieur des Essarts. Each captain then led his company to the Louvre where the King was to hold his review.

The review over, the guards set forward alone, the musketeers standing by to escort the King. As D'Artagnan was marching off to the front with his company, so absorbed was he that he failed to notice a blonde blue-eyed lady mounted on a light chestnut horse. At her side stood two evil-looking men. As she pointed to D'Artagnan, they drew up close to the ranks in order to get a good view of him. They stared at her questioningly; she nodded affirmatively.

The siege of La Rochelle proved to be one of the great political events of the reign of Louis XIII and one of the Cardinal's great military enterprises. But the honest chronicler is in duty bound to recognize the petty aims of an unrequited lover and jealous rival. Richelieu, as everyone knows, had been in love with the Queen. He knew that in fighting England he was fighting Buckingham; in triumphing over England he was triumphing over Buckingham; and finally, in humiliating England in the eyes of Europe he was humiliating Buckingham in the eyes of the Queen.

For his part, Buckingham, pretending to maintain the honor of England, was prompted by interest as personal as the Cardinal's but diametrically opposed. Buckingham, too, pursued a private vengeance. The true stake of this game, which two of the most powerful kingdoms played for the good pleasure of two hapless lovers, was merely a friendly glance from Anne of Austria.

The Guards reached the camp before La Rochelle on September 10, 1627, to find things at a stalemate. The Duke of Buckingham and his Englishmen were still masters of the Ile de Ré; hostilities with La Rochelle had started two or three days before, over a fortress newly set up close to the city walls.

The King was ill in Paris, but news of his convalescence reached the camp, so a very lonely D'Artagnan looked forward to seeing his friends. Meanwhile he had had two adventures. First, he had been shot at, and the bullet had been no ordinary army bullet. Secondly, while on reconnaissance, he had discovered that two of his soldiers had been employed by Milady to kill him. He spared the life of one ruffian, Brisemont, who showed him Milady's written orders for his murder. On the second ruffian's body, D'Artagnan found a note from Milady chiding the fellow for having allowed Madame Bonacieux to escape to a convent.

D'Artagnan meanwhile had become somewhat more easy, as always happens after a danger has passed. His only anxiety was at hearing nothing from his friends. But one morning everything was explained to him in the following letter, dated from Villeroi:

MONSIEUR D'ARTAGNAN:
Messieurs Athos, Porthos and Aramis having dined well at my establishment, carrying out their orders, I am sending you a dozen bottles of my Anjou wine, of which they thought most highly.

> Your most humble and obedient servant,
> GODEAU, *Purveyor and Steward*
> *to the Musketeers.*

D'Artagnan sent the twelve bottles to the canteen and invited two fellow guardsmen to dinner. The hour of the feast arrived. The two guests took their places; the viands were laid out upon the table. Planchet was to serve them, aided by Brisemont, the ruffian whose life D'Artagnan had spared. The guests, having partaken of soup, were about to lift the first glass to their lips when suddenly the cannons fired full blast. Cries of "Long live the King!" and "Long live the Cardinal!" rang out from all sides as the King's Musketeers came marching up. D'Artagnan, lining the route with his company, greeted his friends with a gesture. Then, the parade over, the four friends were reunited.

"Is there any drinkable wine in your shanty?" Athos inquired.

"Of course, my dear friends, there is the wine you sent."

When Athos denied he had sent any wine, D'Artagnan produced the letter.

"A palpable forgery!" said Athos.

D'Artagnan grew pale and shivered.

"Come," he begged. "Let us go back to the canteen."

There, the first thing D'Artagnan sighted was Brisemont stretched out on the floor, writhing in horrible convulsions.

"Ha!" he cried, "shame on you! You pretend to pardon me and now you poison me!"

"What? What's that, you wretch? *I* poison you?"

"*You* gave me the wine . . . *you* told me to drink it . . . you are avenged upon me and I say it is a dastardly act. . . ."

"I swear by the Bible that I had nothing to do with this!" D'Artagnan kneeled over the dying man. "I never suspected the wine was poisoned; I was about to drink it myself, just as you did."

Guardsmen and musketeers went out, leaving to Planchet the duty of rendering mortuary honors to Brisemont. The two guardsmen took their leave, since obviously this

"I swear that I had nothing to do with this!"

was no longer an occasion for celebration. The steward gave the four comrades another room, where he served them some boiled eggs. They drank water which Athos in person drew from the well. D'Artagnan turned to Athos.

"As you see, my dear friend, this is war to the death."

"I see that quite plainly," Athos agreed. "But do you think it is—er—it is *that* woman!"

"I am certain of it. Remember that fleur-de-lis on her shoulder?"

"She could easily be an Englishwoman who committed some crime in France and was branded for it."

"No, Athos, it is your—*that* woman! Don't you recall how our descriptions tallied?"

"Gentlemen, we cannot go on with a sword eternally dangling over our heads," Athos said. "We must solve this problem."

"But how?"

"Well, D'Artagnan, try to meet her again; discuss things with her; tell her this is a question of peace or war! Give her your word as a gentleman never to say or do anything about her, in return for her solemn oath to remain neutral with regard to yourself."

"The idea appeals to me," D'Artagnan confessed. "But how shall I meet her again?"

"By the grace of time, my friend!" Athos explained.

"Yes—but to wait surrounded by assassins and poisoners—?"

"Pooh!" said Athos, "God has preserved us so far, He will preserve us further."

D'Artagnan paused. "But what of Constance Bonacieux?"

"Madame Bonacieux, of course," Athos sighed. "Excuse me, my poor friend, I had forgotten you were in love."

"Cheer up," Aramis put in. "The letter you found on the dead man proves that Madame Bonacieux is alive and in a convent. As soon as the siege of La Rochelle is over, I promise you we shall take her out of the convent."

"But we still have to know in what convent she is now."

"I think I have a clue," Athos announced. "Didn't you tell us the Queen chose her convent, D'Artagnan?"

"I think so."

"In that case Aramis can help us," Athos suggested.

Aramis blushed.

"I happen to know the Queen's almoner," he explained.

On this assurance, their modest meal finished, the quartet separated, promising to meet again in the evening. D'Artagnan returned to his chores; the three musketeers repaired to Royal Headquarters to prepare their lodging.

Meanwhile, the King, who shared the Cardinal's hatred of Buckingham, was impatient to meet the enemy. He therefore ordered all necessary preparations to be made to drive the English from the Isle of Ré and to press the siege of La Rochelle. To his surprise the English, repulsed, were forced to sail away, leaving numerous casualties on the field.

One evening when Athos, Porthos and Aramis were riding home to camp, very much on their guard for fear of an ambush, they heard the sound of horses approaching. A moment later, they saw two horsemen who stopped in their turn. This hesitation aroused the suspicion of the three musketeers. So Athos, advancing, cried in a firm voice, "Who goes there?"

"Beware of what you are about, gentlemen!" said a clear voice in tones accustomed to command. "Who are you? Answer in your turn or you may well repent of your disobedience."

"Royal Musketeers," said Athos, convinced that their questioner had authority to challenge them.

"Advance and explain what you are doing here."

The three companions advanced rather shamefacedly.

As usual, by tacit agreement, Athos filled the role of spokesman.

The horseman who had spoken so authoritatively sat erect and still in his saddle, some ten paces in front of his companion.

"Your pardon, Monsieur," Athos said, "but we did not know whom we were speaking to. As you saw, we were keeping close watch."

"Your name?" asked the officer, drawing up his cloak to cover his face.

"But yourself, Monsieur," Athos protested, now somewhat annoyed at this inquisition. "I beg you to give me some proof of your right to question me."

"Your name?" The horseman bared his face.

"Monsieur le Cardinal!"

"Your name?" His Eminence cried for the third time.

"Athos."

The Cardinal motioned to his attendant to draw near. "These three musketeers shall follow us," he said in an undertone. "I do not care to have it known that I left camp." Turning to Athos, he added, "I request you gentlemen to follow me for reasons of my personal security. Doubtless the gentlemen accompanying you are Messieurs Porthos and Aramis?"

"Ay, Your Eminence," Athos nodded.

"And now, gentlemen, everything is in order," the Cardinal declared.

Soon they reached a silent, solitary inn. Ten paces from the door, the Cardinal signaled to his esquire and the musketeers to halt. A saddled horse stood by the wall, his bridle fastened to the shutter of the window. The Cardinal tapped against the shutter.

Immediately a man wrapped deep in a cloak emerged, exchanged a few rapid words with the Cardinal, climbed into the saddle again and galloped off.

The Cardinal dismounted, the musketeers did likewise. The Cardinal tossed the bridle of his horse to his esquire and the musketeers fastened their horses to the shutter.

"Have you a room on the ground floor where these gentlemen can wait around a good fire?" the Cardinal asked.

The landlord opened the door of a vast room in which an old stove had recently been replaced by a large and excellent chimney.

"I have this room, Monsieur," he said.

The three musketeers filed in. His Eminence, without more ado, ascended the staircase like a man who did not need to be shown the way.

As Porthos and Aramis sat down at a table and began to play a dice game, Athos paced the room, deep in thought. Moving back and forth, he kept passing by the broken stovepipe which obviously communicated with the room above. Each time he did so, he could hear a murmur of voices. Drawing closer to the pipe, Athos distinguished a few words which appeared to him so interesting that he motioned to his companions to be silent. Then he bent down, his ear glued to the lower end of the pipe.

The Cardinal's voice was familiar—but the other? A woman was saying, "Yes, Monseigneur, I am to tell Buckingham that you have proofs of his visits to France; of his intrigues with Madame de Chevreuse, the Queen's friend, whom you exiled to Tours; of his meetings with the Queen; of the diamond studs, and of his plots with Spain. Also that this war may cost the Queen her honor, her liberty or worse. But if he persists?"

"Well, Milady, fanatics have been known to kill tyrants and England is full of Puritan fanatics."

Athos was shocked when he heard the woman's name but aghast when, as subtly as Richelieu, Milady offered to find the right man. However, she added, she too had enemies and *their* deaths might help *her:* a meddlesome

woman called Bonacieux whom the Queen had transferred
from prison to a convent, and a scoundrel called D'Artagnan who had threatened her life. He was also a proven
enemy of the Cardinal's! Richelieu signed some sort of order she asked for.

"Thank you, Monseigneur," she said, "a life for a life!"

"Good-bye, friends, I'm off," Athos cried. "When the

Cardinal comes down, tell him I have gone to patrol the road because I heard it was unsafe."

Riding around a bend in the road, he hid behind a tall hedge, heard the Cardinal's party gallop by, and immediately returned to the inn.

"Walk right up," the landlord said, recognizing him. "The lady is still here."

Climbing the stairs soundlessly, Athos entered Milady's room, closed and bolted the door. Milady turned, startled.

"Who are you," she demanded, "and what do you want?"

"Yes, yes!" said Athos. "You are certainly the woman I am looking for. Do you recognize me, Madame?"

Milady drew back as though a snake lay in her path.

"So far so good!" Athos went on. "I see you know who I am."

"The Comte de la Fère!"

"Yes, Milady, the Comte de la Fère in person. He has come expressly from the other world in order to enjoy the pleasure of seeing you again. Let us sit down and talk."

Milady, terrified, sat down without uttering a word.

"Truly you are a demon sent to plague this earth!" Athos said calmly. "Once before, Madame, you crossed my path and I thought I had felled you; but either I was mistaken or Hell has resuscitated you. But it has effaced neither the stains upon your soul nor the brand upon your body."

Milady sprang up. Her eyes flashed lightning. Athos did not turn a hair.

"You thought me dead, did you not, just as *I* thought *you* dead? The name of Athos concealed the Comte de la Fère just as that of Lady Clark concealed that of Anne de Bueil. It was under that name that your honorable brother married us, was it not?"

"Tell me, Monsieur," Milady said in a faint, hollow voice, "what brings you back to me? What do you want?"

"I can tell you what you have been doing, day by day, ever since you entered the service of the Cardinal."

A smile of incredulity fluttered across Milady's pallid lips.

"So you doubt me, eh?" Athos smiled ironically. "Well, listen carefully, Milady. I know about the studs, about Madame Bonacieux's abduction, about De Vardes and D'Artagnan, about the two ruffians you hired to kill him, about the Anjou wine, and about the plot to murder Buckingham."

Milady turned livid.

"You must be Satan!" she murmured.

"Possibly I am," Athos replied jauntily. Suddenly he rose, drew a pistol from his belt and cocked it carefully. Milady, pale as a corpse, tried to cry out but her swollen tongue failed her.

"Madame," he said, "you will this instant give me the paper the Cardinal signed or I will blow your brains out. You have exactly five seconds in which to make up your mind."

"Here it is," she snarled, "and may you be accursed!"

Athos took the paper, restored the pistol to his belt, drew up the lamp to make sure it was the proper document, and read:

3RD DECEMBER, 1627

It is by my order and for the service of the State that the bearer of this note has done what he has done.
Signed by my hand at the
Camp of La Rochelle.

RICHELIEU

CHAPTER 15:

The Bastion in No Man's Land

N<small>EXT</small> day the four friends met at a tavern to breakfast and discuss matters. D'Artagnan had been in the trenches the night before. Reveille had just sounded; from all parts of the camp dragoons, Swiss mercenaries, guardsmen, musketeers and hussars appeared.

"Confound it," Athos groaned. "I see what is going to happen. We shall get into some gay little brawl or other. Come, D'Artagnan, tell us about your experiences last night and we will tell you about ours."

Overhearing him, soldiers of a rival corps started belittling the exploits of the Royal Guards who had blown up one part of a bastion in no man's land the night before. Amid the din, suddenly Athos cried:

"Very well, gentlemen, I wager that my three friends and myself will breakfast in the Bastion Saint-Gervais and that we will stay there over an hour, no matter what the enemy may do."

"Breakfast is ready, gentlemen," the innkeeper announced.

Athos signaled to Grimaud to pack the food and wine in an empty basket, and bowing to an astounded company, the four young men set out toward the Bastion Saint-Gervais.

"Now, my dear Athos," D'Artagnan pleaded, "will you kindly tell me where we are going?"

"To the bastion, of course. For breakfast!"

"And why did we not breakfast at the inn?"

"Because we have some very important matters to discuss. There, at least," Athos pointed to the bastion, "no one can disturb us."

Reaching the bastion, the four friends turned round. More than three hundred soldiers of all kinds were clustered around the camp gate.

Removing his hat, Athos placed it on the end of his sword and waved it in the air. As one, all the spectators returned his salute, accompanying this courtesy with loud cheers.

Then the quartet followed Grimaud into the bastion.

As Athos had foreseen, the bastion was occupied by but a dozen dead bodies, some Royalist and some of La Rochelle. Grimaud started to prepare breakfast while our friends collected the twelve guns and hundred cartridges left in the bastion and started loading the guns. Porthos suggested throwing the corpses into the ditch but Athos vetoed this.

"They may be useful," he said mysteriously. "And now to table!" he added briskly.

The four friends sat on the ground, their legs crossed.

"Now, Athos, your secret?" D'Artagnan suggested.

"The secret is that I saw Milady yesterday."

D'Artagnan's hand shook so violently that he put his glass on the ground.

"You saw your wi—"

"Hush!" interrupted Athos. Then he told Porthos and

Aramis how Milady wanted revenge of D'Artagnan, how she had tried to have him killed twice and poisoned recently.

"Look!" said Aramis suddenly, pointing.

"A troop coming toward us. About twenty men!"

"Sixteen sappers, four soldiers, five hundred paces away!" Athos smiled. "We have time to finish breakfast!"

Presently, as the troop appeared along a communication trench, Athos scoffed at them as mere prisoners and dismissed their armed escort blithely, insisting he would warn these ditchdiggers.

Paying no heed to D'Artagnan's remonstrance, he mounted the breach, his musket in one hand, his hat in the other, and saluting courteously, shouted:

"Gentlemen, your attention, please!"

Amazed, the troop halted some fifty paces from the bastion.

"Gentlemen," Athos continued, "we are breakfasting in this bastion. Please do not bother us unless you come to drink the King's health."

Four shots rang out and the bullets flattened themselves out against the wall around Athos. Four shots answered them immediately, but these hit their mark.

"Grimaud, another musket!" Athos called. A second discharge followed. The enemy corporal and two sappers fell dead. The rest of the troop took to their heels.

The four friends rushed out of the fort, picked up the soldiers' muskets and the corporal's short pike, and calmly returned to the bastion.

"Let us return to our breakfast," said Athos.

"We were discussing Milady," D'Artagnan prompted.

"She is going to England," Athos said coolly, "to murder the Duke of Buckingham." Then he bade Grimaud fasten a napkin to a pike and plant it on the top of the bastion to prove to the rebels that the King's loyal servants were there. Across the plain a thunder of applause greeted its appearance.

After further discussion about Milady, Athos produced the precious paper and read it aloud.

"We must destroy this paper," D'Artagnan urged.

"On the contrary, we must keep it preciously," said Athos.

"Fortunately, Milady is far away!" Porthos spoke consolingly.

"Her presence in England makes me just as uncomfortable as her presence in France," said Athos.

"Her presence anywhere makes me terribly nervous," D'Artagnan confessed.

Suddenly: "To arms, gentlemen!" Grimaud shouted. A small troop was advancing toward the bastion. There were about twenty-five men. This time they were garrison soldiers. Athos refused to go back to camp, because they had not finished breakfast, they had important matters to discuss and they had been there only fifty minutes. The crumbling wall could be tumbled over to crush the attackers.

"Gentlemen," Athos called, "let each pick his own man."

"I have mine covered," said D'Artagnan. "Mine is as good as dead!" Porthos boasted. "Mine is marked!" said Aramis. "Fire!" Athos commanded.

Four shots rang out as one, four men fell. The drum immediately beat and the little troop advanced at the double. From then on, the volleys followed irregularly; yet on every three shots from the bastion, at least two men fell.

When the assailants reached the foot of the bastion, they still numbered a dozen or more.

"Now, lads, to the wall," cried Athos. "One good push—"

The wall bent as if rocked by the wind, then fell with a deafening crash. A horrible clamor arose, and all was over. Athos looked at his watch.

"Gentlemen," he announced, "we have stayed here for

A horrible clamor arose, and all was over

an hour and thus won our wager. But let us be good sportsmen and stay on awhile. We have more to discuss."

Each of them had plans, all of which were vetoed. Finally it was decided that the Queen must be informed and Buckingham warned. Aramis, blushing, said he knew a clever person at Tours. Athos smiled, knowing it to be Madame de Chevreuse, the Queen's exiled friend. Athos suggested a letter to Buckingham. Their valets would deliver two messages.

Suddenly: "Look, gentlemen!" Athos pointed toward La Rochelle. "What can be going on in the city?"

"It's a general alarm!"

"You watch!" said Athos. "They will send a whole regiment against us."

"You don't propose holding out against an entire regiment, do you?" Porthos asked.

"Why not?" Athos answered. "I have a plan!"

"Let's have it, Athos."

"We will prop up the corpses against the wall, their muskets in their hands."

Which Grimaud proceeded to do, while our friends decided to write to Lord Winter, Milady's brother whose life D'Artagnan had spared and who was a friend of Buckingham's. For to communicate personally with Buckingham while at war with England would have been treason.

As they filed out of the bastion, suddenly Athos cried:

"Our flag! We must not leave it even though it is only a napkin."

And he rushed back into the bastion, mounted the platform and seized the flag. Just then, the enemy opened a murderous fire. Far from being perturbed, Athos seemed to delight in exposing himself to danger. The bullets whizzed all around him. Athos waved his flag proudly, turned his back on the enemy and calmly saluted the men in the camp. Then, coolly, he joined his friends.

"Come, Athos, hurry up!" D'Artagnan begged him, but Athos continued to walk at a slow, stately pace despite all urgings of his comrades. Suddenly a furious fusillade thundered across the air.

"What in Heaven's name is that? What are they firing at now?" Porthos asked. "No one is in the bastion."

"They are firing on our dear departed enemies," said Athos.

"But corpses cannot return fire."

"Perhaps. But the rebels will imagine an ambush, and by the time they have found out how we duped them, we shall be well out of range."

Cries of relief and cheers of approval kept rising from the camp as the French observed the four friends returning at a walk. For a moment all was silence, then a fresh volley of bullets spattered among the stones about our friends and whistled past their ears. The rebels had at last occupied the bastion.

"Bunglers, those rebels!" Athos remarked. "How many did we shoot down?"

"Fifteen!"

"And how many did we crush?"

"Eight or ten."

"And not a scratch in return."

Returning to camp, they discovered that more than two thousand spectators had been watching every move in this exploit as avidly as though it were a rousing drama produced for their entertainment. Cheers and huzzahs rose on every side. Their entrance was a triumph.

The same evening the Cardinal spoke to Monsieur de Tréville of the day's exploit, which was still the sole topic of conversation throughout the camp.

"Splendid," he said. "Pray have that napkin sent me. I will give it to your company as a standard."

"Monseigneur, I fear that would be doing the Royal Guards an injustice. Monsieur d'Artagnan is not one of my men."

"Well then, take him!" said the Cardinal. "When four brave men are so attached to one another, they should not serve in different companies."

CHAPTER 16:

The Council of the Musketeers

L<small>UNCH</small> with Monsieur de Tréville, to celebrate D'Artagnan's appointment as a Musketeer, was a gay affair. Aramis, who was exactly D'Artagnan's size, equipped him fully, for Aramis had two of everything.

Then the friends met to plan their campaign.

Athos discovered the phrase "family affair"—anything kept secret from the Cardinal; Aramis discovered the idea —the lackeys; Porthos discovered the means—to have D'Artagnan's diamond sold, and D'Artagnan discovered nothing at all.

It was decided that D'Artagnan must sell the diamond the Queen had given him. After all, was not money needed to save the man the Queen loved?

Next, what valet was to be sent to Tours, what valet to England? Finally they decided that Aramis' Bazin should go to Tours, D'Artagnan's Planchet to London. Next, there was much debate about how the letters to Lord Winter and to Aramis' friend in Tours were to be composed.

"Hand the pen to Aramis," advised Porthos. "He writes theses in Latin."

The greatest difficulty was how to communicate with England, an enemy country, and how to communicate with Aramis' friend in Tours, without the letters falling into the hands of cardinalist spies.

Finally, amid much excitement, Aramis wrote one letter:

MY LORD:

The person who writes these lines had the honor of crossing swords with you in a duel in which four Frenchmen and four Englishmen participated. Since then, you have several times declared your feelings of friendship toward the writer.

Accordingly he considers it his duty to repay you in kind by sending you some urgent advice.

Twice already you have almost fallen victim to a close relative of yours whom you believe to be your heir because you do not know that before contracting a mariage in England she had not dissolved a previous marriage in France.

She will make a third attempt upon your life very shortly. She sailed from La Rochelle last night, bound for England.

Pray be on the alert for her, she has vast and terrible plans. If you would be convinced of her wickedness, you have but to read her past history upon her left shoulder.

And another, to the "clever person," whom Athos knew to be Madame de Chevreuse, the Queen's best friend, exiled from Paris.

MY DEAR COUSIN:

The Cardinal, whom God preserve, is about to put an end to the heretical rebellion of La Rochelle. Probably the succor of the English fleet will never arrive within sight of the city. I venture to say I am certain Buckingham will be prevented by some great event from even setting out.

As you know, the Cardinal is the most illustrious and determined statesman of times past, present and to come.

Pray give these happy tidings to your sister, my dear cousin. I dreamed that this accursed Englishman was dead. I cannot remember now whether it was by steel or poison but I can well remember I dreamed of his death. As you know, my dreams never deceive me.

You may be sure, then, of seeing me return soon.

Aramis folded the letter and wrote:

TO MADEMOISELLE MICHON, SEAMSTRESS, TOURS.

Bazin and Planchet were very proud of their missions; the former was given eight days to accomplish his task, the latter sixteen. The anxiety of our four musketeers is indescribable; Aramis was on tenterhooks, Porthos blustered nervously, D'Artagnan was in agony. Athos alone remained cool.

Punctually on the eighth day, Bazin brought back the following letter:

MY DEAR COUSIN:

My sister and I are skillful at interpreting dreams and we are terrified by them anyhow.

In the case of yours, I hope we will be able to say that dreams are but lies and illusions.

Farewell. Take care of yourself. And act in such a way that we may from time to time hear of your prowess.

AGLAE MICHON

On the sixteenth day all but Athos could not contain themselves; singly or in pairs they wandered like lost souls along the road by which Planchet was expected. Athos, cool as a cucumber, remained aloof.

"Planchet is a sound fellow," he insisted. But D'Artagnan kept grieving and insisting Milady would foil them in the end. Here they were, four humble musketeers, staking their little all against the Cardinal's power and all the forces of civil and international war.

The sixteenth day crawled on, evening came very slowly. At seven o'clock, the drums beat the retreat. And suddenly, miraculously, out of Heaven, appeared a sweaty, dusty, grimy Planchet with a note which read:

Thank you, rest easy.

CHAPTER 17:

Captivity

MEANWHILE, raging with fury, Milady was sailing away
from France without having had revenge on D'Artagnan
and Athos. As she entered the harbor of Portsmouth, she
found the town in a state of extraordinary excitement because of war conditions. The vessel was drawing to anchor
when suddenly a coast-guard cutter, formidably armed,
drew up. A naval officer came aboard, conversed with the
skipper, questioned the passengers, pointed to Milady's
baggage and invited her to join him. He explained that he
had orders to escort her ashore.

Though mystified, Milady knew better than to ask questions. When they reached the dock, there was a carriage
waiting. Milady, believing that this was the Cardinal's doing, offered no objection. An adventuress, she knew better
than to engage in conversation with the officer, except casually. And he answered only "yes" and "no."

The carriage passed under two arched gateways and at
last drew up in a square, gloomy court. Almost immediately

the door of the carriage swung open, the young man sprang lightly out and offered his hand to Milady.

"So I am a prisoner!" she commented lightly, glancing at the young officer with a gracious smile. "But surely it will not be for long."

They passed through a vaulted passageway, climbed a flight of stairs and reached the chamber Milady was to occupy. The door swung heavily upon its hinges. Milady suddenly realized that she was *really* a prisoner.

"In the name of Heaven, sir, what does all this mean? Where am I and why am I here?"

"You are here in the apartment that has been prepared for you. My mission is at an end," the young officer replied.

Milady involuntarily recoiled. Then, as a tall figure appeared in the doorway, she cried in amazement:

"What, brother, is it you?"

"Yes, fair lady!" Lord Winter bowed. "You are my guest here." He closed the door, fastened a loose shutter and drew up a chair close to his sister-in-law. "So you decided to return to England? What brings you to England, sister?"

"The desire to see you. But how did you know I was coming, brother?"

"Quite simple. The skipper of your vessel entered this port. I am Governor of the Port."

"Tell me." Milady, terrified, paused for a moment. "Didn't I see His Grace of Buckingham on the jetty?"

"Very likely. In France, I hear, there is much talk of British preparations for invasion. Apparently this disturbs your friend the Cardinal."

"My friend the Cardinal!"

"We can discuss this some other time. Meanwhile I hope to make you comfortable during your visit. I am sure I can do as well as your first husband—who is still alive. I mean your *French* husband."

A battle of wits ensued. Lord Winter made it clear—

though not brutally—that he knew everything about Milady. And Milady, aghast, pretended she was innocent. But presently they dropped all pretense when he told her that, as the bigamist and murderess she was, he could readily have her hanged.

"In five days from now," said Lord Winter, "I shall have an order of deportation made out in the name of Charlotte Backson. You may choose your destination, provided it be three thousand miles from London."

"Backson?" Milady objected. "I bear your brother's name."

"Tell me your French husband's name," said Lord Winter, "and we will fill in the deportation blank accordingly."

With which, he left her, a prey to helpless fury. Presently she calmed down and studied systematically the possibilities that lay before her. She had five days; she was not strong enough to break her prison bars. Besides, against the rocks far below her window the surge of surf rose, growled, roared and spent itself. She must use her wits. It was impossible to move Lord Winter, and the turnkeys were constantly changed. Her only hope lay in Felton, the officer who had brought her here in courtesy but in silence. He was young, she was beautiful; she would try her wiles on him. But Lord Winter, in each of the visits he made twice daily, repeated:

"Your warden, Felton, is practically my son; he owes me everything. Besides, he is a Puritan. So do not try to win him over; he is granite!"

Yet that is exactly what Milady determined to do. Her desire to punish D'Artagnan and Buckingham and Athos stirred up a witch's brew of hatred in the cauldron of her heart. And Felton would be her instrument; Felton, a Puritan and therefore a foe of Buckingham's. She must go free and revenge herself on all who were her enemies.

Felton was present when all her meals were served; he

also made a tour of inspection every three hours. During the five days of her captivity, Milady followed a plan, step by subtle step, whereby she hoped to win him over. The first evening, at suppertime, hearing steps, she rose hastily from her bed, flung herself into her armchair and let her beautiful hair fall disheveled over her shoulders. But Felton paid no attention. The second evening, she pretended to be asleep, but watched Felton through her long lashes.

"Are you awake, Milady?" he asked solicitously.

"Oh, how I have suffered!" she moaned in that melodious voice which enchantresses of old used to charm those whom they would destroy. "I am ill."

"We could send for a physician," Felton suggested, pitying her.

"I want nothing of life except to die," Milady whispered.

The third day, Milady made a point of crooning Puritan hymns in low tones, and when Lord Winter sent Felton with a Roman Catholic Bible, she brushed it away.

"This book is not for me," she exclaimed. "I hate Popish idolatry."

By the third day, she found that Felton came more often and that, though shy and seemingly cold, he lingered as long as possible. Also, she noticed he looked at her fixedly; it was as though he could not take his eyes off her. On the fourth day, when he called in the morning, Felton found Milady standing on a chair, holding a kind of rope, which she had fashioned out of cambric handkerchiefs which she had twisted into strips. When he chided her for attempting to hang herself, she begged him for a knife. He insisted that suicide was no solution; indeed, it was a crime in the eyes of God. And, playing with the consummate skill of a genius among actresses, Milady told him a story she invented about how Buckingham had betrayed her.

By the fifth day, Felton was wholly hers and she had talked him into rescuing her from prison. The lies she told him about Lord Winter infuriated him although he should have known better; and, within a period of one hundred and twenty hours, Milady had succeeded in arousing this young fanatic to set her free and to call Buckingham to account.

CHAPTER 18:

Escape

THERE could be no doubt that Milady had convinced Felton: he was now wholly hers!

Though she had eaten nothing for breakfast, dinner was brought at the usual time. Milady was horrified to notice that the uniforms of the soldiers who guarded her had changed. When she asked what had become of Felton she was told he had left on horseback an hour ago. She inquired whether Lord Winter was still at the castle. The soldier replied that he was. So Felton had been sent away, therefore Felton was obviously under suspicion. This was the last cruel blow Lord Winter had reserved for her.

At six o'clock Lord Winter entered, armed to the teeth. One glance at Milady told him what was on her mind.

"I see," he said. "You had begun to influence my poor Felton. But I will save him. He will never see you again. Get your belongings together and pack them up. Tomorrow you go! Tomorrow, by twelve o'clock, I shall have the order for your exile, signed, *Buckingham*."

And he left her.

A terrible storm burst at about ten o'clock. Milady derived a consolation of sorts as she saw Nature partaking in the disorders of her heart. The thunder growled in the air like the anger and fury in her mind. It was as if the blast, whirring across the earth to bow the branches of the trees and to strip them of their leaves, were lashing her very head.

Suddenly she heard a tap at her window and, as the

lightning flashed, discerned a man's face behind the bars.

"Felton!" she cried. "I am saved!"

"Yes," said Felton, "but hush, hush! I must have time to saw the bars. Just shut the window. When I have finished, I shall rap at the window."

An hour later, Felton rapped again. Milady sprang off the couch and opened the window. The removal of two small bars formed an opening through which a man could pass comfortably.

"Are you ready?"

"Yes. Shall I take anything with me?"

"Money, if you have some!"

"Yes! Take this," Milady urged, placing a bag in Felton's hands. He took it and dropped it to the foot of the wall.

"Now," he said, "will you come?"

"I am ready."

Milady mounted on a chair and passed the upper part of her body through the window. She saw the young officer suspended above the abyss on a rope ladder. The yawning emptiness frightened her.

"Put your two hands together. Cross them. That's right." Felton bound her wrists together with his handkerchief, then knotted a cord around the handkerchief. "Put your arms around my neck."

Felton descended the ladder slowly, rung by rung. At last he reached the last rung. Hanging on by the strength of his wrists, he touched the ground. Stooping down, he picked up the bag of gold and placed it between his teeth. Then he took Milady in his arms and set off briskly, climbed down across the rocks, and reaching the sea, emitted a swift, shrill whistle.

A similar signal replied. Five minutes later a rowboat appeared.

"To the sloop!" Felton ordered, "and row smartly!"

A black dot was floating on the sea. It was the sloop.

Felton descended the ladder slowly,
rung by rung

While the boat was advancing Felton untied the handker-chief which bound Milady's hands together.

"You are safe!" the young officer told her.

"Oh, thank you, Felton, and God bless you!"

The young man pressed her close against his heart. They drew near the sloop. A sailor on watch hailed the boat.

"This vessel will take you wherever you wish, provided you first put me ashore at Portsmouth."

"And so you are going to Portsmouth?"

"I have no time to lose. Tomorrow Buckingham sails for La Rochelle."

"He need not necessarily sail!" Milady cried.

"He will not sail," said Felton.

They put Felton ashore in a cove near Portsmouth, ar-ranging that if he did not return by ten in the morning, Milady was to sail and they would meet in France.

Reaching Portsmouth at eight, he found the whole popu-lation astir. Drums were beating in the streets and in the port; the troops about to embark were marching toward the docks. Covered with dust and streaming with perspira-tion, his face purple with heat and excitement, Felton sought to enter the Admiralty Building. The sentry refused him access; Felton called for the Orderly Officer, and produced the deportation order and a letter Lord Winter had written to Buckingham. The officer motioned to him to pass and Felton darted into the palace, and proceeded down a cor-ridor to a dressing room where Buckingham, just out of the bathtub, was putting on his clothes.

"Lieutenant Felton with dispatches from Lord Winter," Patrick announced.

Felton entered into the presence of a minister who, hav-ing tossed a richly gold-embroidered dressing gown over an armchair, was trying on a sky-blue velvet doublet stud-ded with pearls.

"Why did not My Lord come himself?" Buckingham demanded. "I expected him this morning."

"What I have to tell Your Grace is extremely confidential."

"You may go, Patrick," Buckingham told his valet. "But keep within reach; I shall be ringing for you presently."

"If Your Grace recalls, Lord Winter wrote recently requesting you to sign a deportation order for a young woman named Charlotte Backson."

"Certainly; I asked him to send me the order."

"Here is the order, My Lord."

Taking the paper from Felton, Buckingham glanced casually at it and prepared to sign it.

"Begging Your Grace's pardon," Felton said, stepping forward, "Your Grace knows that Charlotte Backson is not the real name of this young woman."

"Certainly, sir, I know that," the Duke replied.

"And knowing that—" Felton's voice trembled, "Your Grace will sign this order all the same?"

"Certainly. With the greatest pleasure, twice or thrice over!"

Felton's voice grew sharper and though low-pitched, assumed a certain shrillness. His words came increasingly staccato.

"Does Your Grace realize that the deportee is Lady Clark?" he asked.

"Of course I do."

"I cannot understand how Your Grace dare sign this order for deportation—"

"I shall sign this order without a qualm. The woman is a criminal. She is lucky to get off with deportation—"

Felton took two steps forward.

"You will not sign that order, My Lord!" he said.

"I will not sign that order? And why not, pray?"

"Your Grace, Lady Clark is an angel, as you well know, and I demand that you set her free."

"You demand—look here, man, are you mad?"

"I implore you to think of what you are about to do. Let Your Grace beware of going too far!"

"What? I believe the fellow is threatening me!"

"You shall hear me out, My Lord. Let her go free and I shall require nothing."

"You will require—?" Buckingham stared at Felton.

"My Lord—" Felton grew more and more excited as he spoke. "Beware! All England is weary of your iniquities. Your Lordship has almost usurped the royal power, and you stand an object of horror to God and man. God will punish you hereafter, but I will punish you here and now! Beware, My Lord!" His eyes blazed. "You are in the hands of God!"

Buckingham sprang for his sword, reached it but could not draw it; Felton was upon him. From under his shirt, Felton drew a knife. Suddenly Patrick appeared.

"A messenger is here with a letter from France, My Lord."

Buckingham looked up . . . Patrick advanced, letter in hand . . . Felton lunged . . .

"Thus die all traitors, villains and scoundrels," said Felton solemnly.

"Ah, you have killed me!" Buckingham gasped.

Patrick rushed to his support. Felton, seeing the door free, took to his heels. He crossed the antechamber rapidly and was about to dash down the staircase when on the top step he ran into Lord Winter. Seeing how pale and confused Felton was, his face and hands spattered with blood, the nobleman seized him, crying:

"God have mercy on me, I knew it. And I have come just one minute too late! Fool and wretch that I am!"

Felton offering no resistance, Lord Winter placed him in the hands of the guards, then hastened to Buckingham's apartment.

Meanwhile, close upon the Duke's cry: "Ah, you have killed me!" and Patrick's appeal for help, the gentleman with news from France entered Buckingham's dressing room.

"La Porte!" the Duke whispered. "Do you come from her?"

"Ay, Milord, and perhaps too late."

"Hush, La Porte, not so loud," Buckingham spoke effortfully. "We might be overheard." He coughed. "Patrick, let no one enter. Ah, I am dying and I shall never know what message she sent!" And the Duke fainted.

Just then Lord Winter and the leaders of the expedition all made their way into His Grace's presence. Exclamations of surprise, horror and despair filled the little room. A moment later the report of heavy cannon announced that something new and unexpected had taken place. Lord Winter tore his hair in an agony of self-reproach.

"Too late," he groaned, "too late by one minute! And I was warned that this might happen!"

"Gentlemen," the Duke said faintly, "I beg you to leave me alone with Patrick and La Porte."

Kneeling beside the Duke's sofa, Anne of Austria's faithful servant said tremulously:

"Your Grace will live, I know it. Your Grace will live."

"What has she written to me, La Porte?" Buckingham inquired feebly, covered with blood and overcoming the most atrocious pain in order to speak of the woman he loved. "What has she written? Read me her letter."

La Porte read:

MY LORD:

By what I have suffered through you and for you since I have known you, I beg you, if you have any regard for my well-being, to interrupt those great armaments you are preparing against France. I beseech you by the same token to cease this war which is generally said to be due to religious causes but privately whispered to spring from the love you bear me.

Pray watch carefully over your life, which is threatened and which will be dear to me from the moment I no longer have cause to regard you as an enemy.

Your affectionate
ANNE

"Have you nothing further to tell me, La Porte?"

"Yes, Milord. Her Majesty charged me to beg you to be very careful. She had learned recently that a plot was afoot to murder Your Grace, and to tell you that she still loved you."

"God be praised, I can die in peace!"

La Porte burst into tears.

At this moment the Duke's physician arrived, much distraught. He approached the Duke, took his hand, held it for an instant in his and let it fall.

"All is useless," he said. "His Grace is dead."

At this cry the crowd returned to Buckingham's apartment to mourn the passing of their master. Lord Winter ran to the terrace where Felton was still under guard.

"You traitor, you wretch, what have you done?" the nobleman cried.

"I have avenged myself!"

Suddenly Felton started. His glance, ranging over the harbor, had become fixed on a tiny speck out at sea. With the eagle eye of a sailor he had identified the white sail of a sloop heading for France.

Felton turned ashen, placed his hand upon his heart, which was breaking, and suddenly understood the full extent of all her treachery. Milady had sailed more than an hour before the time stipulated.

"God has willed it so, God's will be done!" Felton sighed.

Though one part of the Musketeers' effort had failed, their other mission succeeded. The beautiful seamstress of Tours (Athos knew it was Madame de Chevreuse) wrote twice to say in riddles that Madame Bonacieux was in the Béthune convent and that the Queen sent them, enclosed, an authorization for her to leave it.

At just about the same time, the King decided to go to Paris and the Musketeers, of course, accompanied him. Arriving in Paris, they obtained a furlough and rode with all speed to Béthune. On the evening of September twenty-fifth, they entered Arras. D'Artagnan had just alighted before the inn when a horseman, emerging from the posting yard, galloped off toward Paris. As he was passing through the gateway, a gust of wind blew open the cloak in which he was muffled and unsettled his hat. D'Artagnan turned deathly pale.

"That's the man!" he cried. "My enemy! The man of Meung! To horse, gentlemen, to horse; let us pursue him."

But Aramis prevailed upon him not to turn aside from their present purpose.

Suddenly a stableboy came running out of the posting yard in search of the stranger.

"Ho, Monsieur, ho!" he called, "here is a paper that fell out of your hat!" And he looked vainly about him.

"My friend," said D'Artagnan, "a half-pistole for that paper."

"With pleasure, Monsieur, here it is."

"Well?"—"What is it?"—"Read it!" asked the friends.

"Nothing. Just one word! Armentières. The name of that town or village is in *her* handwriting!"

As for the woman who had written this note, she must obviously now be in France. In point of fact, Milady landing at Portsmouth was an Englishwoman driven from La Rochelle by the persecutions of the French; landing at Boulogne she was a Frenchwoman driven from Portsmouth by the persecution of the English.

Traveling rapidly, she spent one night at an inn on the road, and after a journey of three hours next morning, reached Béthune at eight o'clock. At the Carmelite convent, she was received by the Mother Superior, produced her order from the Cardinal, was immediately assigned to a chamber and given a hearty breakfast. After breakfast the Mother Superior paid Milady a visit. The good nun sought her out with anticipatory relish for she welcomed all manner of Court gossip. Milady therefore made it her business to amuse the worthy nun with an abundance of anecdotes about the French Court. As the conversation continued, Milady hinted that she was a victim of the Cardinal's persecution.

"We happen to have a young woman here at this very moment who has suffered from the vengeance of the Cardinal," the nun said. "But, after all, perhaps the Cardinal has sound reasons for acting thus. Though this young woman looks like an angel, who can tell?"

"Who is she, Reverend Mother?"

"She was sent to me by a person of the highest rank. I know her only under the name of Kitty."

Milady shrugged her shoulders and smiled. "When may I see this poor young woman?" she asked.

"You may see her this evening. But you must rest, my dear."

Milady took the nun's advice. Presently she was awakened by a gentle voice. Starting up, she saw the young novice. The novice, seeing that Milady remained in bed, made to go out of the room.

"Come, my dear, we have barely met and you seek to deprive me of your company. I must confess I had looked forward to chatting with you and making friends—"

"I beg your pardon, Madame. I thought I had come at the wrong time. You were sleeping; you must be very tired."

"No, I beg you to stay. Let us talk."

Then began a cat-and-mouse game in which Milady, posing as a victim of the Cardinal, learned Madame Bonacieux's life history in a few moments.

"If only I could escape!" Milady sighed. "But who can help me? I am so alone."

Milady was quick to judge that by talking of herself, she could probably get the novice to reply in kind.

"When I said I was alone," she said, "I did not mean to say that I had not powerful friends in high places. But even the Queen does not dare to oppose the fearsome Cardinal."

"So you know her, Madame? You know our noble Queen?"

"And I know Tréville," Milady said.

"You must have met some of his Musketeers, then? Do you know Athos, Madame?"

Milady turned white as the sheets in which she was lying.

"I know him through stories D'Artagnan has told me."

"D'Artagnan? You know him? What is he to you?"

"A friend—just a casual friend—yes, a friend."

"You are deceiving me, Madame."

"It is *you* who are in love with him," Milady retorted. "Yes, you are Constance Bonacieux! Do you deny it?"

"No, Madame. But are we rivals?"

A savage and malign joy blazed over Milady's features, which she quickly masked.

"Child," she said, "I know all about how you were carried off from the cottage at Saint-Cloud . . . how D'Artagnan was plunged in despair . . . how he marshaled his friends and how they searched for you in vain . . . how at this very moment they are worrying about you. . . . Monsieur d'Artagnan and I have spoken so often of you, he told me all the adoration he had for you and he made me love you long before I ever laid eyes on you. And so, we meet!" she concluded.

"Forgive me." Constance, locked in Milady's embrace, wept over her shoulder. "I was jealous. But I *do* love him so!"

"What a poor, pretty, devoted creature you are!" Milady said unctuously.

"You know what I have suffered," the novice said, "and you know how unhappy he has been!"

"Quite so!" Milady replied mechanically.

"But my troubles are over," Madame Bonacieux continued. "Tomorrow—or perhaps this very evening—I shall see him again."

"Tomorrow? This evening?" The words roused Milady from her reverie as she repeated them. "What do you mean, child?"

"I expect *him*—himself—in person!"

"Impossible, D'Artagnan is at the siege of La Rochelle."

"Read this, Madame," the young woman cried in an excess of pride and joy as she handed Milady a letter.

Milady recognized the handwriting of Madame de Chevreuse.

"I always suspected some secret intelligence in that quarter," she mused. Then avidly she read the following:

My dear child:

Hold yourself in readiness. Our friend (and of course you know whom I mean) will be seeing you soon. His sole purpose in coming is to release you from the imprisonment to which you had to be committed for your own security. So make ready to leave the convent and never despair of us.

Our charming Gascon has just proved himself to be as brave and faithful as ever. Tell him that certain parties are very grateful to him for the warning he has given them.

"Well, the letter is clear enough," Milady commented. "Do you happen to know what D'Artagnan's warning referred to?"

"No, Madame, but I can guess. I suppose he warned the Queen against some fresh trick of the Cardinal's."

Suddenly the echo of a horse's hoofs sent Madame Bonacieux darting to the window.

"It is probably D'Artagnan!" she cried, wild with joy. Then: "Alas, no!" Madame Bonacieux peered through the window. "It is not D'Artagnan!"

Milady sprang out of bed and began to dress.

"Where is this man now?" she asked.

"He is coming in here."

"Oh, I am so nervous," said Milady.

"Hush, Madame, someone is coming!"

The door swung open and the Mother Superior appeared on the doorsill.

"Did you come from Boulogne?" she asked Milady.

"Yes, I did, Reverend Mother."

"A gentleman who refuses to give his name wants to see you."

Madame Bonacieux and the Mother Superior withdrew.
An instant later the jangling of spurs resounded on the
staircase, the sound of footsteps drew near, the door
opened, a man stood on the threshold. . . .

Milady uttered a cry of joy. It was the Cardinal's de-
moniacal tool, the Comte de Rochefort.

"His Eminence was worried and sent me in search of
you," Rochefort explained.

"I arrived only yesterday and I have not wasted my time.
Do you know whom I met here?"

"No."

"The young woman the Queen freed from prison. I am
her best friend!" she explained coolly.

"Upon my honor, only yourself, dear Milady, can perform such miracles!"

"Little good it does me, Monsieur. Tomorrow or the day
after, this woman is being withdrawn from the convent on
orders from the Queen."

"How and by whom?"

"By D'Artagnan and his friends."

"The Cardinal seems to entertain a certain weakness in
regard to these four men. I scarcely know why."

"Well, tell him this, Rochefort, from *me*. Listen carefully.
Those same four men overheard the conversation His Eminence and I held at the *Sign of the Red Dovecote*. After the
Cardinal's departure, one of them broke into my room. The
fellow abused me and seized the note His Eminence had
given me. The four of them warned Lord Winter of my
journey to England. Once again, they almost foiled my
mission, just as in the affair of the diamond studs."

Rochefort asked, "But how—?"

"Tell His Eminence that of the four, two only are dangerous: D'Artagnan and Athos; that the third, Aramis by name,
happens to be a friend of Madame de Chevreuse; and that
the fourth, a fellow called Porthos, is a fool."

"But these four men must surely be at La Rochelle?"

"So I thought, too. But Madame Bonacieux showed me a letter which leads me to believe that all four are on their way here to remove her from this convent."

"Confound it! What are we to do?"

"What did the Cardinal say about me?"

"He ordered me to ask you to communicate to me any desires you have. When he learns what you have done, he will consider what you are to do hereafter."

"So I am to stay here?"

"Here or in the neighborhood. And be sure to tell me where you settle, so that the Cardinal's orders can reach you promptly."

Milady explained that she would probably be unable to stay at the convent because her enemies would be arriving at any moment.

"So this little woman is to slip through the Cardinal's fingers?" Rochefort asked.

Again Milady smiled an enigmatic smile all her own.

"You forget I told you I was her best friend," she answered.

They then planned that Rochefort should send his coach and valet to take Milady away on the Cardinal's orders. She would go somewhere in the region—anywhere, just to escape D'Artagnan.

"Do you want a map?" Rochefort asked.

"No, no, I know this part of the country quite well. I was brought up here. I will stay at Armentières!" Milady decided.

"Where and what is Armentières? Do write that name on a piece of paper, Milady."

Rochefort took the paper she gave him, folded it and placed it in the lining of his hat.

"You forget to ask me whether I need money?"

"Do you? How much, Milady?"

"All the gold you have on your person."

"Here you are, then."

"Splendid! When do you leave?"

"Within an hour."

"All is settled, then. Farewell, Monsieur."

"Good-bye, Milady."

"Pray commend me to the Cardinal."

"Pray commend me to Satan, Madame."

CHAPTER 19:

The Man in the Red Cloak

Rochefort had scarcely departed when Madame Bonacieux returned to face Milady, who was wreathed in smiles.
Milady explained that her caller was her brother; he had
slain a cardinalist emissary and stolen his credentials.
Within two hours, Milady said, a coach would come to
fetch her. Why should not the novice, pretending to say
farewell to Milady, drive off with her? Madame Bonacieux
objected that D'Artagnan might be coming at any moment.
Milady replied that it was a race between the Cardinal's
Guards and the Musketeers. The safest thing was for Constance to accompany Milady and lie low somewhere in the
neighborhood. Suddenly there was the sound of a clatter
of hoofs and, at the bend of the road, Milady espied eight
horsemen. In their leader, she recognized D'Artagnan.

"Ah, what is it?" Constance asked.

"The Cardinal's Guards," Milady lied. "Let us fly immediately."

But Constance stood there, rooted to the spot. Meanwhile the horsemen clattered by under the window. Mi-

lady, with no coach to drive her off, planned to pass through the convent garden into the woods, and stop the coach when it came.

"For the last time, will you come?" she insisted.

"You must flee alone. I am too weak. I cannot walk."

Milady poured a glass of wine, opened the bezel of her ring, and emptied a reddish pill into it. The pill dissolved immediately.

"Here, drink," she urged, pressing the glass to the novice's lips. "Ah, well," Milady said to herself, "this is not the revenge I planned, but we do what we can!" And she rushed from the room.

Dully, Madame Bonacieux watched her disappear; she was like the victim of a nightmare. Several minutes passed but she did not move. Then there was a great tumult at the convent gate, she heard the grating of hinges, there was a trampling of boots, a rattling of spurs and a hubbub of voices on the stairs.

"D'Artagnan, D'Artagnan! Is it you?" she cried.

"Constance, where are you?"

The door of the cell sprang open.

"Oh, D'Artagnan, my beloved D'Artagnan!"

The others followed close at our Gascon's heels.

"Ay, Constance, we are together again!"

"*She* told me you were not coming but I knew you were."

At the word *she*, Athos started up.

"*She?*" D'Artagnan asked. "Whom do you mean?"

"Her name, her name! Can't you recall her name?" Athos cried.

"Yes, I think so. The Mother Superior told me, but I forgot. It is a strange name. Oh, my head swims—I cannot see—"

"Help, help, my friends, her hands are icy cold," said D'Artagnan. "She is ill. Dear Heaven! She is fainting."

While Porthos bellowed for help, Aramis moved toward

the table for a glass of water. Athos suddenly stared into a wineglass on the table.

"No, no, it is impossible," he muttered. "Who gave you that glass?" he asked the novice.

"Milady," Constance answered, choking. "D'Artagnan," she moaned. "Don't leave me, my love. Where are you? You see I am dying."

"Constance, Constance!" D'Artagnan begged.

"Farewell, my love," Constance whispered. And then her eyes closed, her heart had stopped beating.

Suddenly a man appeared in the doorway. Looking around him, he noticed Madame Bonacieux dead and D'Artagnan in a faint.

"I was not mistaken," he said. "This is Monsieur d'Artagnan and you three are his friends."

The musketeers looked up in surprise at hearing their names.

"Like yourselves, gentlemen, I am in search of a woman —" he gave a bitter smile, "—a woman who must have passed this way, for I see a corpse here."

The friends remained silent. Surely they had met this man, but where?

"Gentlemen," the stranger continued, "don't you recognize a man whose life you have saved twice? I am Lord Winter. I have come to chastise *that* woman!"

"I have a prior and more valid claim," Athos said coldly. "She is my wife!"

Athos despatched the four valets, each along one of the four roads leading out of Béthune. The most promising clue was Planchet's, as he followed the tracks of a coach through the forest toward Armentières.

While his friends waited for the lackeys' reports, Athos disappeared on a mysterious errand. Later, as, having talked to Planchet, they were about to set off in pursuit of Milady, Athos said, "Wait for me, I will be back in a moment!" And he galloped off. Within a quarter of an hour he returned, accompanied by a tall man who wore a mask over his eyes and was swathed in a vast red cloak. At nine o'clock, the little cavalcade set off along the road the carriage had taken.

It was a dark, tempestuous night. Vast tenebrous clouds raced across the heavens, obscuring the light of the stars. Now and then, thanks to a flash of lightning on the horizon, the cavalcade could see the road stretching out before them, white and solitary. Lord Winter or Porthos or Aramis tried several times to engage in conversation with the red-cloaked stranger. At each effort they made he merely bowed.

They broke into a fast trot. The storm burst in great fury and the horsemen put on their greatcoats. Presently a man stepped out onto the road. Athos recognized Grimaud, who pointed toward a small lonely house. By the light of a lamp within, Athos distinguished a woman wrapped in a dark-colored mantle, seated on a stool close to a dying fire. Her elbows rested on a mean table and she held her head between her hands, white as ivory.

Suddenly one of the horses neighed. Milady looked up. Realizing that she had recognized him, Athos pushed the pane in with hand and knee and leaped into the room.

Milady rushed to the door and opened it; at the threshold stood D'Artagnan.

Milady fell back into a chair, her hands outstretched as though to conjure away this terrible apparition.

"What do you want?" she screamed.

"We want Charlotte Backson," Athos replied impersonally, "who was first called the Comtesse de la Fère and subsequently Lady Clark. We want to judge you fairly according to your crimes. Monsieur d'Artagnan, it is for you to accuse her first."

D'Artagnan stepped forward.

"Before God and before man, I accuse this woman of having poisoned Constance Bonacieux."

"We bear witness to the truth of it!" said Aramis and Porthos.

"Before God and before man, I accuse this woman of having tried to poison me, too. Brisemont died in my stead," D'Artagnan continued.

"I saw him die!" said Aramis.

"Before God and before man, I accuse this woman of having sought to make me kill the Comte de Vardes. I have finished," D'Artagnan concluded.

"Before God and before man," said Lord Winter slowly, "I accuse this woman of having caused the murder of George Villiers, Duke of Buckingham. And there is more," Lord Winter pursued. "My brother bequeathed his all to this woman. Within three hours after he had signed his will, he died of a mysterious illness. For the murder of

Buckingham, and of my brother, I demand that justice be done."

"It is now my turn," Athos declared impassively. "I married this woman when she was a young girl. I gave her my name and my wealth. One day I discovered that she was branded."

Milady rose indignantly to her feet.

"I defy you," she said fiercely, "to find any tribunal which passed this infamous sentence upon me. No court in France could have branded me."

"Silence, it is *my* turn to speak."

From the depths of the room, the man in the red cloak rose to his full height, dominating the others.

"Who are *you?*" cried Milady, choking.

Her spell of coughing done, her disheveled hair streaming above the hands that held her head, with increasing fright Milady stared up at him. Then, noting his haggard face framed by sable-black hair and beard, she shuddered. The stranger maintained an icy impassiveness. His audience looked raptly at him, eager for the solution of the enigma. Staring straight before him, the man in the red cloak stated in a monotonous voice that the accused had been a nun and that she had tempted a candid, sincere young priest. She tempted him to steal the sacred vessels of the church and sell them. But as the pair were preparing to abscond, they were apprehended. A week later, the woman persuaded the jailer's son to allow her to escape; the young priest was condemned to serve ten years in irons and to be branded.

"I was the executioner of Lille," the speaker insisted. "I was forced to brand the guilty man, and the guilty man, gentlemen, was my own brother. But this woman was the real criminal. I found her where she was hiding. I marked upon her shoulder the same brand my brother bore. It was an unofficial sentence executed by the official executioner of Lille. Later, they *did* escape and the woman married a lord. My brother hanged himself! I have stated why I punished this woman before and why I seek to punish her again."

When he had moved aside, Athos turned to D'Artagnan.

"Monsieur d'Artagnan, what sentence should be passed upon this woman?" he asked.

"I request the penalty of death."

"Lord Winter?"

"On two counts, the sentence of death."

Athos looked at Porthos and Aramis. "You two gentlemen are judges," he stated. "What punishment do you please to impose upon this woman?"

"Death!" they answered in one voice.

It was now almost midnight. The waning sickle-shaped moon rose ruddy and as though emblooded by the last vestiges of the storm. It soared slowly over the village, its wan light etching the dark line of the houses and the silhouette of a tall belfry against a darkling background. The river rolled by like a river of molten lead. Beyond it, a black mass of trees standing out against an angry sky heavy with fat coppery clouds, re-created a sort of twilight amid the fullness of the night.

Grimaud and Mousqueton led Milady forward, her arms pinned under their hands. The executioner followed hard by.

When they reached the riverbank, the executioner advanced to tie a cord about Milady's hands.

"Cowards! You are all miserable cowards! Ten murderers against a defenseless woman!" she screamed.

As the executioner bound her, Milady uttered piercing cries that echoed and were lost, dismally, in the depths of the wood.

"I do not want to die," Milady sobbed, writhing in her bonds. "I am too young to die."

"So too was the woman you poisoned at Béthune," D'Artagnan put in. "She was younger than you, yet she is dead!"

"I swear to enter a convent—I will become a nun—"

"You were cloistered and you were a nun," the executioner replied. "You left the convent to bring ruin upon my brother."

Athos took one step forward and faced Milady.

"I forgive you the evil you have done me," he said. "God rest you, may you die in peace!"

Lord Winter said, "I forgive you for poisoning my brother, for murdering the Duke of Buckingham, for causing the death of young Felton and for your attempts upon my own life. May you die in peace!"

"For my part," said D'Artagnan, "I beg *your* forgiveness. By trickery unworthy of a gentleman, I provoked your anger and moved you to vengeance. In return for such forgiveness, I forgive you that cruel vengeance and the death of my poor Constance. God grant you die in peace!"

"I am lost!" Milady cried. "I must die!" Then, unaided, she rose, stood erect and glancing about her, her eyes shining in the night like a flame.

"Where am I to die?" she asked.

"Across the river," said the man of Lille.

Slowly the boat followed the ferry rope under the shadow of a pallid cloud that descended very gradually over the waters. Milady, reaching shore, jumped lightly from the boat and took to her heels. But the ground was wet. Having scaled the bank, she slipped and fell to her knees. She stayed very still there.

The executioner raised his arms very slowly . . . a ray of moonlight illumined the blade of his broadsword . . . his arms fell down again smartly, and, after one terrified shriek, his victim fell. He took off his red cloak, spread it out on the turf and placed the body upon it. Then he gathered it up and, his grisly burden over his shoulder, returned to

his boat. Midstream, he swung his boat round. Raising his red cloak and its contents over the water:

"God's justice and will and mercy be done!" he cried in a loud voice.

Then he dropped the cloak overboard and the waters closed up about it. . . .

Returning soberly to Paris, our friends arrived in time to escort the King back to the battlefield. A few miles from La Rochelle a horseman galloped up to them. Glancing up, D'Artagnan uttered a cry of joy. It was the man of Meung!

"So, Monsieur, we meet at last," said the Gascon. "But *this* time you shall not escape me!"

"I have no intention of doing so, Monsieur," the stranger replied. "*This* time, *I* am after *you!* In the name of His Majesty the King, I have the honor to put you under arrest."

"And who may you be, Monsieur?" D'Artagnan inquired.

"I am the Chevalier de Rochefort, the equerry of Monseigneur le Cardinal de Richelieu."

Next day, Richelieu received the prisoner.

"You have been arrested by my orders, Monsieur," the Cardinal said. "Do you know why?"

"If Monseigneur will be kind enough to tell me what crimes I am charged with, I shall then inform him of what I have already done."

"You are charged with crimes which have brought down loftier heads than yours, Monsieur. You are indicted for correspondence and intelligence with the enemies of the Kingdom, for violation of secrets of State, and for attempting to thwart the plans of your general."

"But by whom were these charges preferred, Monseigneur? By a woman whom the justice of our country has branded. By a woman who married one man in France and another in England. By a woman who poisoned her second husband and who attempted both to poison and to slay me."

"What in the world are you saying, Monsieur? What woman are you talking about?"

"I am talking about Lady Clark."

"If Lady Clark has committed these crimes, Monsieur, you may be sure she will be duly punished."

"Monseigneur, she has already been punished."

"By whom, pray?"

"By my three friends and myself. She is dead."

"Dead!" the Cardinal exclaimed incredulously.

"Thrice she attempted to kill me and I pardoned her," D'Artagnan said. "But when she murdered the woman I loved, my friends and I seized, tried and sentenced her."

"So you and your friends dared to sit as judges!" the Cardinal declared in a tone that contrasted strangely with the severity of his words. "Do you realize that those who punish without license to punish are guilty of murder?"

"I swear to you, Monseigneur," D'Artagnan answered. "I have never held life so precious as to be afraid of death."

"Monsieur, I know you to be a brave man," the Cardinal said almost affectionately. "I can therefore tell you immediately that you will be tried and probably convicted."

"Another might assure Your Eminence that he had his pardon in his pocket. For my part, I am content to say: 'Command as you see fit, Monseigneur, I shall obey.'"

"Your pardon in your pocket?" said Richelieu, surprised. "A pardon signed by whom?"

"By Your Eminence."

"By *me*? You are insane, Monsieur."

"Surely Monseigneur will recognize his own handwriting?" D'Artagnan said. And he handed over the precious note which Athos had seized from Milady and had given him to serve for a safeguard.

*The Man
in the Red
Cloak
297*

3RD DECEMBER, 1627

It is by my order and for the service of the State that the bearer of this note has done what he has done.
Signed by my hand at the
Camp of La Rochelle.

RICHELIEU

Richelieu remained plunged in thought. At length he
raised his head, fastened his eagle glance upon the other's
loyal, open, intelligent countenance, and on that countenance, furrowed by tears, read all the sufferings D'Artagnan had endured for the last month. For the third or
fourth time the Cardinal reflected what a brilliant future
lay before this youth of twenty-one. Recalling, too, how the
infernal genius of Milady had more than once terrified even
himself, he felt a kind of secret joy at being relieved of her.
Slowly, he tore up the paper.

The Cardinal moved over to his desk and wrote a few
lines on a parchment.

"This is the order for my execution," D'Artagnan thought.

"Here, Monsieur," the Cardinal told him, "I have taken
a document from you, so I shall give you another. The name
is wanting on this commission; you can write it in yourself."

D'Artagnan took the paper hesitantly and looked it over.
It was a lieutenant's commission in the Musketeers. He fell
to one knee before His Eminence.

"Monseigneur, my life is yours," he declared, "do with
it what you will. But I do not deserve the favor you have
bestowed upon me. I have three friends all of whom are
worthier and more deserving—"

"You are a gallant lad, D'Artagnan," the Cardinal interrupted, tapping him on the shoulder and savoring the pleasure of having at last overcome this rebellious nature. "Do
with the commission what you will. But remember, though
the bearer's name is blank, it is to you I give it."

"I shall never forget it, Your Eminence may be certain
of that!"

Overjoyed, D'Artagnan sought out Athos, who refused
the commission saying, "Keep the commission. Heaven
knows you have bought it all too dearly."

Porthos, too, was unwilling.

"A certain lady having returned at last to Paris," he explained, "I am trying on my wedding clothes."

And Aramis: "No, my friend. When the siege is over, I shall take Holy Orders."

"Well," D'Artagnan announced, returning to Athos, "the others refused too."

"That is because no one deserves it more than you," said Athos. Then, taking up a quill, he wrote D'Artagnan's name boldly into the blank in the commission.

Epilogue

AFTER a year's siege, La Rochelle, deprived of the assistance of the British fleet, surrendered. The King returned to Paris the same year, receiving as triumphant a welcome as if he came from conquering an enemy rather than his fellow-Frenchmen.

D'Artagnan assumed his lieutenancy. (Eventually Planchet obtained a sergeancy in the Piedmont Regiment.)

Porthos, having left the service, married the following year. Since the lady he married possessed eight hundred thousand pounds, Mousqueton, clad in a magnificent livery, enjoyed the satisfaction of his supreme ambition: to ride behind a gilded carriage.

Aramis, after a journey into Lorraine, suddenly vanished without a word to his friends. Later they learned that he had retired to a monastery—no one knew where. Bazin became a lay brother.

Athos remained a musketeer under D'Artagnan's command until 1633 when, after a journey to Touraine, he too quitted the service, under the pretext that he had inherited a small property in Roussillon. Grimaud followed him.

D'Artagnan fought with Rochefort thrice and thrice he wounded him.

"I shall probably kill you the fourth time," he declared as he helped Rochefort to his feet.

"We had therefore best stop where we are," the wounded man answered. "In truth, I am a better friend than you imagine. After our first encounter, by saying one word to the Cardinal, I could have had your throat slit from ear to ear."

This time they embraced heartily, all malice spent; indeed, it was Rochefort who found Planchet his sergeancy.

As for Monsieur Bonacieux, he lived on very quietly, wholly ignorant of what had become of his wife and caring very little about it. One day he was rash enough to recall himself to the Cardinal's memory. His Eminence replied that he would provide for the haberdasher so thoroughly that he would never want for anything in the future. In fact, Monsieur Bonacieux, having left his house at seven o'clock in the evening to go to the Louvre, never set foot there again. In the opinion of those who seemed best informed, he was thereafter lodged and fed in some royal stronghold at the expense of His Generous Eminence.

THE BEAUTIFUL
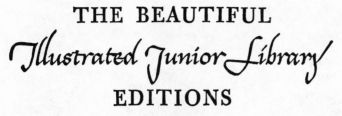
Illustrated Junior Library
EDITIONS